HEATHER BLACKWOOD

CAT'S PAW

A TIME CORPS NOVEL

CHAPTER 1

December 24, 1863
New Orleans, Louisiana

A T THE PRECISE MOMENT THE grandfather clock began to chime noon, there was a knock on the laboratory door. Seamus Connor pushed himself away from his table covered in assorted mechanical parts and equation-covered papers and rose to answer it. Mrs. Washington, his housekeeper, stood in the hallway bearing a lunch tray with a small pot of tea, a thick slice of cornbread and a covered bowl.

Mrs. Washington always arrived precisely at noon, per his instructions. Seamus knew that he was not an orderly man, and having Mrs. Washington bring his lunch at noon every day reminded him to eat regularly and ensured that he didn't get so wrapped up in his work that he neglected to eat, sleep, or make the trip to Tulane University where he taught physics classes a few days a week.

Once again, he was surprised to discover that it was lunchtime already. If he had to guess, he would have said it was still mid-morning. Seamus thanked the housekeeper and took the tray, but she didn't turn and leave. Instead, she looked past him, into the disastrously messy laboratory, as if assessing if she could safely enter. As a rule, she refused to enter the room, which Seamus found a satisfactory arrangement as it kept her from disturbing his things.

"I already took yesterday's tray down to the kitchen," he said, wondering if she was searching for yesterday's dishes. Occasionally, things became buried.

"It's not that," Mrs. Washington said. "It's just that it's Christmas Eve."

"I know it is. Did you want to go home for the afternoon? Hazel and I can manage on our own until your return."

"No, I said I could stay until two, and I will. It's just—I thought I ought to speak to you. It's about Miss Dubois."

Hazel Dubois was Seamus's ward. The girl had been a street urchin, sleeping in the abandoned buildings of New Orleans and playing her violin for money on street corners. Back then, she had dressed as a boy and had gone by the name of Henry. Before he knew she was a girl, Seamus occasionally hired Henry to run errands, retrieving packages or picking up items for Mrs. Washington. And beyond that, he had never given the lad much thought.

But then Felicia Sanchez had come into their lives, arriving from another time in another world through a time rip that Seamus himself had accidentally created. She was a young woman in training to become a doctor in the early twenty-first century. Aside from being strange and unaccustomed to dressing and behaving in a civilized manner, she had been the one to discover that Henry was really a girl. She had encouraged Seamus to take in the child, and he had done so.

Naturally, the poor woman had wanted to return to her home. Aside from missing her former life, Miss Sanchez had a nephew dying of a rare form of consumption, which Felicia called cancer. Before slipping through the time rip, she had been in contact with a doctor from Brazil who might have been able to help the young boy. Without Miss Sanchez present to speak with this doctor and put him in contact with her sister, the child's mother, the little boy would surely die.

Six years had now passed since Miss Sanchez had

unwillingly fallen through another time rip accompanied by Seamus's former research partner and enemy, Oren McCullen. It was Seamus's duty to find her and then get her home to her own time, for her sake and for her nephew's. He had worked in his laboratory every day for six years, hoping that eventually he would discover a way to find her.

In that time, Hazel had gone from a scrawny eleven-year-old to an educated young woman. Occasionally, it struck Seamus that she was a different person than the girl he had known. It pleased him that she was sensible and good-hearted, but he sometimes missed the little girl who preferred trousers to dresses and liked to sit on a stool in the corner of the laboratory, asking him endless questions.

"Does Hazel need anything? Is she all right?" he asked Mrs. Washington.

"She's well enough. It's just that she'll be home any time now and tomorrow is Christmas."

"A fact of which I am well aware."

Mrs. Washington looked uneasy, which was rare. She was usually composed and certain of herself. She ran the house almost single-handedly and knowing how much he depended on her, she was not shy about stating her opinions. "She's almost grown now, you understand. Her birthday is in two weeks."

"Another fact of which I am aware."

"Have you gotten her anything?"

Seamus had the feeling that Mrs. Washington had wanted to say something else, but studying her, he could not discern what it could be.

"Not yet," he said cautiously. "But I was thinking I would drop by one of the shops and buy her a new pair of gloves."

"It's Christmas Eve, Mr. Connor."

"There's still time. The shops won't close for another hour or two."

Mrs. Washington sighed and looked like she was deciding on something. "Firstly, you would not have remembered at all had I not reminded you. Miss Dubois is alone in the world, but for the two of us, and you're her only real family. She's a good girl, but she could use a little guidance here and there."

"But you provide wonderful guidance for her."

It was true. Mrs. Washington was steady, practical and patient. Seamus knew that he was none of these things.

"You're her guardian. And she's close to being a grown woman. She needs someone to look after her, to meet the family of her gentlemen callers—"

"She has gentlemen callers?" said Seamus in alarm. "Why wasn't I told?"

"Just the one. Mr. Ross."

"Well, that's all right then," he said, relieved. "I know about him already. A decent enough young fellow. I have no problem with him courting our Hazel."

"It's not him that's the problem. You're up in this laboratory at all hours. Or else you're at the university working."

"I have to make a living."

"I understand that. But the girl needs to understand the ways of the upper classes."

Seamus, through the patents of his inventions, his employment as a professor at Tulane University and with a little help at the riverboat gambling tables, had been able to bring the household into a financial position in the upper class. Hazel was his sole heir and if the patents were renewed and the investments carefully watched, the income would last Hazel a lifetime. But fortune-hunting men might find the girl easy prey. Though clever and street-smart, she was young and naïve in the ways of high society. Mrs. Washington, however much she loved Hazel and however good her intentions might be, was black and a housekeeper. She could not help Hazel navigate

4

the treacherous waters of the wealthy white families of New Orleans.

"What she needs is a mother," said Seamus, and immediately regretted it. He knew that Mrs. Washington had done her best to provide feminine guidance for Hazel, but a kindly housekeeper couldn't ever replace a mother.

He thought of Felicia Sanchez again, and wondered if she would have been able to assist with the situation. She was too young to be Hazel's mother, and she was from a time in which women wore masculine clothing and held men's jobs. She was nothing like the coquettes and social darlings of the wealthy New Orleans set. No, she would not have been of any assistance.

"But she doesn't have a mother," said Mrs. Washington. "What she has is you and me. And you need to get cleaned up and quit drinking in this wreck of a laboratory."

He opened his mouth to object, but she put up her finger.

"And another thing. There's a war on, and Miss Dubois takes a streetcar or a hansom cab home, sometimes after dark. There are Union soldiers who might think to have some sport."

"Our Hazel can take care of herself," he said, but then thought better of it. Hazel had been a scrappy street urchin once, able to run and fight. And once she had moved into Seamus's house in the Garden District, he made sure she knew how to throw a proper punch as well as fight dirty enough to disable any man who tried to harm her. But it wasn't enough.

He had seen enough violence done to women who couldn't fight, both back home in Ireland and here in New Orleans. Women were vulnerable and he wouldn't have Hazel harmed again. Not after all she had been through as a child. There was a reason she had lived on the streets, having fled from her uncle and aunt. If her uncle hadn't died mysteriously on a train bound for New York, Seamus thought he might have liked to hunt the man down himself. Any man who preyed on children to slake his lust was vermin, and like vermin, he should be exterminated without mercy.

"She's a small girl," said Mrs. Washington. "And if there were more than one soldier ... it wouldn't matter how well she could bite and kick."

"Maybe I should give her a handgun to carry in her bag."

"No, what you need to do is see that she gets home before dark and has someone with her when she goes to teach her music students."

"There's no one who would go with her, unless that Mr. Ross would like to."

"I meant you." Mrs. Washington wasn't smiling.

"I have to work. I have to keep food on the table."

"You only teach a few afternoons a week."

"But I also have to find a way to get to Miss Sanchez. I can't stop working on these equations. For her sake. From my readings, I can tell she's stranded in 1961. We're fortunate that she's in our universe. It makes it easier to find her."

"Miss Sanchez isn't here now," said Mrs. Washington. "And Miss Dubois is."

"But Miss Sanchez needs me too. I promised to get her home, and I intend to keep that promise."

Miss Washington held up a hand. "I've said what I came to say. Miss Dubois needs you to look after her and you need to get her a Christmas and a birthday gift. That's all."

She turned and went downstairs, her head high and her posture stiff. Seamus cleared a place on his worktable for the tray and ate while he worked. Mrs. Washington went beyond herself in telling her employer what he should and should not do. It wasn't as if he didn't care for Hazel. He had given her a place to live, an education, and up until the war forced her back to New Orleans two years ago, he had paid for her to attend the Boston Women's Conservatory to study violin. She had food, a place to live, and the sort of life most young women would envy. Besides, she knew where he was if she ever wanted to speak with him.

And it wasn't as if he would be of much use to her anyway. He was a poor Irish farm boy, an escaped convict who lived under an assumed last name. His knowledge of upper class society was most likely on par with Mrs. Washington's. On further thought, he decided that he probably knew less. He had been to various functions and had held his own, but many of his rougher traits were forgiven because he was a wealthy bachelor who was known to be eccentric. Society would not be so kind to Hazel.

Even with their money, there was no way that she would ever gain admittance to the higher echelons of the upper class. She had no family, no connections, and her money came from his inventions and occasional gambling trips. They had no land, aside from what was under their house, no plantation and no slaves.

The last word stayed in his mind. Slaves. Miss Sanchez had told him that in her world, the Union won the war and the slaves were all freed. He had never owned a slave, nor would he, even if he could. Besides, there was no telling if the North would win the war here. Miss Sanchez came from another world in which a man named Jacob Lincoln was president.

He finished his beef and vegetable soup, poured a cup of tea and eyed his bottle of whiskey. It was empty. He couldn't remember having drunk it, but the bottle didn't lie. In the wee hours of the night, he sometimes had a bit. Not too much. Now, how long had it been since he had purchased that bottle? Had it only been two days?

His equations required his full attention. It was the only way he would ever work out how to get to Miss Sanchez. After a terrifying night six years ago, she and Oren McCullen, the man who had stolen Seamus's peroxide engine designs, had both been swept through a rip in time that Seamus had created to stop McCullen's monstrous machine from destroying New Orleans. He had taken readings at the site, so many readings, and he knew that they had gone to the year 1961. He had even narrowed it down to the middle part of June of that year.

After nearly seven years, he had only managed to make a few time rips into years closer to his own. The farthest he had ever managed was 1939. He had not stepped through the rip, as that would have been foolish, but he took readings. Pages and pages of readings. Leather journals packed a bookshelf on one wall, and boxes filled with papers stood to one side.

Oren McCullen had caused numerous tiny time rips throughout New Orleans. They were mostly stable. But every few weeks Seamus and Hazel made a circuit around the city with their equipment to ensure they were closed. When the rips passed a mathematical instability threshold which Seamus had determined, the two of them reclosed the doorways.

He wondered how long it could continue. As long as he was alive, he could reclose the rips. And Hazel was highly intelligent and could already handle most of them on her own. But years from now when Hazel was dead, what then? Perhaps she could train an assistant. The safety of the city and the other versions of New Orleans in other worlds depended on it.

He ran his hands through his black hair, not caring that the action would make it stick out even more than usual. The whole situation was impossible. The equations to take him farther into the future, toward 1961, were simply not solvable. Perhaps he should begin again and get a fresh perspective. Pulling out a sheet of paper, he licked the tip of his pencil and set to figuring.

CHAPTER 2

December 24, 1863
New Orleans, Louisiana

HAZEL DUBOIS ENTERED AUGUSTUS'S MUSIC Shop through the alleyway door, using the key Mr. Augustus himself had given her two years earlier. The place was warm, but she didn't remove her shawl or bonnet, as she wouldn't be staying long.

"Mr. Augustus!" she called. Then she noticed the line of light under the door of the small office. It opened off the room that Mr. Augustus used for storing and repairing instruments. "It's Hazel!"

"Come on back!" Mr. Augustus called, and Hazel pushed open the office door.

The man was bent over the desk, sorting through a stack of papers. He turned his slanted green eyes to her. His hair was still the same mixture of gray and orange that it had been when she had first met him and his snub-nose and round face gave him an elfin appearance. He was a stocky man with short fingers, but he could play every instrument in the shop well.

"I apologize, Miss Dubois. But I won't have your pay for another few days."

"I didn't come for my pay," said Hazel. She didn't need the small salary that he paid her, and so did not mind that Mr. Augustus was late with it. It was not the first time.

After she had been forced to return to New Orleans

when the war had started, she had visited Mr. Augustus and through him, found employment teaching violin and viola to pupils whose parents could afford the lessons. It was not the first time she and Mr. Augustus had met. She was never sure if he had recognized that the young woman offering to teach lessons was the same boy who had represented Mr. Augustus's music business at the steamboat festival or offered to sweep his shop and make deliveries. Mr. Augustus had never mentioned it, and she certainly never would.

She enjoyed playing violin, and liked helping youngsters learn to love the instrument as much as she did. It kept her occupied, so the money was not critical. She also taught both alto and tenor viola and was fairly competent on the cello, though she did not enjoy it as much as she did the smaller stringed instruments.

"If you didn't come for your pay, why aren't you at home? It's Christmas Eve."

"I wanted to bring you your Christmas present," she said and pulled a few papers from her handbag. They were the sheet music to two new musical pieces, "When Johnny Comes Marching Home" and "Oh My Darling, Clementine." They weren't classical, but Mr. Augustus loved all music, and Hazel was fairly sure that he had not heard these new pieces.

Mr. Augustus took the pages. She knew that, like herself, he could hear the music in his mind as he read it, and she waited for him to finish.

"Delightful," he said, looking up from the pages. "Sad music for sad times." But he did not look sad, but rather wistful.

Hazel had not thought that "When Johnny Comes Marching Home" was a sad song. It was all about how Johnny's town would celebrate his safe return at the end of the war. But then, there were many soldiers who would not return home, or would return maimed. For every Johnny who came home, how many others would not?

"I have something for you as well," said Mr. Augustus. "I got some new horsehair bowstrings. The Italian ones."

"They came?"

"I only managed to get a few, but one of them is yours."

"I couldn't. You need to sell it."

"I ordered an extra specifically for you, and I'm not even sure I can sell the other ones."

Hazel hesitated while Mr. Augustus went into the storage room. The shop was struggling, and she didn't want to take inventory, even as a gift. But she also didn't wish to insult Mr. Augustus. He was sensitive about rejected gifts. He returned with a length of horsehair and held it up for her inspection.

"It's beautiful," she said. The mixture of hairs included both black and white, all of them straight and strong.

"They're from Mongolian stallions, and the dealer in Italy is reputable. I noticed that your current bow needs re-hairing. That violin of yours is so fine, and it deserves a bow that equals it."

A man named Neil Grey had given her a beautiful violin and matching bow when she was eleven. Her wicked uncle had destroyed the violin that her father had given her before he died, and she was distraught at its loss. Mr. Grey was a time traveler from a time close to that of Miss Sanchez and had only appeared around the same time she had, vanishing with as little fanfare as he had come. Mr. Grey had been confident that the Professor would figure out a way to make a functional device that would allow them to travel through time, but it had not happened yet and he had been working for six long years.

She thought about Mr. Grey now and then. He had been in his forties, as near as she could guess, a man in a long black duster who was of medium height and build and who wasn't physically remarkable in any way. But he was intelligent and resourceful, and he had taken a special interest in her. He had given her the violin because they would be good friends in her future and his past.

"Thank you," said Hazel, winding the horsehair into a loose circle and wrapping it in a piece tissue paper from a shelf above the worktable before putting it into her bag.

"You're more than welcome. Although, I don't know how much you'll get to play it once you're a married woman." Mr. Augustus chuckled when he caught her shocked look. "I'm not so old that I don't know what a young man in love looks like. Your young man is going to ask you to marry him, mark my words."

"I'm not sure," she muttered. "Well, Happy Christmas!" She hurried toward the door, decidedly uncomfortable with Mr. Augustus speculating about her marriage prospects.

"Happy Christmas to you also!" called Mr. Augustus after her.

Hazel hailed a hansom cab and gave the driver her home address on St. Charles Street. As the horse clopped down the street, she thought of Mr. Wesley Ross. They had been courting for six months, and she liked him. They had been friends, and then the friendship had changed into something more. He was the son of an ink manufacturer and his family's fortune was new and was earned in trade. Economically and socially, they were a good match. He was kind, honest and earnest. She enjoyed his company. And yet, she was terrified that Mr. Augustus might be correct and that Mr. Ross might propose marriage. She would be eighteen in two weeks, old enough to marry, certainly. And though she liked Mr. Ross, how could she know if she should spend her life with him? Practically speaking, she supposed the wise course would be to marry him, but perhaps she ought to wait and think it over more. She wasn't sure.

The cab passed Jackson Square where St. Louis Cathedral stood white and magnificent against the pearl gray December sky. The cathedral would not have an automaton display on Christmas day as in years past. On some holy days, Ash Wednesday, Easter and Christmas, the cathedral became a gathering place for the citizens of New Orleans. The cutout doors on the front of the cathedral parted and life-sized automatons slid out on tracks to reenact religious scenes to the delight of the crowds. The Professor worked with one of the local monks to create the automatons, and when she was younger, he even let her assist them.

Hazel hadn't watched an automaton display since the Union army had begun their occupation of New Orleans in early May of 1862. The prevailing thought among the Union military was that any large gathering would give the residents of New Orleans a rallying place which might lead to disturbance and rebellion. They might be correct, but Hazel wished that they would allow a display this year. If nothing else, it would give the Professor something to occupy his time other than working on finding Miss Sanchez.

The city had rebuilt itself after Oren McCullen's six-legged machine had destroyed so many buildings. But though the Union occupation had left the city architecturally unharmed, the war had left its heart broken and its people hurting. Even now, she knew she should get home before dark, as soldiers and other men were likely to accost a young woman alone.

This evening, there weren't any steam carriages traveling the streets with her. Only the very wealthy could afford them, and those families were already at their homes, feasting on duck and pheasant and opening lavish gifts. The Professor could have built a steam carriage for the two of them to use, but it would require a driver. The only full-time employee they had was Mrs. Washington. They also had a gardener and a laundress who each came once a week and a girl who came to help Mrs. Washington clean the house. As a rule, the Professor liked privacy. He did not want to risk anyone but Mrs. Washington knowing about his time experiments, and if Hazel's guess was right, he was never entirely comfortable hiring help at all.

The Professor had grown up as a poor farmer's son in Ireland and had killed his sister's husband. The brute had it coming after beating the Professor's older sister and killing the child she was carrying, but that didn't matter to the law, and the Professor had been imprisoned. He was a young man then, and his cellmate was Oren McCullen, who was also mechanically inclined. The two of them worked together in the prison and later escaped while being transported to New Zealand. They had made a home in New Orleans and Seamus Doyle had become Seamus Connor. The pair of them obtained professorships at Tulane and while McCullen had pursued fortune and power, the Professor had sought a quieter life.

Their friendship had come to an end when McCullen had stolen the Professor's peroxide engine designs, had improved upon them and had sold machines with these new and powerful engines, making himself very wealthy. The only problem was that the engines were dangerous. They sometimes exploded. And perhaps even worse, they punctured holes between universes, using matter from other worlds as a catalyst to power themselves. Thus, New Orleans was dotted with time rips which required monitoring lest people like Miss Sanchez accidentally pass through. Other rips had been caused by the Professor, and those needed monitoring as well.

Hazel maneuvered her hoop skirt to exit the cab and paid the driver. She pushed open the iron front gate and went up the brick walk of the house she shared with the Professor. Compared to the modest house where she had grown up outside of New Orleans, their Garden District home was grand. It was painted white with a dark green door and matching shutters. Two galleries ran along the front of the house, supported by white columns with tendrils of ivy winding up their sides.

The long windows were closed now to keep in the warmth, but in summer, all of them would be open and the humid, fragrant air would pour through the house like a sweet fog. At night, her bedroom curtains would billow out and in and she would lie in bed, inhaling the sweet scent of the night-blooming jasmine that grew outside her window.

It was almost supper time, and Mrs. Washington was with her own family for Christmas Eve. Hazel found a plate of cold roast chicken that Mrs. Washington had left for them and sliced off pieces to make two sandwiches. Hazel could have cooked a proper Christmas Eve supper for them both, but it was only the two of them and the Professor didn't care about such things. She supposed he was in his laboratory. He seldom left it.

The years since Miss Sanchez and Oren McCullen had slipped from 1857 through the time rip into the twentieth century had been hard on the Professor. He blamed himself for Miss Sanchez being brought to their world in the first place, and he blamed himself for losing her. He was not a naturally responsible man, often forgetting to pay bills or take care of mundane tasks, but Hazel knew that the weight of his duty to Miss Sanchez pressed heavily upon him.

She brought the sandwich and a glass of water up to the Professor, setting it on an old stool in the corner where she used to sit with him when she was younger. He muttered a thank you and she left to eat her supper alone in the kitchen.

The Professor was a man obsessed. Her schoolmates and people around town called him the Mad Irishman, usually mocking but sometimes with a touch of admiration. He was a brilliant man, known for his inventions and his exceptional luck at gambling, but also for his reclusiveness and eccentricity. Long ago, Mrs. Washington had explained to Hazel that the Professor's focus on his work did not mean that he didn't care for her. The housekeeper felt sorry for her, an orphan, one of many on the streets of

New Orleans. Part of Hazel hated the pity, but she liked having Mrs. Washington's motherly care.

Once in her bedroom, she took off her shoes and put on a more comfortable dress without a hoop skirt. She would only be spending time around the house and perhaps opening gifts with the Professor later that night.

On her dresser sat a tiny black mechanical jackal. The Professor had long ago confiscated the tiny engine inside that had not only made the creature's eyes glow green and its head nod up and down, but had been part of a plan to rip many holes in time and send energy for McCullen's monstrous machine. Now, the jackal was little more than a hollow figurine, but she kept it anyway. Aside from the beautiful violin, it was the only other thing Neil Grey had given her.

That and a promise to return on her eighteenth birthday.

CHAPTER 3

February 23, 1857
Tuscaloosa, Alabama

N
EIL GREY SHOVED HIS HANDS into his coat pockets and kept his eyes low as he walked down the center aisle of the train on its way north to Birmingham. He had purchased his outfit, a loose gray coat, plain wool trousers, linen shirt and top hat at a secondhand shop in Tuscaloosa. He had stuffed pieces of cloth into the toes of his new shoes, as people in this world had feet not unlike those of apes, with large big toes growing out sideways from the balls of their feet. Their feet were so dexterous that they could almost be used as hands. No one in polite society would ever do such a thing, of course, but it was something he had to keep in mind: never allow anyone to see him barefoot.

There were minor differences like this between different worlds. In some, people's eye colors were much lighter than in his world where his medium brown eyes were considered typical. In another world, people had no canine teeth. These differences between worlds were part of the fun of his job, as were the food, the landscapes, the technologies and the people. He tried to keep these things in mind in the quieter moments when he questioned his work.

"Pardon me," he murmured to a man blocking his way. The man noticed him and moved aside.

Neil knew that he moved almost silently and he was

easy to miss, but sometimes it was inconvenient. Most people didn't feel him come up behind them or notice him unless he spoke to them. Typically, this worked to his advantage, as did his appearance. From his own time in the mid 1990s throughout every time and world he had visited, a man with his build and presence drew no attention and his sort of ordinary face was easy to forget.

He had boarded in Tuscaloosa and would leave the train at the next stop in Birmingham. It was a short trip, and there was no reason for him to stay on the train any longer unless something in his plan went awry. He had no luggage and carried only two items in his coat pockets. One was a billfold with enough currency from this era to pay for expenses. The other was a tiny syringe, no longer than his finger. It was from the twenty-second century, and a safety cap covered the small injection pad. A few milliliters of transparent fluid waited inside.

He reached the dining car and took a moment to have a look around from the doorway. Three barstools were bolted to the floor in front of a long countertop. Regular tables ran along the wall, a few of them occupied by passengers having their breakfasts of pastries or soft-boiled eggs. Rose-colored curtains swayed over the windows as the green and yellow landscape flew by. The tables were real wood, not the hybrid plastic materials that things were made of in his own time, and the cups and plates were real ceramic, not safety plastic. The whole place felt warm and homey and smelled like polished wood and coffee. Delightful.

Though he was here to do an unpleasant job, there were always a few things that were enjoyable on any job, and a trip on a train could be one. The Civil War was still four years away, so travel between the South and North was easy. There was peace, for now.

He spotted the man he had been sent to find, Andrew Dubois, and took a seat at the table behind him.

"May I get you anything?" asked a man in a waiter's uniform.

"Just a coffee, please," Neil said. And then, as an afterthought, "and a newspaper."

He enjoyed the innumerable ways he could compare this time to his own. The land was different. There were no highways, no shopping malls, no stadiums or skyscrapers. Just huge, open expanses of land. He had vague memories of attending school, and knew that people of this time period thought that the land's resources were inexhaustible, that the space was unlimited. He understood now. Here were these people, on this luxurious modern conveyance of a train, taking only days to traverse a continent. It was a little miracle to them.

And here he sat, a twenty-year-old man who had soared through the sky in impossibly heavy planes, had sailed the seas in ships yet unimagined and had traveled through time itself. And now, he was on a train in 1857 having coffee. It almost made him smile.

Andrew Dubois sat alone, reading a newspaper and taking occasional bites of a pastry. Neil noticed that he rarely looked out the window. Had he made this journey before, or was his mind elsewhere? It was not his job to speculate, and past experience had taught him not to try to understand or empathize with his targets.

According to Mr. March, this man had robbed numerous families of their land and livelihoods through legal maneuverings involving land ownership disputes. Worse than that, he was a child molester and left unstopped, he would victimize others.

Mr. March knew these things. He was the one who made all of Neil's trips through time possible. He was a thin man with pale skin and white hair who saw it as his duty to use his ability to travel through times and worlds to make those worlds better. Neil was, as Mr. March told him often, his right-hand man. He was the one Mr. March called when there was a hard job, like the removal of a person.

It was always a bad person, a murderer, rapist, someone the world needed removed. And it was only done when the justice system failed or society wasn't advanced enough to protect its people. That was the case with Andrew Dubois. Mr. March could see future possibilities, things that Neil could not, and told him that left alive, Dubois would harm others. There were no laws to protect children in this time. But Mr. March and Neil could take the place of the law.

It was almost time. Mr. Dubois finished his pastry and tossed his white cloth napkin to one side. Neil sipped his coffee and then pulled out a dollar bill. He didn't know how much the coffee and paper would cost, and he had no coins. Let the waiter think he was a big tipper. He did not want to be held up for failing to leave enough money.

Mr. Dubois rose from his table, and Neil kept his eyes on his newspaper as he passed, vaguely registering news of trade disagreements between North and South involving steamships and airships. A few seconds after Mr. Dubois passed him, Neil set down his paper, slipped the dollar under his half-empty coffee cup and followed him.

Andrew Dubois was an ordinary-looking man. In that way, he and Neil were alike. But evil hid behind every sort of face, the young and old, the beautiful and the homely. The teeth or eyes or feet of the people in various worlds might be different, but their capacity for cruelty and viciousness did not vary. It was another constant throughout all times and universes. Mr. March had once said that the human race had a peculiar genius for evil. Neil had to agree.

Mr. Dubois slipped into a seat in the passenger car. The man was already guilty of molesting his niece and a neighbor girl two years before that, but for whatever reason, Mr. March had waited months after the last incident to send Neil to end the man's life. If Neil had been the one to decide, then after one crime the man would be removed. But tampering with time was a delicate dance, and Neil was intelligent enough to know that he didn't have the skill to foresee possible futures or to understand how events wove together to lead to other events.

Mr. March had that skill. He could make paths between times and worlds, but more than that, he understood the interconnections of births, decisions and, of course, deaths. Sometimes they had to wait, and other times they had to act. Mr. March always knew the correct course to take.

Neil took the seat behind Mr. Dubois and looked out the window. He wished he had taken the newspaper from the dining car, but then, taking in some scenery was not such a bad way to pass the time. The man before him had not brought anything to read either, and twenty minutes later, his head tipped sideways, leaning against the window frame.

There were a few other people in the car, but most were reading, embroidering or chatting quietly. Neil could feel the people and where their attentions were focused. It was like a sixth sense. Their attention was not on him or Andrew Dubois. A porter passed through the car and out the back. A woman with a young boy hurried in the opposite direction. They were all caught up in their own lives.

He drew the syringe from his pocket and removed the safety cap from the administration pad. The device was small and completely anachronistic. The fluid within was deadly, but this particular type had a time release of approximately twelve to fourteen hours. He had used other types of drugs in his jobs, but he wanted to be long gone by the time Mr. Dubois's body was discovered.

He thumbed back the plastic safety cover that protected the trigger button. Careful not to touch the administration pad, he moved the syringe around the side of Mr. Dubois's seat. The tiny pad was no larger than a dime, white, sterile and as soft as the sole of a kitten's paw. Through it, the drug would pass through Mr. Dubois's skin and into his bloodstream, leaving no mark and causing no pain.

The drug was illegal in its own time, naturally. And in the twenty-second century, forensic scientists could identify the drug in autopsies. But here, it was undetectable.

He pressed the pad gently, so gently, like a kiss, against the side of Mr. Dubois's neck and pressed the little button. Soundlessly, the drug entered the man's system, and Neil placed the cover back over the syringe's pad. He would take the used device with him, leaving nothing for even the garbage collector to find.

An hour later, when the conductor announced the Birmingham stop, Mr. Dubois stirred and woke, but then settled back into sleep. By midnight, he would have a heart attack, or what would pass for one, and die.

The train hissed to a stop and Neil stepped out onto the covered platform where families and friends embraced and greeted each other. He had no such people, in this world or any other, except, perhaps, for Mr. March who would be meeting him in two hours. A cool wind whipped through the crowd and people grabbed their hats and pulled their coats tighter.

Neil did what he always did. He kept his eyes down and passed through the crowd.

CHAPTER 4

December 24, 1863
New Orleans, Louisiana

"W HAT IS IT?" SEAMUS GROWLED, not bothering to turn toward the laboratory doorway.

"It's Christmas Eve," said Hazel. "Did you want to come downstairs and open presents?"

"Presents?" muttered Seamus, looking up from his papers and blinking. Yes, it was Christmas Eve. What time was it, anyway? He glanced at the clock. Eight fifteen in the evening. "Aw, Hazel, I'm sorry, but I didn't get you anything. I was going to get out earlier today, but I forgot."

"It's nothing," said Hazel airily.

"I got caught up ..." he said, but he felt like a fool. What imbecile forgot Christmas?

"I have a fire started in the front parlor. And I already got a fine present from Mr. Augustus—new horsehair for my bow."

He should have bought her some new rosin, or new sheet music or some gloves or something, but he thought he had gotten closer today, closer to solving the equations. He followed her downstairs where she had a cheerful fire crackling away in the fireplace. A few packages sat in a neat pile on the center table, and Seamus remembered other Christmases, when Hazel was younger, and she'd plop herself into the stuffed chair and fold her hands in her lap, trying to be patient.

Today, she arranged her skirts and seated herself gracefully in that same stuffed chair. She was on the short side for a woman, with a petite frame, and her brown eyes twinkled with pleasure as he took his seat across from her.

He was glad she was enjoying herself, but for his part, Christmas always made him feel gloomy. His family was in Ireland: his mother and father, brothers and sisters, nieces and nephews. He would never see them again. For him to reveal his whereabouts to them would bring trouble to them and arrest for him. They had to believe he was dead, for all their sakes. Sitting in their front parlor, he felt like his Christmas was a shadow of what Christmases were like in other houses with puddings and punch and scores of children scampering about.

"What is it?" asked Hazel. "You look sad."

"Not at all," he said, forcing himself to brighten. "It's Christmas, and here we are, with comforts and fine company. In fact, I might even make us hot chocolate later."

"Do you mean it?" Hazel laughed.

He hadn't made her hot chocolate since she was a girl, but at that moment, he decided he would do it that night.

"Certainly. Why not?"

He thought of that little girl, a frightened slip of a thing, distrustful but with a touching optimism that her situation would improve. He had liked her when she was Henry and had run short errands for him. But when they had discovered that Henry was a female, he had felt more protective of her. A little girl, even a tough and scrappy one, should not have to live on the streets.

Her mouse-brown hair was no longer short and wild, but was parted down the middle, smooth on top and caught up at the back of her neck in the style that many of the young women wore. Her railroad cap and scruffy trousers were replaced with a high-collared blue dress and when she had come back from the Boston Women's Conservatory, she had carried herself differently.

Perhaps this was how fathers felt, watching their children grow up. Seamus was thirty-one years old, old enough to be married with children. But he had not married, and though Hazel was only fourteen years his junior, she was as close as he thought he would ever get to having a daughter.

She handed him the first gift, a new lapel pin from Mrs. Washington. Then she unwrapped an embroidered bookmark that Mrs. Washington had made for her. On the table sat a small red box tied with a gold bow.

"Who is that one from?"

"It's from Mr. Ross."

Seamus thought it was an expensive-looking package, and he had not even seen the contents yet. Hazel unwrapped it and lifted a silver bracelet from inside, set with nine dangling pearls that quivered in the firelight. Both of them looked at it in astonishment as it hung from her hand. The gift was extravagant, more extravagant than one given from a young man to a girl he fancied. It was the sort of gift one gave to a fiancée. Or a wife.

"He's going to ask you to marry him," Seamus said softly.

"No," said Hazel, setting the bracelet in the open box on the table between them.

"It's too expensive a gift for a mere admirer."

"He hasn't asked, and I haven't accepted."

"But would you accept him if he did?"

Hazel stood and walked out, her footsteps fading down the hall. Seamus considered leaving her alone to her thoughts. It's what he would have wanted. But Mrs. Washington wasn't there, and it was only the two of them in the big, dark house. The bracelet rested gleaming in its box, next to the long, thin box holding whatever Hazel had gotten for him. She had wanted to save his gift for last.

He found her in the kitchen, standing in the open doorway to the backyard, the cold winter air blowing her skirts. She was looking upward, at the sky, and was leaning forward slightly as if she was a bird about to fly off into the night.

"Going somewhere?" Seamus asked.

"I want to take a walk. I need some air. To clear my head."

"I'll go with you."

"It's foolish. I know I can't run to get away from things. That only worked when I was a girl."

"It brought you here, so perhaps it wasn't so foolish after all."

"Look at the two of us," she slouched against the door frame. It was unladylike and when she rubbed her eye with the heel of her hand, he saw the little girl who came to the back door, dressed as a boy, bearing letters or packages for him. "The two of us ran, didn't we?" she said. "Ran from where we came from, from troubles and now here we are, neither of us knowing what we ought to do."

He wasn't sure what she meant. He knew what he needed to do: find a way to get Miss Sanchez home, look after Hazel. It wasn't complicated. But then, he wasn't a young woman being courted.

"Do you love him?" he asked, moving beside her to look out into the night. The sky was cloudless and clear, the stars sharp and white.

"I like him," she said. "Mr. Ross is a good man and a good friend. He would make a good husband. And let's be honest, Professor. I'm no beauty."

"You're very pretty."

"You say that because you love me. You can't see me objectively. I'm no beauty. I know it. It was painful when I was younger, to know that I would never be beautiful. But I am at peace with the idea now."

"You are too hard on yourself."

"I am trying to be realistic. I am thinking of my marriage prospects, as any young woman of my station should do. What are the odds of me having a better offer from a better man? Slim."

"You sound like a spinster, steeling herself for a marriage of necessity. You are too young to be so cynical," he said.

"But you must have thought of it as well. You have cared for me for all these years, educated me, housed me. Surely you have thought of it."

"Hazel!" He looked her full in the face. "You don't need to marry anyone if you don't want to. You can stay here forever, be a spinster, marry at fifty, never marry at all. I don't care."

"But wouldn't you rather see me off?"

"The only way I would be pleased to see you go is all smiles, leaving on your wedding day with a man you loved. You need not leave for my sake."

"You aren't weary of supporting me? It's been so long, and you're not blood kin and I'm nothing but a burden to you." Tears stood in her eyes, glittering in the soft light.

"My sweet lass," he said, touching her cheek. He could count on one hand the times he had seen her cry. She was strong, for a female. "You're no burden to me. You're my joy and delight. Without you, this house would be a dank old prison. You've kept me sane these years."

She embraced him then, and rested her head against his chest. He was a tall man, six feet and three inches, and she would never grow any bigger than she was now. She would always be his wee lass, his precious girl. He placed a kiss on the top of her head. Then, she released him and they moved into the kitchen so she could shut the door.

"Do you still want some hot chocolate?" he asked.

She nodded. "There's still time for that, before midnight Mass."

"Oh, I'd forgotten about that."

"I thought you might have. You make the chocolate and I'll get your present."

While the milk heated, he opened the box.

"A new set of pencils," he said. They were of excellent quality with leads that would make clear, dark lines.

"I thought you could use them with all the figuring you do."

"Thank you."

She stood on her toes and kissed him softly on the cheek. "Happy Christmas, Professor."

"Happy Christmas."

Seamus awoke in the night and he fumbled in the dark to find the gas lamp that sat on his bedside table. He had dreamt it. The equation and the solution.

There were an uncountable number of mathematical curves that satisfied the known boundary conditions to the problem of time travel, but only a finite number were elliptical. He had only just realized that any solution *must* be elliptical. And finitely many curves just might be calculable.

He lit the lamp with trembling fingers.

The numbers had floated before him in his dream, touching one another, forming new strings, revealing their secrets. Barefoot and in his nightshirt, he sorted through the things on his bedroom desk, found Hazel's pencils, pulled one from the box and made notes, desperate to capture everything before his sleep-clouded mind cleared and he couldn't remember anything. When he was done, he paused and looked over the numbers.

He had it. He had a way to find Felicia Sanchez.

CHAPTER 5

May 24, 1982
Las Vegas, Nevada

THE BRUTAL LAS VEGAS HEAT hit Neil Grey like a wave as he stepped out of the office building where Mr. March still sat three floors up. As Neil walked down the sidewalk, he stuffed his top hat into a trash can. He stopped at a phone booth to look up a thrift shop in the phone book and after calling them and getting directions, he headed off.

With the money Mr. March had provided for him, he would buy some less anachronistic clothing. He occasionally purchased brand new clothing for jobs, but he found that people seemed to notice him more when he did. He was sure they themselves had no idea why. Used clothing made him less conspicuous and the trick was to find something that looked worn, but also fit with the time he was visiting.

He found the thrift shop and pulled open the glass door. The interior smelled musty, like old cigarettes and dust, of attics and garages, aging newspapers and mothballs. He sorted through the men's clothing racks, looking for something to wear that wasn't some polyester nightmare or something a grandfather would wear. Along the back wall of the shop sat furniture, boxes of toys and other non-clothing items. A gold sunburst clock hung on the wall next to a landscape painting of a sea coast. On one shelf sat a metal Bionic Woman lunch box, a set of ceramic praying hands and a ship in a bottle. The last item was small, no larger than a soda bottle from a vending machine. The glass was clear and smooth, and the dragon-headed Viking ship inside was incredibly small.

This could be fun. He liked visiting times far different from his own, but traveling within his own lifetime could be interesting as well. He would only be seven years old this year, living in California. And now, he was twenty and could look at things with new eyes. He left the clothing area and browsed the books, Reader's Digests, eight-track tapes and other items, things he had vague childhood memories of, or no memories at all. But here they were, these artifacts of a time not so long before his own. In a century, they would be antique treasures, but now they were just junk.

A blond man in his fifties wearing a tweed jacket and blue jeans flipped through a box of records, pulling out a few and then sliding them back in. He moved on to look at the shelves, and paused at the ship in a bottle. Neil watched as the man leaned forward, examining the interior, and then jerked back.

"Holy hell," muttered the man.

"What?" asked Neil.

"Monkeys," said the man with a grin. He picked up the bottle and headed to the cash register.

Well, it takes all kinds, Neil thought. He returned to the men's clothing section and found a pair of blue jeans and a white polo shirt. He would keep his shoes. Though out of fashion, they would serve.

After changing in the back of the shop, he found a homeless man down the street and offered him his clothing from 1857. The pants and shirt were not too bad and a coat was a coat, after all. Nights in the desert could get cold. Neil also gave him a twenty-dollar bill and walked the few final blocks to the famous Las Vegas strip.

It was still daylight, so the strip was not illuminated in all its glory. The May sun was harsh, and he was soon damp with sweat. The Rabbit's Foot Hotel and Casino was one of the older establishments, opening in the 1950s. Now, according to Mr. March, it was barely clearing expenses. It was 1982, and Neil knew that in 1997, this casino would be purchased, torn down and replaced by the Bellagio with its dancing fountains. But for now, the Rabbit's Foot's neon sign blinked out front, advertising its winning slots and titillating shows while a few guests moved in and out through the sliding glass doors.

He crossed the street, admiring the long, boxy Lincoln Continental and the white Oldsmobile Cutlass Supreme idling at the stoplight. He hadn't seen either car in years. He supposed if he could turn on a radio, he would hear tunes he had forgotten too.

It was strange. Some of his childhood memories were clear, but most were hazy, or he only had an impression, like a set of information about the past. Very few memories were distinct. There were memories of various foster care families, and then, when he was older, Mr. March. It was only the last three years or so that were plain in his mind, but he supposed that was what it was like with childhood. Memories were hazy.

The lobby of the Rabbit's Foot stank of cigarette smoke, but at least it was cooler inside. For a moment, Neil worried that he might be asked for his identification. He wasn't twenty-one, and so could not legally be in the casino. And even if he was old enough, he did not have any identification to prove it. But no one asked and he followed the signs to the back where women in skimpy outfits performed their stage show, Girls of the Wild West. A bar ran along the back of the room, and small, round tables filled the rest of the floor space. Most of them were occupied by individual men, although there were a few couples.

A standing sign informed him that a show would begin in fifteen minutes and Neil ordered a rum and Coke. His target wasn't here yet, but according to his profile, he would be.

Rick Gallo was a murderer. He ran the Girls of the Wild West show, which employed sixteen women ranging in age from eighteen to twenty-seven. Some were runaways or locals trying to earn money to leave town, some were hoping that this would be a first step to a career on the stage. And some of them, three to be exact, had been murdered.

The Las Vegas desert was large and hard to search. A body could be buried anywhere in its thousands of square miles and would never be found. Especially in times like these, without global satellite monitoring or implantable identification, it was nearly impossible to find a body that had been hidden.

And there he was. Rick Gallo came in and sat near the front, setting his cigarette in the indentation on the edge of a black glass ashtray. He was overweight, balding, with a round, red face. Neil watched him, and then the curtain parted.

The rum and Coke was heavy on the rum, which was how he liked it, and the girls were good looking. They played cowgirls and Indians with three blondes in tiny denim shorts singing while shooting at three dark-haired "Indians" who wore fringed vests and brown suede miniskirts. He tried to enjoy himself. He had a nice drink, no one was bothering him and the girls were easy on the eyes.

But he knew that most of them were there for money, not because they enjoyed men leering at them. They were around his age, which made him wonder. He didn't remember much of high school, but he must have had a female friend or two. How would he feel, knowing a friend was doing something like this? He studied a girl with straight black hair, imagining it, but then she pulled off her tiny fringed vest and shook her tasseled breasts, and the thought left his mind.

Rick Gallo was looking over some paperwork now, occasionally glancing at the girls. Neil knew that he had seen all this before. He thought about it. Should he wait, or go forward now? No time like the present.

He took his drink and moved along the edge of the room, plastering a big smile on his face and sitting down across from Mr. Gallo. The man was twirling his pen, pausing to write things now and then. It brought forth another memory in Neil's mind, one of learning coin tricks. Moving the coins from hand to hand, undetected, palming them, doing little flourishes. Something was wrong in the memory, something about the hands, but Mr. Gallo was now looking at him expectantly.

"I'm Neil Grey. I was talking with one of your girls earlier, and she said I should come and find you."

"Yeah? What about?"

"My employer, Michael Gorski, is known for choreographing some of the big shows in Paris, New York and Tokyo. You've heard of him?"

"Can't say as I have," said Mr. Gallo.

Neil lied to him without a qualm. This man had murdered three girls, and he deserved no better. Neil regaled him with tales of his fictional employer who had made barely profitable shows into highly profitable ones. He reached into his pocket, pulled out the syringe and while keeping it out of sight, pulled off the safety cap and pushed back the button cover. He palmed the syringe, like he would a coin, in his left hand.

He gave Rick Gallo a made-up phone number and then stood, his right hand out. Gallo shook it, and Neil moved his left hand to enfold Gallo's hand in both of his own. The gesture was too familiar and intimate for this time and culture, but it didn't matter. He touched the syringe to the back of Gallo's hand, pressing his left thumb to the administration button while keeping the syringe concealed. The job was done.

Today's poison was not a time-release formula. Mr. March had said that Gallo having a heart attack within a few minutes would not be a problem. It was only a matter of time now.

Taking his rum and Coke, Neil returned to his seat for the grand finale which involved the girls marching in a patriotic military display in sequined white bikinis with red, white and blue feathered headdresses. They were safe now, all of them. He felt a little flush of pride. All the beautiful girls would live. They would keep dancing and go on with their lives.

Mr. Gallo fell from his chair, pulling it down with him, and there was a commotion up front. The show was almost over anyway, and two of the girls hurried down to help their boss. The bartender and a waitress soon joined them, and Neil watched. He supposed he should leave, but he didn't. He wasn't done with his drink.

Someone ran to call an ambulance, there was shouting, and the girls on the stage crowded around, whether out of sympathy or curiosity, Neil could not tell. One girl started crying, and she backed away, leaning up against the wall. It was the busty girl with the tassels and straight, black hair who had pulled off her vest.

He had seen her nearly naked, and now, standing in a tiny white bikini, she seemed small and vulnerable. Something about this was wrong, he thought. Her emotion was raw, and now he saw that some of the other dancers were crying or had their hands pressed to their mouths or throats, as if this man was a good friend. Neil approached the black-haired girl.

"Was he your friend?" he asked.

"Mr. Gallo was the best," she said. "He helped us so much." Her eye makeup was a black mess under her eyes and she looked younger up close.

"I heard that he wasn't good to the girls, that he hurt them."

"What?" she said, looking up at him in bewilderment. "No, not Mr. Gallo. He was not like the other guys who run the shows. He was good to us."

This wasn't right. But maybe she didn't know about the three murdered girls. "I heard there were three girls, Clara Barnard, Sally Polanski and Brandy Ito who all disappeared. Rumor had it that he killed them."

It was a very risky thing to say, but it wasn't as if he would be lingering here, and he couldn't afford to beat around the bush. If something was wrong about this job, he needed to know so he could report it to Mr. March.

"I didn't know Clara very well, other than seeing her around. But I know that Sally went to school in Boston and Brandy moved up north with her boyfriend."

No, how could that be? Mr. March couldn't have been wrong. He was never wrong. Mr. Gallo must have lied to the girls to explain the disappearances of their fellow dancers. Naturally, there would be turnover in a show like this. People moved on, and no one would think anything of a girl moving away.

"Have you heard from any of them?" he asked.

"No, but Denise," she pointed to a blonde woman, "shared an apartment with Brandy. They still write to each other."

Denise, upon hearing her name, looked up at them. Neil motioned her over.

"I heard you're friends with Brandy Ito. Is that true?"

"Yeah, we used to room together," said Denise, glancing at the black-haired girl in concern.

"Where is she now, and how long has it been since you heard from her?"

"She's up in Carson City. And I got a letter day before yesterday. Why?"

"No reason," Neil said. "Was Mr. Gallo good to all of you?"

"He was great," said Denise. "Some of the girls, if they can't make rent when they first get here, he loans them money. They have to pay it back, it's not a gift, you understand. And I know what you're thinking about how they pay it back, but that's not how he is. He doesn't make you do anything you don't want to. He's not like some of the other creeps in this business. Why are you asking about those girls anyway?"

"I'm a private investigator. There have been rumors." Let them interpret that however they pleased. But now both women were studying him, which was not to his liking. "Is Mr. Gallo going to be all right?" he asked.

"I saw you talking to him," said the black-haired girl. "What were you talking about?"

The paramedics rushed through the door, and the women both stepped forward to see what they would do. Neil moved away, slipping out into the casino.

Mr. March had the data. He had profiles on people, including Mr. Gallo. There must have been more to this. Maybe he had made a mistake with the names of the girls, and it was other girls he had murdered. Or maybe the letter from Brandy to her roommate was written by Gallo himself, meant to keep anyone from suspecting that the girl was dead. The black-haired girl didn't say that she had regular contact with the other two girls. It was only someone's word that they had happily moved on.

He walked fast through the casino, past the card tables and through the rows of jangling, ringing slot machines until he was outside, blinking in the bright light of day.

CHAPTER 6

December 25, 1863 and June 14, 1961
New Orleans, Louisiana

S EAMUS ROWED THE SMALL BOAT out into the Mississippi and opened the wheeled trunk containing the time-ripping device. The thing was still crude, just a rectangular housing containing its components and a tiny vial of bluish liquid that he had harvested from all of the tiny mechanical Mardi Gras toys Oren had invented. A brass sphere sat on top of the machine, and various knobs, dials and buttons ran along a control panel. Some day, he would like to add a few artistic touches, just to make the machine look nicer, but for now, it just needed to get him to 1961 and back again.

He checked and double-checked the coordinates, turning the appropriate knobs and sliding the panels on the brass sphere to the corresponding locations, just as he had taught Hazel to do. When he was satisfied that the panels were properly configured to amplify and direct the signal and the coordinates were correct, he waited for a synchronicity. Ships had traveled past this location on the Mississippi for centuries, and one, surely, would be passing in 1961.

This location existed at a soft spot, an unstable area of time that he and Hazel monitored regularly to ensure that it remained safely closed. There were a number of such spots throughout New Orleans, caused by the time rips

Oren McCullen had created with his engines. Seamus had created the original rip to 1961 by using some of the power that was intended for McCullen's monstrous machine that had destroyed much of the city. Unable to generate such power again, he was dependent upon the soft spot in time to make a doorway.

After nine torturous minutes, the air shimmered. And then, at the center of the shimmering area, the light changed. It was brighter, which meant that the time on the other side of the doorway must be closer to noon. On this side, it was still morning. He rowed with all his strength, sliding through the opening, and then he pulled in the oars and shut down the device as quickly as he could. He didn't want to take a chance on anyone else coming or going through the time rip.

As he floated, he checked the readings on the time rip: 1961. Excellent. The rip was also unstable on this side, just as it had been in his own time. That meant that the doorway might shift, and without his equipment, it might take years to find a way back. He needed to hurry.

Seamus rowed the tiny boat to the bank, hopped out and, fighting a wave of dizziness and nausea, pulled it the rest of the way onto shore. He latched the wheeled trunk and turned to take in New Orleans in 1961. He had done it!

He felt sick again, as if he might vomit, and he paused for a moment to breathe deeply. His head hurt, and the world tilted and whirled. He fell to his knees, grabbing onto the trunk, and then, when he had recovered, he rose. He remembered that Miss Sanchez had experienced similar symptoms upon her arrival in his world. Well, she had weathered them, and so would he.

He thought of Hazel for a moment, how she would have clapped and been so glad that he had succeeded. But he had to leave her behind. Traveling in this way was dangerous, and he would not risk her safety. Besides, he planned to return to her very soon.

The time machine was heavy, but not unmanageable, and he dragged it up the riverbank to the cement sidewalk. Miss Sanchez had described many things of her world, and although she was from 2015 and this was 1961, he could identify the automobiles, the paved roads and the men without hats. Excellent.

Now, to find Miss Sanchez. He pulled off his bowler, so as to blend in with the locals. He had not come unprepared. In his pocket were a few pieces of gold jewelry, and gold would work as currency, once converted.

He stopped a man. "Excuse me, but where can I trade gold for money?"

"You mean a pawn shop?"

He hesitated. "Yes?"

"Up this street, right on the next and it's on the far corner."

Seamus thanked him and turned to go, almost running into a small woman standing in his way. She smiled at him but did not move aside. She was older, with grey streaked hair and wore loose trousers and leather boots.

"Aren't you going to say hello?" she asked, and when Seamus looked her full in the face, she broke out laughing.

"Hazel?" No. How could it be her? But though age had changed her face, he knew her.

"The very same. May I ask what brings you here?"

"I'm here for Miss Sanchez, of course. Why else would I be here?"

"Just checking. It isn't as if this is the first time you've come through town. Well, for you I suppose it is the first time."

He rubbed his eyes and swallowed. The nausea was intensifying, and he felt dizzy.

"You'll get more used to that," said Hazel. "With time, your body adjusts and you won't feel so bad when you travel."

"I'm glad to hear it," He muttered and tried to swallow. His mouth was dry and the implications of meeting an older Hazel raced through his mind. He wanted to ask her a hundred questions, but he knew his time was limited and he needed to find Miss Sanchez. He took a deep breath. "Do you know where Miss Sanchez is?"

"I do. She's at LSU Medical Center. She and McCullen are both alive, though Miss Sanchez was unconscious for days. I've been posing as her aunt and the doctor says she'll recover."

"Then take me to her. I need to get her back to our time. My time. And then work on getting her back home."

"That's my Professor," she said. "I know how you can be when you get fixated on an idea. I have a car this way."

She led him to a long, lavender automobile with no top. He made a circle around it, and then studied the interior controls.

"It's a Buick Electra, and you can study it later," said Hazel, unlocking the trunk. Seamus put the time machine inside while Hazel slipped into the driver's seat. "Hop in."

He seated himself, and Hazel pulled a safety belt across his lap and latched it. Then she started the car and drove. If he had felt sick before, it was nothing compared to the sensation of barreling down the streets of New Orleans at this pace. The scenery was a sickening blur and the air roared past his ears.

"Do slow down!" he said.

"I'm going the speed limit," she said in an offended tone. "Do you want me to put the top up?"

He leaned forward and held his head in his hands, wondering if he was going to vomit all over the inside of Hazel's automobile, but he felt her reduce their velocity and take turns more slowly. When she stopped the car, he looked up.

"It's our house," he said.

"It's still in my name, well, after some legal maneuvering

40

it is. According to city hall, there have been a number of mothers and daughters going by the same name for the last century. I live here, for now."

"Why did you bring me here? I need to get to the hospital immediately. Miss Sanchez is there."

"And she's receiving the best medical care this time has to offer. I know her doctor, very well, in fact. And he's looking after her."

"That's well and good, but I can't get her home unless I can get both of us back to my time and my laboratory."

Hazel pulled the time machine out of the car and rolled it up the front walk, essentially forcing him to follow her. The house had been repainted, and the plants were different. But it was unmistakably their home.

"And that's where you're wrong," she said. "What you need to do is to take McCullen with you and leave Miss Sanchez here."

"Have you taken leave of your senses?"

"Far from it. Come on in."

He wasn't sure what he ought to do, turn on his heel and find the hospital? He knew where Mercy Hospital was in his world, but not this LSU Medical Center. And Hazel wasn't a flighty or silly person. She would not mislead him. He followed her inside.

"I'll make this fast, seeing as there's not much time," she said. "You came yesterday. A future you. To deliver a time machine. It's in the attic, and Miss Sanchez is going to use it to get back to you in 1863. McCullen, on the other hand, needs to go with you, that is, current you, back to 1863."

He waited for her to go on, but she didn't. "Is that all?" he asked.

"Yes. That's all."

"And how do I know you're correct? How do I know that if I leave Miss Sanchez here, she'll come back?"

"Because in eight minutes, Oren McCullen is going to knock on our front door."

"Show me this machine upstairs."

"No, sir. You know how Neil—Mr. Grey—wouldn't tell us about his time machine but kept insisting that you'd figure out a way to make one? He couldn't show it to you because if you saw it and looked inside, then you'd never invent it. You'd just recreate what you had seen."

"And how is that problematic?"

"Because then the information, the device itself, has no stable origin and its existence forms an unstable time loop. You invent it by imitating what you had already seen, and then see it because you invented it. If you invent it on your own, then the machine has a stable origin."

"So what happens when there's an unstable time loop? How is that so bad?"

"Bad things happen. You know how you and I went around closing up those time rips in New Orleans? That was child's play. Us messing with time destabilizes entire worlds. So we need to be careful and not create any unnecessary instabilities."

She dragged the time machine into the kitchen, which had completely transformed in the last century. There was a white ceramic sink with a shiny spigot, a stove that didn't seem to burn wood and a large rounded white cupboard, five feet tall with a small upper door and a larger lower door. Hazel opened it and pulled out a pitcher. "Would you like some tea?"

"Yes, please," he said, and as she poured tea and added ice cubes, he explored the kitchen. She explained the refrigerator and freezer, showed him the stove and then the telephone. He remembered Miss Sanchez describing things, but seeing them was something else entirely. He wanted to try placing a phone call, but the doorbell rang.

"You ought to get that," said Hazel.

"I'm not going to take McCullen with me, and I'm not leaving Felicia behind, no matter what that lying snake says to me. Do you remember, he wanted a war? He tried to destroy the city. I'm leaving." He went for the time machine, thinking he could take it out the back kitchen door and avoid McCullen.

"Now you listen to me!" Hazel pointed a finger into his chest. She was still small, but the years had not taken anything from her. Instead, age had made her more formidable. "I remember every single thing that McCullen did. I was right there next to you. I did what you said, and we made that time rip and lost Miss Sanchez. And now you listen to me. I've been traveling for a long time, a very long time. And I understand the way instabilities work, and the way to fix them. And I know our personal histories. Miss Sanchez will come to you, I promise."

"How can you be sure?"

"Because I can."

She left the kitchen, and the doorbell rang again. Seamus went to answer it, and just as Hazel had predicted, Oren McCullen, his former friend, partner and cellmate, stood on the doorstep.

"Oren," said Seamus. "Why are you here?"

"Are you going to invite me in?" said McCullen. He was dressed in modern clothing, but he had the tired, puffy-eyed look of someone who had been in the hospital recently. His nose was darkly bruised and a red line on his lip showed that it had been split. For Seamus, six years had passed. For McCullen, it had only been a few days.

"No, you can't come in," said Seamus. "Not until you tell me why you're here."

"I came to find you."

That was strange. "How did you know I'd be here?"

"Either you'd come for Miss Sanchez or you wouldn't. And I know you. You'll move heaven and earth if a woman or a helpless child is involved. I thought you'd show up at the hospital. But then I noticed that this woman was claiming to be Miss Sanchez's aunt, and I knew that couldn't be true. I got her phone number from the hospital. Then I had the telephone operator give me the related address, and lo and behold, it was your old address."

"So this is a social visit?"

"Don't be daft. I'm here because this isn't my world. I fell through that shimmering doorway from my world to yours in 1947, and though I'm closer to my own time here than in your time, this is an entirely different world, so it's no use to me."

"So you came to me for help." Seamus gave him a smug look, happy that, for once, he had the upper hand. His time machine was inside, and here McCullen was, stranded without him.

"I did," said McCullen. "I can help you as well."

Seamus laughed. "Help me? You're here, penniless and homeless in some strange world, and you're going to help me?"

"I know how the little blue vial inside my engines works. I know how to punch holes to other universes and use the matter from there as a catalyst."

"You know how to make engines that explode and make unstable time rips. If you know so much, then invent your own machine and go back to your own world."

"It's what I intended to do, but I'm not currently able to do so."

Seamus knew he was hiding something. McCullen was resilient and resourceful. He took control of situations and turned them to his advantage. If he could make a machine in 1857, then why not in 1961?

"There's something else you're not telling me," Seamus said.

"I had just hoped we could work together."

"No lies, Oren. Or I'll slam this door right in your face. I've no patience for this."

McCullen sighed, and Seamus imagined him in the hospital, injured and alone. He also remembered their time together in Mountjoy Prison, and later years when they shared a laboratory as professors at Tulane University. Whatever they may have shared, it was over, and McCullen was a villain of the blackest kind. Seamus could not forget or forgive.

"Please, Seamus. I came through when I was only twenty. I was in Ireland, at one of Epona's temples. She's our horse goddess. It was a naturally occurring time rip, and I can only assume it closed itself. I tried to get back, but to no avail."

"But if you thought you could find a way to go back home with my machine, why didn't you come to me before?"

"You didn't have a time machine before. You were just an inventor of engines and gadgetry."

Fair enough, Seamus thought. But there had to be something else. Seamus paused, looking at McCullen and then into the distance, not encouraging him to elaborate but simply waiting. He ought to break the man's nose, but his curiosity as to why McCullen had come to him was stronger than his anger.

"And the person who was supposed to fetch me didn't do so," sighed McCullen.

"Person, what person?"

"His name is Mr. March, and he's left me here, stranded in this world for days without coming for me."

"Is he some kind of time traveler too?" Seamus asked.

Seamus thought that time must be getting a wee bit crowded. McCullen had no knowledge of the man, Mr. Neil Grey, who had given Seamus some modest assistance when Miss Sanchez had come into his world. But Seamus had not heard of this March person.

"He's a time traveler, of a sort," said McCullen. Seamus knew he was hiding something, he knew his old partner well enough for that. And he also could tell that McCullen had been humbled. It was killing him to admit to being wrong.

"And?"

"And, he helped with the engine design. He didn't do

it to rip any time holes. It was simply assistance with the blue vials, with the catalyst that made the engines able to produce so much power."

"And this man was supposed to find you and help you?"

"I thought he would. Since he can travel between worlds, he promised me that he'd take me back to my own world, if I wanted to go. But I was having such a grand time in old New Orleans."

"Smashing it up and starting wars."

McCullen opened his hands and shrugged, as if to say, "What of it?"

Seamus continued. "And you thought he'd fetch you when you found yourself here?"

"I did."

"So you were betrayed by someone you trusted, eh? A partner?" Seamus crossed his arms.

"You're enjoying this."

"I have to admit that I am. A little. Yes. You had a person you trusted, and he left you high and dry. You reap what you sow, old friend."

McCullen looked away, and Seamus felt an instant of pity for the man.

"He used me, Seamus."

"Used you. How?"

"To keep an eye on you. And now I understand why. You did it. You made the machine."

All the pleasure that Seamus had felt at McCullen's misfortune evaporated. If this Mr. March person was interested in him, it couldn't be for any good reason.

"Why don't you come inside?" Seamus said.

Once inside, he led McCullen to the kitchen instead of the front parlor, perhaps because it was the only room with which he was familiar. Hazel was nowhere to be seen. They each took a seat at the kitchen table.

"He wants to stop you, you know," said Oren.

The kitchen clock chimed half past noon and Seamus

remembered how little time he had before the time rip might shift.

"I need to get Miss Sanchez back to my time. I don't have time to chat with you. I'm sure Hazel can see that you have something to eat, and then you'll have to go."

"Why are you taking her back to your time? Why not to her own?"

"I haven't found out how to get to other worlds yet. I can only travel in a limited way within my own."

"That is where I can help you. I understand how the power systems work in my engines. You're better with time and space calculations, it seems, since you're here, and I excel at power generation and delivery systems. The two of us, we could do it. We could figure out a way to travel between worlds. Take me back with you."

"Out of the question. Besides, it's been six years in my time. Your company is gone. The manufactory building is being used as a Union barracks. New Orleans is occupied."

"Even more reason for me to find a way back to my own world."

If McCullen wanted to start wars and build terrible machines in his own universe, then Seamus couldn't stop him. And in his home world, McCullen wouldn't have ever spent time in prison. He could return to his old life, perhaps to a life of peace.

"Tell me more about this Mr. March," said Seamus. "Why was he interested in me?"

"Because you were going to learn how to travel like he can. That's all I can figure. He can travel between times and worlds, just like that." He snapped his fingers. "He simply thinks about it. And you, some Irish convict, managed to figure out how to do the same."

"So he had to watch me, waiting for when I'd invent the machine?"

"I didn't know why he wanted you watched. But when I learned that your machine could make doorways in time, I decided that it was the likeliest reason."

"And in trade for watching me, you were willing to take Mr. March's assistance in developing those wretched McCullen engines."

"Of course I was. He wanted to help people, give us a power source that would allow technology to advance at great leaps. It was a humanitarian gesture, helping me. I decided to do a little more with the knowledge, admittedly. All I had to do was tell him what you were up to, which was mainly teaching your classes, drinking, gambling and puttering about in your laboratory. It wasn't until Miss Sanchez arrived that the situation changed."

"I still don't understand why this Mr. March was interested," said Seamus. "If he can already travel between worlds, I'm no use to him."

"I was never sure. I wondered if he meant to kill you, or steal the machine, but seeing as that never happened, I don't know."

"Maybe it was just a distraction to get you to start a war."

"I decided to do that all on my own."

"Did you?" Seamus really wanted to know. The man he had known in prison and with whom he worked at Tulane was not so mad as to start a war. Or was he? Oren's hatred of the English was deep, very deep. And he had never displayed too much concern for others.

"The hexapod was entirely my idea."

"You destroyed half the city with your hexapod, as you call it."

"I didn't kill anyone, and I had good reason to destroy those buildings."

"Spare me your reasons," said Seamus, shooting out of his seat. "You wanted to start a war that would not only involve the Americans, but the Irish people, the English, the French and God help us, the Welsh! Thousands would die."

"We've had this discussion before. The English deserve to be wiped off the map."

"You're mad. Are you aware of that?" Seamus knew he was pacing back and forth across the width of the kitchen, but he didn't care. "Completely and utterly mad."

"I'm as sane as you are."

Seamus snorted and then laughed. "I've spent the last six years of my life locked in my laboratory inventing a time traveling machine. Perhaps you're right. But of the two of us, at least I wasn't used as a cat's paw."

"What do you mean?"

"A cat's paw. It's an old fable. The monkey wanted some chestnuts that were roasting in the hot coals inside the fireplace. So he convinced the cat to get them out for him, promising to share them. The cat reached his paw in and scooped out the chestnuts one by one. And as each chestnut was removed, the monkey gobbled it up. The cat was left with nothing but a burnt paw. He was used by a cleverer creature at great expense to himself."

"Now see here!" McCullen stood up, outraged. He was a proud man, and saying that he had been duped was too much for him to bear. "I wasn't his puppet."

"Then why did he leave you stranded, though he could easily help you? He could take you back to my time or back to your own world where you have no criminal record. And yet, he didn't."

"Understand this. When I meet him again, and I will, there will be a reckoning."

"Now, I might like to see that."

"So you'll take me with you?" asked McCullen.

"Why would I want to?"

"Because without me, you can't ever get Miss Sanchez home."

Miss Sanchez. Felicia. He had worked so hard to find her, and yet he was still unable to get her home. A part of him didn't mind the thought of her being with him forever. He was fond of her. More than that. His feelings went beyond mere fondness. In the cold, dark hours in his laboratory, sometimes he had admitted as much to himself. He loved her. But when the next day dawned and his head cleared, he always reconsidered. The woman had many admirable qualities. She was intelligent, kind and brave. She was also beautiful. Nothing more. There was no need to lose his head with fanciful thoughts. And yet, the night always came again, and the circle of yellow light from his desk lamp felt so small and lonely. Without her, he was bereft. And yet, his duty, his sacred mission was to return her to her own time, far from his own.

And after all this time, he couldn't even accomplish that.

Curse the scoundrel McCullen. He was correct. Though he could travel through time, barely, Seamus still was unable to travel between worlds, no matter how much he had tried to figure it out. Even though he had been the one to create the time rip through which Miss Sanchez had come, he had never been able to recreate the doorway into another world. He needed McCullen, and he despised it. But if McCullen helped him to make such a machine, then he could send McCullen back to his world and be rid of him. Then, he could help Miss Sanchez.

"Very well. I'll take you," Seamus said, "but only if you understand this: It makes us even. You got me out of prison, and I got you out of the twentieth century. Agreed?"

McCullen agreed, though Seamus knew it pained him.

"Now, if you'll give me a moment," said Seamus, "I need to speak with Miss Sanchez's supposed aunt."

McCullen waited in the front hallway and Seamus found Hazel in the library.

"Do you give me your word that Miss Sanchez will find her way back?" he asked her.

She set down the book she was reading. "I do. And it won't be long. Only a few days."

"I'm going to trust you."

"Most likely the smartest thing you'll do all day, you madman."

"Don't you sass me," he said, and then Hazel jumped up and hugged him.

"I'll call you a cab," she said. "And Professor?"

"Yes?"

"It was good to see you again. Real good."

CHAPTER 7

December 25, 1863
New Orleans, Louisiana

HAZEL REREAD THE LETTER FROM the Professor and then sat down in front of the cold, empty fireplace in the library. He had gone to find Miss Sanchez in 1961. And should he not return for a period of one month, all of his assets would become hers.

He might not return.

The address of his solicitor was included. She was his sole heir, and if he did not return, she was to notify Tulane University so she could receive his pension. He asked her to make sure that Mrs. Washington received a yearly stipend upon which to retire when she grew too old to work for Hazel. He also asked that Hazel send some money to his family in Ireland, and he gave their names and the name of the town in which they lived.

She reread the last line:

I assure you that these are merely prudent precautions, as I fully expect to return to you within a few days, as nearly as I can figure.

Hazel crumpled the letter and tossed it into the fireplace, where it sat, white against the blackened bricks and the ashes. She would burn it later. It would not do for anyone to discover the Professor's family's name or whereabouts. She knew his real last name was Doyle, but there were many Doyles in Ireland. There was no need to associate his family with an escaped killer.

And what if the Professor did not return? She would own this big, empty house and have the income from his patents. She would be materially comfortable. And if she chose to marry, it would not be for financial security. She would be an independent woman of modest fortune, a position most women would envy.

The Professor was infuriating, moody and frustrating. And she missed him terribly.

It was Christmas Day, and Mr. Ross would be with his family. She needed to thank him for the silver and pearl bracelet, but she would prefer to do it the next time he called. If she married him, she realized, she would be a part of his family. His parents were pleasant people, and he had two sisters who would then become her sisters. Their children would be her nieces and nephews. And then, when she had children, she would have even more family. The thought had its appeal. It would mean a place to belong and people to belong to.

She spent some time reading, but found it impossible to concentrate. She re-haired her bow and played her violin, playing slow sad songs, and then fast pieces, sawing almost violently at the instrument. Damn the Professor. How could he do this to her, knowing she'd be alone?

She ate sliced cheese with bread for supper, not bothering to heat anything on the stove. It would be too much trouble for one person. She considered calling upon Mrs. Washington to wish her a happy Christmas, but the housekeeper would be enjoying Christmas with her daughter and grandchildren. Hazel would be out of place.

She got ready for bed early, knowing she couldn't sleep, but not knowing what else to do aside from pace through the house like a caged cat. Her mind would not be still and kept returning to the world Miss Sanchez had once described, where white and black people lived together, intermarried and where there were no slaves. She looked out the window into the night sky. That world was where the Professor was now, the world where women could be doctors and a man could walk on the moon.

It was before dawn when she heard the voices. She leapt out of bed, recognizing the Professor's, and ran downstairs. The two men stood in the entryway with a wheeled trunk resting between them. She knew it was the time machine, as she'd seen the thing in all of its stages of development.

The Professor was disheveled, his hair sticking up at all angles, but that was nothing new. What was strange was that he was grinning from ear to ear while standing next to his enemy and adversary, Oren McCullen.

"You're back!" said Hazel. "But how is he here? And where is Miss Sanchez?"

"Miss Sanchez will be coming along in a few days on her own," said the Professor. "McCullen and I are going to figure out how to travel between worlds. He'll be assisting me with the machine."

"I am not your assistant," said McCullen darkly.

"Very well. We're collaborating."

There was an uneasy moment of tension between them, and then they both looked up at her. She was still standing halfway down the stairs in her nightdress.

"So you two will make the machine that will take Miss Sanchez home?" she said, addressing the Professor and ignoring McCullen.

"That's it exactly," said the Professor, who proceeded to drag the trunk up the stairs. She backed against the railing to let him pass.

"And Miss Sanchez is going to get here on her own?"

"Not entirely, but she'll come."

"How do you know this?"

"I have it on good authority." He smiled and winked at her, as if sharing a joke.

"Mr. Grey? He told you?"

"A little birdie."

She wasn't sure what he was insinuating. Had he seen Mr. Grey? The Professor rolled the trunk down the hallway, toward his laboratory.

McCullen followed, but paused beside her. "A pleasure to meet you, Miss Dubois."

She knew McCullen. She had once broken into his house and had hidden in his conservatory, eavesdropping on him and his nefarious planning session with another man. But she knew he had never seen her.

"A pleasure," she said, but too coldly for either of them to mistake it for anything but the required response.

McCullen gave a curt nod and followed the Professor up to his laboratory. She trailed behind.

"Professor?" she said. He turned. "You are never, ever to leave me behind again. Do you understand?"

"It was too dangerous, lass," he said, opening the trunk and pulling out the machine within. "I didn't want to put you in any danger."

"I'm grown now, and I can decide what's too dangerous for myself." She was being too forward, too unfeminine, but she couldn't tell him how frightened she was, or how alone she had felt, especially not in front of McCullen.

"As you say," the Professor said, but he didn't seem to be paying attention to her. McCullen knelt beside the machine, and the Professor started to explain something to him.

Hazel turned to go.

"Oh, and Hazel?" called the Professor. "Could you make us something to eat? I'm famished."

She went to her room to dress. It was not yet dawn, but she would never be able to get back to sleep. The Professor was back, accompanied by that hateful McCullen man. But if the Professor, who had been betrayed by McCullen, felt he was trustworthy, then perhaps she should exercise her Christian charity and give him the benefit of the doubt. Perhaps.

She stopped by the library to take the crumpled letter from the fireplace. In the kitchen, she tossed it into the stove. Then she lit a fire. She could make eggs and there was some leftover sliced ham that she could fry with them. The Professor was back home, and though her mind was in turmoil, she held onto the hope that all would be well.

CHAPTER 8

April 17, 2032
Boston, Massachusetts

NEIL GREY SWIPED HIS FALSIFIED badge at the identification pad at Boston Applied Robotics and once the glass panel of the turnstile slid aside, he passed through and took the elevator to the fourth floor.

This was a floor full of offices, some in cubicles and some along the walls. He knew that Trevor Grant's office was at the far back corner. And he knew where his shared laboratory would be, stretching along the back wall.

The syringe sat in his pocket, along with a slim card, like a credit card from his own time. It allowed him to purchase what he wished. He touched the syringe lightly. Today's formula would kill the victim in four to six hours, enough time for Trevor Grant to get home, have his dinner and be dead before bedtime.

Mr. March had told him about this man. Boston Applied Robotics was a corporation that contracted with the military. They also had a division that worked on independent projects, presumably profitable ones. A company had to weather the years when defense spending was cut and funds were scarce, and the two-pronged approach had served them well. The business was thriving.

He thought of Rick Gallo in Las Vegas. He had palmed the syringe then, like a coin. He stopped in his tracks, and a woman walking behind him almost bumped into him. A memory was troubling him, the memory of the coin tricks he had learned as a teenager. He needed to stop and think for a minute. Turning in to an employee break room, he poured cold water into a cup and drank.

He knew he should go to find his target, but he would only be a few minutes. Why was it that so many of his memories were so indistinct or strange? The memory of the coin trick, it was a little clearer now. The coin was a silver half dollar with John F. Kennedy's profile on it. The trick was a simple one, but the hands—the hands. They were older than his hands, with shorter, hairier fingers and calluses. And yet, in his memory, they were his. He could feel the coolness of the coin, its worn shape and the movement from one hand to the other.

How could this be? How could he feel the coin, see it, remember it, and yet the hands were not his own?

A young woman was watching him while eating a cup of pink yogurt at a break table.

"Are you new?" she asked.

"Yeah," he said, and topped off his glass of water. Then he took the seat across from her, angling his chair so he was not facing her directly and would not seem threatening, even on a subconscious level.

"I'm going to be working with Trevor Grant," he said. "Do you know him?"

"Trevor? Sure. He's nice. You'll like working with him." She spooned yogurt into her mouth. It clung to her lips and she licked them.

"I haven't been briefed on anything yet. What projects is the team working on?"

"Wow, you really are new. They work on implantables. I hope you have a good background in genetics."

That confirmed part of what Mr. March had told him. The military contracts sometimes involved modifications for soldiers, and implantable devices could be a part of that. Trevor Grant was working on a terrible invention, something that, in a decade, would lead to the death of thousands of innocent people. Mr. March had not given him the specifics.

"Tell me about these implantables."

"You'll have to ask Trevor. I'm sure he'll brief you. We're all very proud of his team's work. Exciting stuff."

She stood and tossed her empty yogurt cup into the trash. "Well, good luck, and I'll see you around."

Something was wrong about this. The way the woman had said that the research was exciting was not the way people normally spoke of weapons. Unless she had become dulled to the idea of killing people, or was convinced of the guilt of the enemy and of their well-deserved death. That was possible. Just because she seemed like a nice girl didn't mean that she wasn't hardened inside.

This was a government-funded weapons facility. Neil had no moral opposition to the production of weapons, nor was he particularly bothered by them being used, if necessary, for a nation's protection. But he trusted that when Mr. March said that the thing Trevor Grant was creating would cause the deaths of innocents, it was the truth. At least, he had thought it was the truth.

Neil walked the rest of the way, scanning his badge to enter the long laboratory that was shared by five or six of the researchers. It was empty but for two people: a woman in her sixties and Trevor Grant, who sat at a computer.

Neil smiled easily at both of them. "I'm from network security. We got a virus report from one of your machines." He motioned toward the desktop computer where Mr. Grant was seated. He waited for an instant, allowing the two of them to have the impression that they could refuse him, and then he headed for the machine. "I'll only be a few minutes."

Trevor Grant got up without objection and pulled a stool up to the counter just a few feet from Neil. It would be simple to reach over and touch him with the syringe.

He could pretend to reach for something on the table, or he could shake his hand after pretending to do work on the computer.

Mr. Grant had not bothered to log out of his computer. How trusting people were sometimes. Neil looked over the open documents and then slid them to the side of the screen.

"So, how has your work been going?" asked Neil. "Word has it that you're on to something."

"It is going well," said Trevor Grant. "And if we get the funding, we should have something to show for our efforts by the end of the year."

"What do you think you'll have to show?"

"The leg implantables are still our most popular devices. But the upper body devices are significantly more difficult, especially the hand systems. That's where the big breakthroughs are coming."

How monstrous. To replace a soldier's hands to make him a more effective killer was grotesque. It was no wonder that Mr. March wanted this man stopped. Still, he wanted to be sure. He didn't want to have any doubts later, as he had with Rick Gallo in Las Vegas.

After he had left Las Vegas, he asked Mr. March about it, only to receive assurances that he had removed the right man, and that additional murders had been prevented. Mr. March had waved away his concerns, applauded his devotion to acting in an ethical manner, and sent him on his way.

Neil went through various files, reading as quickly as he could, scanning, opening documents and closing others. There were tables of data, long documents, research logs, so many research logs, some of them dating back years. It was overwhelming, and Neil understood little of what he read. There was a proposal written for upper management. Now, that could be useful. Management types typically needed things broken down into simple, easy to understand tidbits. He opened the file. The top few paragraphs gave a summary of its contents.

It stated that Mr. Grant and his team sought an increase in their department's funding to pay for research on implantable devices. The implantables were to help people who had lost function in their arms and hands. Some of the voluntary test subjects were elderly arthritis sufferers. They made up most of the hand implant recipients. There were others, people who had lost hand or arm function in accidents or from nerve deterioration.

This was no military operation. He remembered that Boston Applied Robotics had two divisions. One was the private, for-profit division and one worked on military contracts. But what if the for-profit division did not exist simply to enrich the stockholders as he had assumed? What if it made something less profitable? Or something profitable but charitable as well?

He kept reading. The proposal stated how much the devices had helped the recipients and how, with practice, they had gained a significant measure of manual dexterity, even to the point of being able to write and feel the touch of a feather on their fingertips.

He read the alphabetical list of recipients, from Rosa Becerro all the way to Dennis Wasserman. They had all received medical implants to help them regain physical function. It listed their birthdays and occupations. These were not soldiers, forced into physical modifications to become better weapons. These were civilians, some as young as fourteen years old.

CHAPTER 9

December 26, 1863
New Orleans, Louisiana

S EAMUS AND OREN MCCULLEN SAT on opposite ends of the table in Seamus's laboratory at Tulane University. Seamus typically preferred to work in his home laboratory, but since McCullen was working with him, he had decided that they were better off on neutral ground. As far as Seamus knew, the university staff was unaware of McCullen's presence, and that was for the best.

Once, years ago, the two of them had blown up most of the building that had housed their shared university laboratory. But that was before McCullen stole his peroxide engine. Seamus still didn't know if he could trust him. Scratch that. He knew he couldn't trust him. McCullen could easily give this Mr. March information about the time machine, steal plans or even kill Seamus in his sleep. But then, he could do the latter whether or not they were working together. For now, it was to both their advantages to act as allies.

At the moment, McCullen was bent over some disassembled parts. He flipped through his notes, pulled out a page, and then wrote something down.

"What is it?" asked McCullen without looking up. He must have felt Seamus watching him.

"It's nothing. I'm just hungry."

McCullen pulled out his pocket watch. "And no wonder.

It's supper time. Let's get something to eat at my old club. I'm certain they'll remember me."

It was as good an idea as any. Seamus didn't want to go home, as they could still get a good amount of work done that night if they stayed late. A quick supper would be ideal.

They took a cab to Bouchard's, the gentlemen's club where McCullen had once been a member. Even though he had been absent for six years, Seamus knew that within one day, McCullen had sent notes to various businesses and personal connections to try to restore his place in New Orleans society. Seamus had not asked, but he was certain that a note to his former bankers would have been among the first McCullen had written. By the end of the week, McCullen would probably have his own place to stay, money and some new mischief up his sleeve.

At Bouchard's, they were taken to McCullen's favorite table. They were only just removing their coats when the host appeared.

"I'm so very sorry, Mr. McCullen," he said. "There must be some misunderstanding."

"What do you mean?"

"Your membership—it has been so long, you understand."

"And I will pay my dues promptly, I assure you." McCullen held out his coat for the man to take, but the host did not oblige.

"But that's not the only issue. There is a small problem. If you would just come with me for a moment."

"We've come for supper," said McCullen. "Surely this can wait."

"I'm afraid not. If you would only come with me."

The club was not crowded, but the few men present were now watching. None of them looked amused or sympathetic. If anything, Seamus thought they appeared hostile, disgusted even, as if they could see that McCullen and he were really nothing but filthy Irish refugees, playing at being a part of the upper crust.

"Oren, why don't we go with the man?" Seamus said.

"I most certainly will not." McCullen took a seat and arranged his napkin in his lap. "Now, a glass of claret, if you would."

The host wrung his hands and looked to Seamus, who he must imagine had more sense.

"Let's step into the back room," muttered Seamus, and the host cast an anxious glance at McCullen before walking beside Seamus.

"Now speak plainly," said Seamus once the door was shut. "Why can't McCullen be here?"

"It was assumed he fled because of the problem with his engine designs."

McCullen, Miss Sanchez and the hexapod machine had all vanished on the night of Mardi Gras in 1857. But even before that, the engines had been dangerous, exploding now and then without warning. Without McCullen to defend his company and arrange for bribes and threats, the police had shut the company down for creating dangerous machinery. The existing engines had been confiscated, and the manufactory building had been left empty until Union soldiers took occupancy.

"But now he's back," said Seamus.

"He isn't exactly the sort of clientele we pride ourselves upon."

"You mean he has no money. I'm sure he'll remedy that soon enough."

"It's not simply a financial matter," said the host. "His name is not uttered kindly, here or elsewhere."

So, McCullen's bad deeds had caught up with him at last. The townsfolk would not have known that it was McCullen who had piloted the hexapod in destroying parts of the city, but once his former company was investigated and his involvement in the explosive engines was revealed, Seamus could understand how he might be ostracized. He had been condemned in absentia, but the verdict was fair. Under other circumstances, Seamus would have been pleased.

"I think I understand," said Seamus.

"Now you, sir, if you yourself wished to become a member, you would be most welcome."

"I'll consider it," said Seamus. "Could I have supper tonight with Mr. McCullen as my guest?"

The host thought it over. "I suppose no one would have an objection to that."

Seamus would explain McCullen's situation to him later, when he wouldn't rant and fume and cause a public scene. He wondered if McCullen's other former connections were rejecting him as well. Perhaps it would not be so simple for him to reestablish himself.

A young woman came through the doors that led to the kitchens. It took a moment to register, but she looked like she had been crying.

"I'm sorry to interrupt," she sniffed, looking up at the host. "But it's urgent." The girl had an Irish accent. Another immigrant girl, working to make a living.

"Later, Noreen," snapped the host. "I'm with a guest."

Bouchard's was an all-male establishment, from the waiters to the hosts. Seamus supposed that women could work in the back, as long as they remained unseen by the male clientele. The club members came to the club to escape wives or simply to be able to discuss business or smoke in peace.

The girl nodded and sniffed. The poor thing, her hands were as red as her nose. She must spend all day scrubbing and cooking.

"It's all right," said Seamus. "What is it you need?"

Noreen's eyes widened when she caught his accent, and she seemed to relax. "My sister didn't come home last night, and my father just sent word that I'm to come home right away to answer questions from the police."

"Didn't come home? Well, where is she?" asked the host.

"If we knew that, then my father wouldn't have called the police. Like I said, she never came home."

"Where was she last seen?" asked Seamus.

"She's a maid at a hotel by the riverbank. We're worried sick about her. What if she was snatched by someone? She's not the only one who has gone missing."

"There have been others?" asked Seamus.

She nodded and sniffed. "Some of the people who work near St. Louis Cathedral and Jackson Square."

"Union soldiers, having a bit of sport," said the host darkly. "Grab a young girl, and she's too ashamed afterwards to return home."

"No," said Noreen. "It's not just young girls. I've heard of two others, an older woman and a man."

"Near the cathedral, you said?" asked Seamus, a dark thought creeping into his mind.

She nodded and her eyes filled with tears. "I don't know what we'll do if we don't find her."

"Where are your people from?" Seamus said gently.

"Ballindooley."

"Ah, County Gallway," said Seamus. "Good people."

"You know of it?"

"I do. How long ago did you come over?"

"Ten years ago. I was just a little girl."

So her family had come just at the end of the potato famine, like countless others.

"Now, you go home to your mother and father," he said. "And don't worry about your work here." He gave a hard look at the host. Noreen also looked warily at the host, but at his nod, she hurried off.

Seamus pulled some bills from his billfold. "That's to give the girl a week off work, you understand? With pay."

The host agreed and Seamus hurried out to the table where McCullen sat, looking sulky.

"We need to go, right now," said Seamus.

"I refuse to leave. I am a legitimate member of this—"

"Never mind that." He dropped his voice. "There have been some disappearances near the river."

"And you think it might be because of the time rips?"

"I do."

"Excellent!" McCullen shot up from his chair. "We can get some valuable readings! We'll go immediately, as soon as we get your equipment from the laboratory."

"Agreed. I hope we can find out what happened to those people."

"Never mind them," said McCullen, walking beside Seamus as they left the club and headed down the street. "If your method of keeping those rips closed is faulty, we're bound to learn something that may help us with the machine."

Seamus was grateful that McCullen hadn't been openly accusatory about his ability to keep the time rips closed. He felt bad enough as it was. He was so sure that he and Hazel had successfully monitored and adjusted the rips to make them safe. He had even asked September Wilde, the colleague and friend of the mysterious Neil Grey, who lived in town. She had told him that he was doing well, and that she had heard no reports of anything amiss. She had also refused to answer any questions about her involvement in the time-traveling group in which she and Neil Grey were both involved. After a few visits ending in nothing but frustration and offers of homemade baked goods, he had ceased visiting her.

After retrieving Seamus's sensory equipment from his laboratory, they hired a cab and rode to the riverfront near Jackson Square. They left the larger sensors on the grass and split up to run the smaller sensors to various points around the square. They had been working for a quarter of an hour when McCullen called Seamus over.

"It's near here," said McCullen. He was at the corner of Jackson Square closest to the Café du Monde, where customers ate pastries and chatted over coffee.

"But this isn't where the largest time rip was," said Seamus. That location was over the river itself, and he had monitored it closely, fearing it would reopen.

"I'm certain. Look." McCullen showed the needles on the handheld device to Seamus, and he was forced to agree. They unpacked the larger sensor array, setting up the receptor devices in a wide arc, facing the location of the presumed unstable time rip. People from the Café du Monde studied them, but it wasn't as if he and McCullen could come in dead of night and do this. If the rips were unstable, it had to be dealt with immediately.

"Flip it," said McCullen to Seamus, who flipped the power switch after checking on a final wire.

They stood shoulder to shoulder to observe the readings on the output panel.

"That's it!" whispered McCullen. "Those readings aren't from this world."

"Are they from yours?" Seamus had the readings from his own world, in 1863 and 1961, but these were different.

"No way to be sure. I wouldn't know what my world's particular readings would look like if I saw them."

"These readings are fresh," said Seamus pointing to one of the dials. "I haven't seen readings like this in years, not since the time rips were new."

"It's like scar tissue," said McCullen. "The old rips are scarred over, not exactly healed, but if they aren't disturbed, they won't break open again. But this—this is a fresh wound breaking open over an old scar."

Seamus rummaged in his bulging pocket for a pencil and a slip of paper and then recorded the readings. McCullen grabbed his shoulder. Seamus looked up to see the air thirty feet in front of them shimmering.

"Did you amplify the signal?" said Seamus. "That could open a doorway!"

"I didn't do a thing. But if we can see through the rip, we can see if it's my world. Or Miss Sanchez's."

Seamus moved closer to the shimmering rip with the handheld sensor. Something flashed past the opening. It was large and white, but a moment later, it was gone. He hurried forward, eager to obtain readings. Perhaps it was a truck or a large automobile. Even a brief look through the rip could yield valuable information.

One moment, the air was shimmering, and the next, the time rip opened wide, revealing an eyeless white head, like that of a giant earthworm. It was at least four feet in diameter, smooth and sickly pale. Then, its mouth opened, but instead of opening at the bottom of the face, it opened in the center, spreading sideways until the head was bisected, becoming a gaping crimson canyon, like a hungry wound.

The air around him slammed Seamus to the ground and he braced himself as he was dragged toward the time rip and that gaping mouth. He wasn't being blown from behind, as with a strong storm wind, but was being pulled, along with the sensors, pieces of gravel from the pathway and hunks of earth and plant life. Things flew into the mouth, but it remained open, waiting as the world was sucked into it.

And then the door shut, the air stilled and he was left, gasping, hatless and covered in dirt on the grass.

"That's another one you owe me," called McCullen. He was kneeling in front of the control panel. The sensors were in disarray, having been knocked down and dragged, but somehow McCullen had managed to close the time rip.

A few of the customers at the Café du Monde had risen and were watching them, but after Seamus dusted himself off, he saw that they had returned to their tables. Yes, there you go. There is nothing out of the ordinary. You did not see anything other than two men with some mechanical devices, and one fell down.

"What in the hell was that thing?" said Seamus.

"It wasn't from my world, that's for certain. Perhaps that's where the missing people went."

Seamus sincerely hoped not, and yet, he knew that McCullen might just be correct.

CHAPTER 10

December 27, 1863
New Orleans, Louisiana

Hazel answered the front door, already knowing who would be on the doorstep.

"Good evening, Miss Dubois. Care for an afternoon out?" said Mr. Wesley Ross. He was a man of medium height, well built with dark blond hair and ruddy cheeks. It was cool outside, and he wore a new wool coat trimmed with thin strips of black satin. Perhaps it had been a Christmas gift. The top hat he held was also new and his shoes were polished. Mr. Ross was a man who took care with his appearance, and in all other aspects of his life, but he usually wasn't quite so fastidious.

"Let me fetch my coat. Where will we be going?" Hazel moved aside to allow him into the front entryway and closed the door.

"I was considering the botanical gardens."

They had visited the botanical gardens the previous May, and Hazel had loved the place. Everything had been alive and fragrant. It had made her feel far from the war and all her troubles.

"That sounds delightful," she said. "Let me get a few things."

She went upstairs, grabbed her handbag, put on her coat and the bracelet Mr. Ross had given her, and told Mrs. Washington where she was going. Then she joined Mr. Ross and took his arm.

Out in front of her house stood his mechanical carriage, trembling slightly as steam puffed from its exhaust pipe. It was shaped similarly to the horse-drawn carriages, with large metal-rimmed wheels and curtained windows along the sides. The driver sat up high in the front, but instead of managing the horses, he operated the accelerator and brake pedals and turned a wheel on a long pole to steer.

The Ross family carriage was black with silver painted accents outside and a royal blue interior. It was not the finest steam carriage in the city, but to own one at all was an accomplishment few families ever achieved.

Mr. Ross handed her into the carriage, and she took the seat facing forward while he took the one across from her. The carriage growled and then lurched forward. Unlike many of the more ostentatious carriages with large windows set low and wide to allow people to see the fortunate passengers, this one had modest windows, and if Hazel sat back, she would not be gaped at by pedestrians. She might be a respectable young woman, but she retained part of her old instinct to remain unseen. There was no sense in making a spectacle of herself.

"Thank you for the bracelet," she said, shifting her arm to let him see that she was wearing it. "It's absolutely beautiful."

"No less than you deserve," he said.

The way he was looking at her made her feel warm inside, but also uneasy. She felt her cheeks flush with heat, and she looked out the window. He loved her. Mr. Augustus and Mrs. Washington and the Professor all thought that he was going to propose marriage. But her eighteenth birthday was still more than a week away, and Mr. Ross still lived in his parents' home. He may love her, but there was still time for her to think sensibly about her future.

They arrived at the botanical gardens. The last time they had come, the plants were lush and in bloom. Today, the place was almost empty, and as they walked arm in arm along the winding gravel pathways, she saw that many of the plants were dormant and the branches of the leafless trees rose gnarled and naked into the air. It was not as lovely as in spring and summer, but still, it was the Christmas season, and Mr. Ross was not only her suitor, but her good friend.

"The business is going well," said Mr. Ross when she inquired. "I have taken over most of the duties my father and uncle have done, but there are still a few things yet to learn. They hope to both retire from their posts this summer."

"So soon? But how will the company get along without them?"

"Well, with me, of course." At her surprised silence, he laughed. "I am capable of running a business, you know."

"Of course, it's just that, well, I suppose I still think of you as being so young."

"I'm nearly three and twenty. My birthday is in May, and they want me to have taken over every duty by then. Of course, both my father and uncle will always be available for consultation."

"It would be a shame to lose all of their wisdom." She must have looked gravely concerned, because he smiled.

"They're retiring, not dying. They'll be around for a few years yet, long enough to see the company prospering under my management. In the areas I've taken over so far, I've managed a seven percent increase in profits."

Talk of profits bored her, but she was proud of Wesley. She knew he had worked hard to learn the business and to make it a success.

"In fact," he continued, "the business is doing so well and prospects are so good, that by summer, I am going to be purchasing my own house. I've already started looking."

"Have you? What neighborhoods are you considering?"

"I was hoping you would help me with that."

"Of course," she said, and then realized what he meant. He was implying that she would assist in choosing a house because she would be living there. Her insides went cold, and then hot.

Did she love Mr. Ross? That was the question, the burning question. Would he make a good husband? Yes. Was he kind, decent and hard working? Would he provide a good home and be a good father? Yes and yes. She would be a fool to let him slip through her fingers.

One of her old school friends, Cassandra, had even said that if Hazel ever tired of Mr. Ross, she should inform her. He was a good prospect in every way.

"Hazel?" he said, and she realized that they had stopped atop a small wooden bridge that arched over a thin stream. The water looked cold and dark below, but the sunlight wavered and played against the submerged rocks in a striking way, and dark tendrils of living plants wavered beneath the surface, like beckoning fingers.

"I need to ask you something," he said. "You know my feelings for you." He touched her cheek, and she looked up into his eyes. She could tell that he was worried, nervous and sincere. He slid his hand down her arm and took both of her hands. She wanted to pull away, to run down the path and keep running. And she remembered the other times she had run, or wanted to run. But she was a grown woman now, and running would not do.

"Hazel, will you marry me?"

At her hesitation and dismayed expression, he added, "Not immediately. I know you are not yet eighteen. And I need to take over the company, purchase a home and get things in order before I can take a wife. Ours would be a long engagement, over a year most likely."

He looked so hopeful, so sweet, and he had been so good to her. He didn't care that she had no family connections and that she wasn't even the daughter of the Professor. She had told him that she was the daughter of country folk, though she had left out the time she had been a runaway. He knew enough of her past to be repelled by it, but he was not. He was a man of integrity, of good humor, and yet, she was terrified.

"I'm not sure," she said. "I'm still young."

"Is there someone else?"

"No! No. No one else. It's simply that the thought of marriage and children still frightens me. I—I'm not sure." Then she had an idea, one that would buy her some time to think things over. "And besides, you're Methodist and I'm Catholic. I need to get a dispensation from the priest in order to marry you. It could take awhile."

"I'll wait," he said. And she knew he would. It was clear that he was disappointed, but he wasn't angry with her. She had never claimed that she loved him, but she thought she might grow to love him, in time. Perhaps she was cold-hearted and romantic love was beyond the scope of her feelings. She wasn't sure.

Later, she undressed for bed, took down her hair and while brushing it, tried to think logically about the marriage offer. The little mechanical jackal sat looking at her with its green jewel eyes.

It was Mr. Grey. She did not have any romantic notions about the man, and he was far, far too old for her. When they had met, she was eleven and he was somewhere in his forties. But she needed to be honest with herself. If it weren't for Mr. Grey and the promise of some other life, would she have accepted Mr. Ross's offer gladly? Yes. Unless some other dashing young man came along and swept her heart away, she would be content with Mr. Ross. Any woman in her position would be.

So that was the crux of it. Mr. Neil Grey had promised to return on January 8, 1864, her eighteenth birthday. And she was waiting for him.

CHAPTER 11

December 27, 1863
New York, New York

"I COULDN'T DO IT," SAID NEIL, dropping two sugar cubes into his coffee. "The man was creating medical implants to help people. He wasn't making weapons implants."

Mr. March sat across from him in the New York coffee house of 1863, a huge change from the polished and sterile establishments of 2032. It was a place with a rough plank floor and bad lighting, but clean cups and decent coffee. It was only six years after he had last been in this time period, and the Civil War was now in full swing.

Neil had allowed Mr. March to take him away from the twenty-first century, presumably to his next job, without telling him that he hadn't killed Trevor Grant. He had feared that Mr. March would do it himself, or somehow force him to do it against his will. It was an odd thought, but he had the feeling that Mr. March could make him do things he didn't want to do. It made a little flame of anger burst to life inside him.

"The medical implants were a front for his true work," said Mr. March, setting down his coffee cup. "It wouldn't do for anyone to know about it. Do you think he would allow some person from their company's network security department to see his work? His real work, that is?"

That might be true, but it still didn't add up. The young

woman in the break room had been pleased with Trevor Grant's work, and the funding request was clear. They had test subjects, many of them, who had benefited from the medical devices.

"Unless I see evidence that the man was making weapons, I'm not going to do the job," said Neil.

"I have the evidence."

"Then give it to me. Let me see it as well."

"Why? Do I need to justify every job to you now? You always trusted me before." Mr. March looked so sad, so disappointed, and though Neil couldn't remember his father, he imagined that this must be how a disappointed father looked at his wayward son. "Look, Neil. Think about that man, Dubois. That was six years ago, and you've saved innocent children. The work you do is good work. You are the hand of justice, the triumph of right over wrong. The justice system fails, society fails, evil men and women go free. But you, you are the counter-balance to that."

"Why don't you do it yourself then, if it's so important." Neil reached into his pocket and withdrew the card with the twenty-first century money on it. To anyone in this time, it would be a strange curiosity, but Mr. March would never allow anyone to have the chance to see it. Neil slid it across the table, and Mr. March took it. It would vanish to the place where the man himself went. And Neil never knew exactly where that was.

"Because I can't do what you do," said Mr. March. "You move silently, you blend. You have a gift. Your kind of justice is not pompous and does not wear either a mask or a star on its chest. You do your work with such precision, a precision I could never duplicate."

Neil wondered if Mr. March was buttering him up, but he didn't feel flattered. He felt tired, worn down and full of a terrible feeling—that he was not some hand of justice, but of something else entirely.

"You need to go back," said Mr. March, patting his pink

lips with the napkin. He looked a little drawn, and his fair skin looked more pasty than usual. He wore a light grey suit with a crisp white shirt, the sort of clothing he always wore, the type that gave Mr. March the impeccably groomed air of wealth without ostentation.

"I won't go back," said Neil. "Find me another job and show me the proof of guilt. All of it."

"And then what? Will you want to investigate the entire thing yourself to verify my facts?"

"Perhaps. You were wrong about Trevor Grant and about Rick Gallo in Las Vegas."

"Have some sense, boy, and listen to reason. It's a waste of your talents to have you investigating crimes, like some common street detective."

Neil disagreed, but he didn't speak his thoughts. Another memory came, of reading about a great detective, a man in London, tall and hawk-nosed. Fiction. It was fiction, and there was a mystery, a dead person. Neil remembered loving the story.

"I won't do another job for you until I see proof."

"No, Neil. This is not how our arrangement works. You do not make demands of me. I make requests of you, which, up until now, you have fulfilled. And in return I have given you a livelihood, and most important, a purpose. A noble purpose."

Neither man spoke, and Neil sat back. He was not going to give in. He sipped his coffee.

"There is something you need to understand. There's a reason I do what I do. I believe in freedom, human freedom. I believe that individuals should not be controlled, not by governments or corporations or religions. Everything I do is ordered toward one goal, that of ensuring human freedom. Sometimes that involves snipping a time thread before something bad grows and begins to have negative effects. Dictatorships, religious monopolies, well-meaning morality codes, all of them impede the right of men and women to do as they please."

"Then why do you end lives? That's taking away the most fundamental freedom of all."

"I only end a life when no other option is possible. You are not the only one who works with me. There are other ways to prevent certain events. Someone slips a condom into the wallet of the father of the next tyrant. A computer file is deleted or a building full of records burns down. Sometimes it's as simple as making someone miss a train."

"You still end lives."

"All for a reason, for a greater purpose. It gives me no pleasure." Mr. March sighed and watched a woman cross the room. "If you could see things as I do, you would understand the necessity of performing smaller acts to prevent greater horrors."

"The ends justify the means. Is that what you're saying?"

"If you want to put it so crudely." Mr. March set aside his cup and stood. "Now, shall we return to 2032?"

"No," said Neil.

Mr. March watched him, and Neil got the feeling that the man was making a decision. Then, he pulled a roll of bills from his pocket. It was currency from this time.

"If that is how you wish it, I will give you this choice. You can stay in this time for now, until you see reason. And when you are ready to return to me, you may inform me." He wrote a name and address on a piece of paper. "You may leave word there, and she will see that I get it. And if, for whatever reason, you decide to remain here, you may tell her that as well. I will not seek you if you do not wish to return."

"What about taking me home? To my own time."

"No. You can do less damage here. You can work as a dockside worker or on a farm somewhere. You're young and so very strong. If you are determined to waste your talents, then let it be on your own head."

And with that, Mr. March tossed enough money onto the table to cover the entire bill and then joined the crowds on the streets of New York. Even now it was a bustling metropolis, the engine of the American dream. Or perhaps Neil was being sentimental. The country was at war, and the city was full of struggling immigrants, the poor, the diseased, and of course, the criminals. Perhaps he did belong here, he thought ruefully.

He opened the slip of paper. The name of the contact was September Wilde, and she lived in New Orleans.

CHAPTER 12

December 28, 1863
New Orleans, Louisiana

"IN A WAY, I ENVY you," said McCullen as they walked down the boulevard on the way to call upon Miss September Wilde. "You haven't had great wealth, but you haven't had great poverty either."

"I wouldn't say you're in great poverty," said Seamus. "You'll land on your feet. You always do. And as I recall, both of us have had a good taste of poverty."

"Yes, yes. But what I mean is that I've had wealth and influence, and now I have none of that. Had I taken a wife, I might still have her. But after a six-year absence, who can say?"

Seamus tried to sneak a glance at him, to assess if he was speaking the truth or having him on. It was impossible to know. McCullen understood that he had lost all that he had spent years building, but he still had his mind, his cleverness, his talents and his way with people. He would not suffer long.

But after spending two days together, Seamus wondered. Could it be that McCullen, stripped of money and power and free of their intoxicating influence, would revert to the decent man Seamus had known when they had been cellmates?

"You've built a life for yourself," continued McCullen. "Granted, it's not a life of prestige, but it's solid. Good and solid."

"Not so terribly solid. I was just almost eaten by a monster living inside a time rip."

"You're willfully misunderstanding me. You have people. Hazel and Miss Sanchez and Mrs. Washington. They would still care about you if you were a beggar on the streets."

McCullen turned his face aside, looking off across the street. McCullen had no one, Seamus knew. If he had taken a wife, she would have been someone from the upper class, a woman of wealth, interested in preserving her social place. When he vanished, she would have had him declared dead and moved on to other prospects. What a change from six years ago. At the Mardi Gras ball, matrons had pushed their daughters to dance with McCullen. Where were his admirers and friends now? He could not even secure a place at his own gentlemen's club.

If he had been corrupted by the pleasures of the world before, perhaps this was his opportunity for redemption.

They turned down the last street toward September Wilde's house. The last time Seamus had come this way, Hazel had accompanied him. Miss Wilde was a black woman living in a middle-class white neighborhood, so upon first meeting her, Seamus had assumed she was a servant. She was not, but somehow she managed to own a house here without being driven out or harassed. She also worked with Mr. Neil Grey, so presumably she was some sort of time traveler, though Seamus had always found her at home whenever he had visited.

At their knock, Miss Wilde pulled open the door. She was in her late fifties or early sixties as close as he could guess, with spectacles and gray hair cropped unfashionably short. Her long features relaxed into a smile when she recognized him.

"Mr. Connor! Delighted to see you."

"Miss Wilde, may I introduce my ... colleague, Mr. McCullen."

The look she gave McCullen was frosty, but she greeted him politely. "Do come in. I have a pie cooling."

They seated themselves in the front room, and Miss Wilde took the chair across from them. A sleek white cat strolled into the room and leapt up onto the stuffed arm of her chair.

"Something has happened," said Seamus, not wanting to waste time on niceties. "Something with the time rips. In the past, you have been reticent to tell me anything about the machine or traveling in time, and I understand that. But this is urgent. Perhaps you should call Mr. Grey."

"He isn't here. Last I heard he was sailing to Peru."

"You might want to call him on your telephone or whatnot. We've seen something, at Jackson Square. There is a rumor that a few people have disappeared in that area, and we went to take readings to see what we could learn. We found a fresh rip, one that had opened recently. And when we got close, it opened and there was this giant serpent-like creature. It was white and eyeless, and it somehow pulled on the air and me and everything around us."

Ms. Wilde looked concerned now, and she leaned forward in her chair. "Haven't you been closing the time rips when they become unstable? I thought you and young Miss Dubois monitored them closely."

"Yes, we have. That's just it. They're becoming unstable despite our efforts. If it wasn't for McCullen closing the door so quickly, the monster would have eaten me."

She looked at McCullen, who had not said a word the entire time.

"Well done," she said.

After a moment's hesitation, McCullen waved the compliment away as if it were nothing.

"Is it because of a time loop?" Seamus asked. The older version of Hazel had mentioned time loops in 1961. "Is this one of the bad things that can happen when there's an instability?"

Ms. Wilde looked at the cat as if she wanted to say something to it, but then turned back to Seamus. "If a void wyrm has come, then I suppose you need to know a few things."

"A void wyrm?"

"An ancient species. A creature that lives in the empty space between worlds. Are you familiar with the creature known as the trapdoor spider?"

"I can't say as I am."

"The spider makes its home in a small space, a hole in a log for instance. It then makes a plug over its home using its webbing. It strings web all around the hole, and waits. When prey comes by, it steps on the webbing and the spider feels it. It opens its trap door, grabs the prey and slips back into its hiding place. The void wyrm is similar. It makes its home in the pockets between worlds, near spaces that are unstable. It doesn't use webbing, of course, but it can sense when prey is near and then open the door and feed. You said some people had vanished?"

"Yes, I fear they were eaten by the thing."

"Most likely they were. Unfortunately. But if the void wyrm has come, it's because this has become a good place to feed. That means that we need to close the door."

"I would if I could," said Seamus. "But I cannot. Neither McCullen nor I have the knowledge."

"And that is why you came to me?"

"Can't you close it, or call one of your time agents and have them do it?"

She smiled. "This isn't a job for an agent, not this time. I need to consult with my siblings. You need not worry about it further. Thank you for notifying me."

"And that's all? It will be taken care of?"

"Yes. Thank you for coming by." She stood. "Would you like to stay for a slice of pie before you go?"

Seamus was about to say no, but McCullen said, "We'd love to, thank you."

She went into the kitchen and left them alone. The white cat folded its paws underneath itself and closed its eyes.

"We need to get home," Seamus said. "We've no time for pie."

"I want to ask her a few things," said McCullen.

Miss Wilde reappeared with plates of warm apple pie. Seamus had not realized how hungry he was, but then remembered that he had skipped supper.

"I'm not from this world," said McCullen. Seamus almost choked at the abruptness of it. "And I want to find out how to get back. And Mr. Connor's friend, Miss Sanchez, will also need to get back to her world. How can I do it?"

Miss Wilde raised her eyebrows. "There's a world that is close to many others, including this world. It's almost like a hub world with other universes, like spokes, touching it in various places."

"Don't tell me," said Seamus. "You can't tell us because giving me the information will form an unstable time loop."

McCullen clearly didn't understand, so Seamus explained. "Information and objects have to have an origin. If we learn the information from Miss Wilde, and then in my future I tell her the information, then it has no origin. Someone has to come up with the idea in the first place."

"Sounds like rubbish to me."

"It's just that sort of rubbish that prevents us from attracting void wyrms," Ms. Wilde said. "And I can, in fact, give you help in getting there. Because you didn't discover it."

"Who did?"

"My people," she said and went to a bureau against the far wall. She opened a drawer, pulled out a pencil and paper and started to write. "Go to this world. People there have narrow feet, like Miss Sanchez, but it isn't her world. From there, you should be able to reach her world, and yours." She looked at McCullen. "But the synchronicities you require to travel are more difficult to manage."

When she approached them, McCullen reached out for the paper, but she handed it to Seamus instead. He opened it, memorized its contents, folded it and put it into his coat pocket.

"Tell me how you'll get rid of this void wyrm," he said. "And who, exactly, are your people? Do you mean the time travelers?"

"Some of us can travel between, yes. The Twelve will want to know about the void wyrm. Only a few of us are able to seal the door with ease. If my suspicions are correct, someone is interfering with timelines, and that is why the doorway became unstable and attracted the wyrm in the first place." Seamus and McCullen had finished their slices of pie and Miss Wilde collected the plates. "I will be going on a trip to speak with my siblings. One brother lives here in New Orleans, and another is in Los Angeles."

She glanced at the cat, who had not moved. "Time is short and I'll need to send a message to June in San Francisco too." The cat stretched and trotted out of the room.

"Were you born in Miss Sanchez's time? Or Mr. Grey's?" asked Seamus. As long as she was being so forthcoming, he wanted to know everything.

She smiled fondly at him. "If I told you my birthday, I don't think you'd believe me."

Miss Wilde moved toward the front door, and both men took her cue and followed.

"If you require anything else from me," she said, "I'll be at Augustus's Music Shop or here."

"Is there nothing else you can tell us? No other help you can offer?" Seamus asked.

They stood on the front steps and put their hats on. Miss Wilde looked up at the sky, as if assessing the weather.

"Only my blessing," she said.

CHAPTER 13

December 31, 1863
New Orleans, Louisiana

IT WAS SUNDAY MORNING, AND Hazel had no music lessons to teach and no obligations aside from her morning Mass attendance. She decided not to stop to speak to the priest afterwards to ask about obtaining a dispensation to marry Mr. Ross. The guilt prickled her as she headed home, but she did not turn back.

She hurried home, changed out of her Sunday best and went to help Mrs. Washington prepare lunch in the kitchen.

"Any hopes or resolutions for the New Year?" asked Mrs. Washington, elbow-deep in flour and soft, white bread dough.

"I don't know," Hazel sighed.

"What's wrong, sweetheart?"

Mrs. Washington knew her moods, and there was no hiding that she was unhappy. She thought of calling on her friend Cassandra. She was a good friend, but her opinions on Mr. Ross were unchanging. She would tell Hazel that she was a fool to reject such a man. Mrs. Washington was a steadier soul.

"Mr. Ross asked me to marry him."

"From the way you sound, I take it you refused him?"

"No." Hazel sighed and looked out the kitchen window at a hummingbird that was flitting around the bougainvillea.

It didn't have to worry about marriages or people disappearing forever through time rips. Its understanding of the world was limited and its choices in life were few. It was content.

"If you've accepted him and you're this unhappy about it, I'd think you might want to reconsider." Mrs. Washington wiped her hands and rummaged through the cabinets for the bread pans.

"I didn't accept him either. I told him I'd think about it."

The housekeeper set the pans down, and after a moment, nodded. "That was wise. It's good to keep a clear head about these things. Consider your future, especially since you're still young."

Mrs. Washington placed the dough into the pans, covered them and set them aside to rise. Hazel sliced cheese, cold pork and apples and filled four plates, two for McCullen and the Professor, and two for Mrs. Washington and herself.

"I don't know that thinking it over is going to help," said Hazel. "It seems like the more I think about it, the more miserable I become."

"I wish I could tell you what to do. I wish I had a good answer for you."

Hazel knew that there was no one to help her but herself. Each choice she made opened one door but closed another. Perhaps it was the loss of options that bothered her. The hummingbird outside was still darting from flower to flower, a rounded iridescent emerald glittering in the sunshine. Its life was almost absent of choices, and it was happy. But something was wrong with that sort of thinking, and she knew it.

"It's nearly noon," said Mrs. Washington, glancing at the kitchen clock. Hazel loaded up the tray along with two glasses of tea. The Professor always liked his lunches at noon precisely, and he was so lax about everything else that Mrs. Washington had once said she felt obligated to do that one thing for him every day exactly as he wished.

"I'll take it up," said Hazel.

When she reached the upper hallway, the clock was already chiming. Then the air all around her shimmered.

"Professor!" she yelled and darted toward the laboratory, hoping to escape the shimmer. The lunch tray slipped from her hands and crashed to the floor.

The Professor had described the void wyrm to her, and she wasn't about to get eaten by it, or pulled into some other world or time. She lunged for the laboratory doorknob, desperate to escape from the air that shimmered on every side of her, filling the hallway from floor to ceiling and wall to wall. Her hand was about to grasp the knob when the door flew open. She landed hard on her hands and knees and then scrambled into the laboratory, her legs tangling in her skirts.

Then strong arms grasped her under the arms and hauled to her feet. It was McCullen. The air inside the room was not shimmering. Had she escaped? The Professor hurried past her and McCullen looked beyond her, into the hallway.

There was a shout, a happy shout in a woman's voice. She knew the voice. Miss Sanchez. She leapt forward and threw her arms around the Professor's neck with a look of pure joy. She held onto him and he gently lowered his cheek to rest against her hair and after a long while, she let him go. Behind her stood a machine. It looked like the Professor's current machine, a trunk with a paneled brass sphere on top, but was much more polished and sophisticated-looking than his cobbled-together device. After glancing between the machine and Miss Sanchez a few times, the Professor was unable to resist its pull. He knelt to examine the thing.

"Hazel?" said Miss Sanchez, and then Hazel found herself the recipient of an enthusiastic hug. Hazel hugged her back. Miss Sanchez seemed so much smaller now.

"How long has it been for you?" said the Professor over his shoulder. He was on his knees, digging into the innards of the machine.

"Only a few days," said Miss Sanchez.

So Miss Sanchez was still in her mid-twenties. Hazel watched as Miss Sanchez pulled herself up a few inches and addressed McCullen.

"Thank you for saving my life," she said. Hazel remembered how Miss Sanchez had almost drowned in the Mississippi because of her huge dress. Once wet, the dress would have pulled her under to her death. But McCullen had saved her, just before they had been swept through the time rip into 1961.

"My pleasure," said McCullen. There was an awkward moment of silence. Hazel wondered if Miss Sanchez was about to rebuke McCullen for returning here without her.

"Where did you get the machine?" asked Hazel.

"We'll talk about that later," Miss Sanchez said. "I can't believe how much you've grown! Look at you. How long has it been?"

"Six years."

"And what's the date today?"

"It's New Year's Eve, 1863," said Hazel.

"And was there a war?"

"It started when you said, in 1861. New Orleans is occupied by the Union now."

"Are you both all right? Have you been safe?"

"Don't worry about us," said Hazel. "I had to come home from school in Boston when the war started, but I wasn't in any danger. And we're safe as can be."

Miss Sanchez looked doubtful, and while McCullen went to sit back at the laboratory table, Hazel went to see what the Professor was doing. The machine Miss Sanchez had used was from the future, a later model of the Professor's own creation, she was certain.

"It's broken," the Professor said, running his hands

through his hair. "It could only make one trip. There was a failsafe. I think it was intentional."

"But it has a little book with all the coordinates," said Miss Sanchez. "It has been used hundreds of times, according to this." She pulled open a small flip-out writing surface and retrieved a hand-written book from the small space inside. The Professor took it.

"I shouldn't look at this," he said. But he opened the cover anyway and paged through.

"Why not?" asked Hazel. "If it has the information to get Miss Sanchez home, you should know."

The Professor closed the book and put it back into the opening from which it had come. But he did it so slowly that Hazel was certain he was going to grab it again. Instead, Miss Sanchez took it.

"If this thing can help us, then we're going to use it," she said.

"There's a problem," said the Professor. "If I wrote that, and it does appear to be in my hand, and I read it now, then I'll be learning the information in an unnatural manner. It's called a time loop. The information has no origin, but will simply be passed from future me to past me and back again unendingly. And, as McCullen and I learned a few days ago, such things have dire consequences."

He described the void wyrm to Miss Sanchez in the same way he had described it to Hazel. But with Hazel, he had made her promise not to try to close any time rips without both him and McCullen present. Apparently, McCullen had saved the Professor's life, and the Professor now trusted him to do the same for Hazel, if faced with the need.

"Professor? Do you think you're the one who set up the failsafe in the machine so it could only make one last trip?" Hazel asked. "That way, we couldn't use it to travel all over creation and make more time instabilities."

"That's what I'm thinking," he muttered. "And yet, I

would have known that I would want to look at it, to learn from it. And I might be able to repair it. This is a delay, not a prohibition on travel. I'll work on it immediately."

McCullen was now standing in the doorway. "Along with taxes and death, the only other constant in the world is Seamus Connor having an uncontrollable need to start digging into an unknown machine."

"So perhaps, looking at that book won't cause an unstable time loop," said the Professor. "I would have known my own nature and planned for it, wouldn't I?"

Hazel shrugged. The Professor was brilliant and worked well under pressure, but he was also erratic, moody, and occasionally irrational. Planning ahead was not his strongest suit.

"Let me look at it," said McCullen. "Then we can use the information. You will originate it in the future, and I'll read it now."

"No, because I'll learn from you. It's still a time loop." The Professor paced to the end of the hallway and back. "Blast it all, I'm going to look. I'm going to trust that I knew what I was doing when I allowed it to come to me."

He took out the book and flipped it open. Then he took it to the laboratory worktable, and McCullen and Miss Sanchez pulled up stools on either side of him. Hazel watched them, bent together and talking. McCullen began writing something.

Hazel dragged the time machine into the laboratory, and picked up the dishes and pieces of food from the fallen tray. Then she thought of Mrs. Washington downstairs. She would want to know that Miss Sanchez had returned.

"Hazel?" called the Professor as she headed down the hall. "I hate to ask, but could you bring up another lunch tray?"

She said she would, but as she did, she felt much younger, still the small girl whose only purpose was to fetch and run errands. That was nonsense, she thought.

If she had wanted to, she could sit at the worktable. Perhaps later, she would. But for now, she didn't feel right sitting with the three of them. She was an outsider to their little group.

She glanced back at the three of them, and the Professor looked sideways at Miss Sanchez. Her finger was on one of the pages, and her arm was touching his. Hazel could only see the side of his face, but it was changed. He was happy.

She hadn't seen him like that in so long.

CHAPTER 14

December 31, 1863
New York, New York

NEIL GREY PULLED HIS HAT on more firmly and shoved his hands into his pockets. Necessity had driven him to purchase warmer clothing, including a scarf and a heavier coat, as New York in winter was painfully cold. He was a little grateful for the insulating cloth stuffed into the toes of his shoes. He could have purchased better shoes, or a complete outfit of finer quality, but he didn't know how long his money would need to last him. He would be prudent and endure the discomfort.

He had spent the day touring the city and thinking. No Statue of Liberty held vigil, torch aloft in the harbor, and Ellis Island had yet to be built. The subway did not exist yet, but there were a few areas of the city connected by elevated railroad tracks where steam-powered engines puffed chains of smoke, trailed by cars filled with people going from one part of the city to another. Commuters, he would call them. But that word did not exist in their vocabulary.

Times Square did not exist, but was simply an area in town that was being gradually developed by various hotels and shops. In his own time, a ball would drop in Times Square tonight and the crowd, decked in glittery hats and light-up necklaces would count down to the New Year. Here, nothing at all would happen. Perhaps somewhere in the city someone hosted a gala event where the rich toasted with champagne. But every other tired soul would work, trudge home, sleep and then do it all again the next day.

Neil reminded himself that this was a city struggling, and a city at war. Still, it was probably one of the safer cities, comparatively speaking. He had seen the future in this world, and the North would win the Civil War. New York was so far North that it wouldn't be attacked.

Yet here he was, hoping to get on a train and leave. He would not stay in New York to make his fortune. No, he would head south, or west, or both and see where fate took him. He refused to return to Mr. March. He couldn't, not with the weight of what he had done in Las Vegas. He wasn't completely sure that Mr. Gallo hadn't murdered those show girls, but it was a safe bet, which meant that he had killed an innocent person. Mr. Dubois, the child molester, and the others, so many others, might have been guilty or innocent. There was simply no way to know.

He wished he could know, if only to clarify things in his mind. If he had killed one innocent, then it was an evil of a different magnitude than to kill five, or ten or twenty innocents. But what would knowing accomplish? In a way, not knowing was the better option. If he knew for certain exactly how many innocent people he had killed, then he might try to atone for it. Wouldn't he? Was that the sort of man he was? The sort to spend a life atoning for his evil deeds? Was he free because of his ignorance? Or did it simply imprison him with the knowledge that nothing he could ever do would erase his debt?

He took a streetcar to the train station and purchased a ticket for the next train to Louisville, Kentucky. From there, he could head west, perhaps to the Dakota Territory or to the Arizona or New Mexico Territories. He was a Californian by birth, and it was a recognized state. Perhaps he could go there. The gold rush was over, but the Central

Valley was full of fertile farmland, and San Francisco and Los Angeles both had ports where he could find work at a dock or on a ship, perhaps.

It was a three-hour wait until boarding time which gave him plenty of time to think as he strolled through the surrounding streets. He decided that instead of heading west from Louisville he would instead travel to New Orleans. He could leave a message with this September Wilde woman. With the war on, he didn't completely trust that she would receive a letter through the regular post. If Neil left a letter with her himself, he would be assured that Mr. March would receive it. Then, Mr. March would not seek him. He would be free.

Still, he knew that Mr. March might not be so easy to escape. Simply telling him good-bye would not be enough. March would pursue him, maybe in a year, maybe two. He would reappear at some unexpected moment, and Neil wondered what would happen then. Would March force him to come with him? Again, he had the feeling that Mr. March might become very persuasive and could make Neil obey him. But how could that be? He had free will, as did any person. He was faster and stronger than other people too.

He knew better than to think that he could persuade Mr. March to bring him back to his own time. If the only choices were obedience or abandonment, he would choose the latter.

If Mr. March left him in the 1860s, then so be it. He had no loved ones in the 1990s, nor did he have a job, money or anything else. It was merely a time familiar to him. But he was a person of flexibility and resourcefulness. Mr. March had been correct to say that Neil was young and strong. He could make a life, not one with a television and a swimming pool and a car. But perhaps he could work on a ship for a bit, find decent work, perhaps buy some land for farming later on.

One thing was certain: He would become harder to find. That was within his control. He made a decision. Once in New Orleans, he would take a ship, whatever ship was leaving the port that day with an interesting destination. Then, if Mr. March accepted his resignation, all would be well. And if not, he would be safe so long as Mr. March could not find him.

He headed back to the station where the train waited. He boarded, and after an hour of looking out the window, he wished he had a book to read to pass the time. Perhaps one of the books about that hawk-nosed detective in London. Now, what was his name? The memory was the same as before, no fresher or clearer. He leaned his head back in his seat and let the jostling movement of the car and the staccato beat of the wheels on the rails become a relaxing rhythm.

His stomach was full from the ham sandwich that he had purchased from the passing cart and the train compartment was warm without being stifling. More than that, he had money in his pocket, was literate and was vaccinated against smallpox, measles, polio and who knew what other deadly diseases. Perhaps life might not be so bad, all things considered. But though his mood improved, he could not recall the name of the book or the detective in it.

"Fancy meeting you here," said a man from immediately beside him, and Neil's eyes flew open.

A man had taken the seat next to him, a blue-eyed blond man in his fifties wearing a tweed jacket. It was the same man who had purchased the little Viking ship in a bottle in Las Vegas in 1982.

"It's you!" was all Neil could sputter out.

"Yes, it's me."

Neil sprang to his feet, cursing himself for being so careless as to relax, become unobservant and then to allow himself to indulge in even a moment's hesitation.

This man was a time traveler as well, and that meant he worked for Mr. March.

"What do you want?" Neil demanded.

The man remained seated, smiling up at him with serene amusement. "Not to harm you, I promise."

"Yeah, right."

A few of the passengers were turning around and craning their necks to see what was happening. Neil was ready to punch this man in his grinning face, but he didn't care for an audience. He also didn't care for being stuck against the wall of the train car with this man between himself and the aisle.

"Please sit down," the man said. "Like you, I don't care to draw too much attention to myself."

"I'll bet. You get your hands where I can see them." If this man had a syringe, Neil wasn't about to let him use it.

"Look, let's take a walk to another car. We can talk quietly."

Neil didn't move.

"And I'll keep my hands where you can see them," said the man.

Without waiting for Neil to answer him, the man headed toward the back of the car. If this man was sent by Mr. March, then Neil couldn't very well wait until he was asleep in his sleeping car or drowsy over his morning coffee to be ambushed. Best to deal with him now. He followed.

The man was already seated in the dining car, leaning back in his chair. He looked completely relaxed, and Neil had to admit, happy. Well, killers could look any way they pleased. Not looking like killers was precisely the talent they needed in their line of work.

"Two sweet teas," said the man to the waiter. Neil took a seat, but kept his eyes on the man's hands. He could have a gun, a syringe, anything.

"I don't believe we've properly introduced ourselves. I'm Elliot Van Dorn." He reached his hand across to shake, but Neil was not so foolish as to touch anything the man offered him, even his own hand. His skin could hold some sort of poison or sedative. The future held wonders, ones at which even he, widely traveled as he was, would marvel.

"How do you know who I am?" asked Neil.

The man did not answer.

"What were you doing in 1982?"

"I had to find something," said Elliot. "I'm making a delivery."

"That ship in a bottle?"

"That's it," said Elliot. "I make deliveries. I do lots of things. But killing people isn't on my resume."

The sweet tea came, and Neil kept hold of his, not allowing this Elliot man to get anywhere near it. In his dying moments, he did not want to feel like an idiot for allowing his drink to be drugged.

"I'd like to offer you a job," said Elliot. "Not killing anyone. Just doing good work. Honest work."

Neil wanted to say that he had heard that line before, but he didn't want to give the man any information he might not already have.

"It pays well," Elliot continued. "It's dangerous, but nothing out of the ordinary for someone like you. And you wouldn't have to kill anyone."

"Who sent you?" Neil asked.

"I came on my own."

"So you know about me? How?"

"Because we're friends and we work together in your future and my past."

Neil wasn't sure what to make of that. Certainly, it was possible, but improbable.

"Prove it," Neil said.

Elliot sighed. "You're not from this world, but another one where instead of Breckinridge being president in this year, a man named Lincoln is. You take your coffee with two sugars and no cream. You love classical music, especially

Baroque. And you appreciate art, with a special love for the Dutch painters, but you never play music, draw or paint. You sleep little, rarely laugh and spend most of the time with the expression you have now, mostly unreadable by anyone who doesn't know you well. Right now, you're angry and distrustful, but that's understandable. You were born in California, though you remember little of your childhood. You like to read, and your favorite author is Sir Arthur Conan Doyle."

That was it. That was the name on the cover of the book about the tall detective. Neil still couldn't remember the title of the story. But he did remember Holmes. That was the detective's name. Like a little burst of light, the memory clarified itself.

"It's a new start for a new year. A new job. New possibilities," said Elliot. "Besides, I doubt you want to stay here and be conscripted into either the Union or Confederate armies."

"Definitely not the Confederate side."

"Right. I don't blame you. Neither of us is a big fan of what they call the 'peculiar institution.'"

"It's an evil institution if you ask me," said Neil. "What time are you from? Originally, I mean."

"Born January 10th, 1993. So I'm not used to slavery either. But even the Southerners in our circle of colleagues who were born in this time agree with you. But don't get it into your mind to try to change anything, like teaching the Union to make better weapons or telling them where the big battles will be."

Neil hadn't actually thought of doing either.

"And don't think of helping the abolitionists or escaped slaves or anything like that. Our job is our job. We do the job and then we leave."

"You talk as if I've accepted your offer. I haven't."

"Well, do think it over. I'll be disembarking in Louisville, so you have until then." Elliot then told him the train car where he would be staying, drank down the last of his tea and left. Neil noticed that he hadn't asked how long Neil would be on the train. Nor had he said where his final destination was with this ship in a bottle.

A job with no killing. A job traveling through time. Now that might be even better than taking a ship out to Cuba or sailing to Argentina or India. He could truly evade Mr. March if he went between worlds. It would even the odds.

CHAPTER 15

January 1, 1864
New Orleans, Louisiana

"NOW YOU LOOK MORE LIKE yourself," said Hazel to Miss Sanchez.

She was back in one of her old dresses which were now a few years out of date, but not terribly so. Many women in town had not been able to update their wardrobes much during the war, and Miss Sanchez would not stand out. At least she was out of the woolen skirt and blouse that she had been wearing when she arrived. The thing looked like the clothing a little girl might wear and with no hoop skirt or even crinolines. The skirt only just covered her knees and clung too closely to her body. And she had no structured undergarments like a corset save for something she called a "bra."

"I'd be more myself back in my jeans and sweaters," said Miss Sanchez. "But I'd rather be here with you and the Professor than in the 1960s."

Hazel and the Professor had saved all of Miss Sanchez's old clothing, including her mobile phone which, oddly, the Professor had never taken apart. Hazel hadn't noted the fact until now, as Miss Sanchez looked at the black screen with longing. The thing could be used to talk to her family or to send them messages. It had lost its electrical power a few days after she had arrived, and had sat in a drawer since then. And yet, as wondrous as the machine was, the

Professor had not disassembled it. Leaving Miss Sanchez's clothing and room as it was had been a simple matter. If he hadn't taken apart the phone, it meant something significant, but Hazel did not know what it was. Could the Professor be in love with Miss Sanchez? Yes, that had to be the reason. It was not simply duty that had motivated him all these years. All of Miss Sanchez's things were as she had left them, down to the hairbrush with a few strands of her hair still in place.

Of course, she couldn't properly wear the jeans or the strange top that went with it. And she would have to manage to wear the shoes from Hazel's world. Miss Sanchez came from a world of people with very narrow feet, so regular shoes would not fit her well. Her big toes were small and stubby and were only slightly larger than the others. Also, her eyes were a shade of brown that was unusually light. They were nearly golden, almost catlike, though not so strange that they drew undue attention.

"Tell me about your world," said Hazel. "What's it like in a hundred years?"

Hazel sat on the edge of the bed while Miss Sanchez looked at herself in the mirror and pinned up her hair. Hazel considered offering to help, but though Miss Sanchez was inexperienced, after having spent a few weeks with Mrs. Washington before she was pulled through the time rip, she had learned enough to fix her hair competently, though slowly.

"I'm originally from 2015 and I was just in 1961. I wasn't even born yet. But in a hundred years, women can vote."

Hazel caught Miss Sanchez looking at her in the mirror.

"And most families have an automobile. Do you remember what those are?"

"I remember," said Hazel. "You drew one for me on a scrap of paper when I was younger."

"You have indoor plumbing, but in my time, almost everyone has it. Everyone in America anyway. And central heating, automatic dishwashers and clothes washers and dryers. Plus, we have chocolate in almost every store. Really, you can buy a chocolate bar almost anywhere. And all different kinds of fruit, even out of season."

Her world sounded like a wonderland of pleasures. But Hazel was old enough to know that no such thing existed. "And what bad things are there?"

Miss Sanchez really appeared to be thinking about it. "Well, manners disappeared. No one calls anyone "Miss" or "Mister" like they do here. Hospitality isn't the same. And people are more on their own. Here, people stay in the same neighborhood, all together, for generations. You know how the Irish all live in one neighborhood? They help each other out. They watch each other's children and take care of the widows and the elderly. In my time, each individual is sort of on their own."

Hazel had been on her own before, so that was not frightening to her. "What would my life be like, if I lived in your time?"

Miss Sanchez gave her a funny look, and Hazel's intuition rang like a tiny bell. Miss Sanchez was hiding something. Or perhaps she sensed that Hazel had an ulterior motive for asking. Well, she did. If she knew what the future was like, it might help her make a better decision about Mr. Ross. Even though Neil Grey was coming, she also could go with Miss Sanchez to her world, if she wanted to.

Miss Sanchez continued. "You could achieve any level of education your talents allowed. You could study physics and invent amazing things that even the Professor would wonder at. You could be a musician and play with the Boston Philharmonic, right alongside men. Or play as a solo artist."

"Sounds lovely."

"It is. But you shouldn't try to come with me when the Professor finds a way to send me home."

"What? Why not?"

"Because, it's not all fun and freedom. Even if we managed to fake an identity for you, you'd have to go to college for years and take out loans that would take forever to pay off. You wouldn't even have a high school diploma. And if you wanted to play violin at a professional level, the competition is fierce. You'd start off without any money and people might think you were crazy since you wouldn't have memories of the same things they do. You wouldn't know ordinary social conventions either."

"I could learn."

"You could. I know you could," Miss Sanchez said. Again, Hazel thought she was hiding something.

"What are you not telling me?" asked Hazel.

Miss Sanchez sighed. "I'm only trying to give you a realistic view. I can imagine being seventeen and thinking that the future is some sort of magical place without problems. And that's not the case."

"I'm not so naïve as that. I'm a grown woman."

"Not at seventeen, you're not."

Her tone made Hazel's anger flash hot. She forced her voice into a polite but firm tone, one becoming a Southern lady of breeding and manners.

"I have to disagree. You come from a world where there was plenty to eat and every opportunity to do what you wanted and to pursue whatever goals you might have. A world very different than mine. I've lived by my wits on the streets, while at the same age, you were still in grammar school. And when I was thirteen, I traveled all on my own to Boston where I studied hard and was at the top of my class. After the war started, I came home and taught music to children. And now, I may be getting married."

Miss Sanchez spun around in her chair. "Married!"

"Mr. Ross asked me."

"Seamus didn't tell me that."

Miss Sanchez sometimes referred to the Professor by his Christian name, usually when she was caught off guard and forgot her manners. Well, Hazel would not forget hers. She was a Southern lady, whatever her age or past might be.

"He asked me the other day," she said. "And I might still accept. I'm trying to decide."

"But you're so young!"

"I'm not that young. I'm not in danger of being put on the shelf, true. Tell me, how old are women when they marry in your world?"

"They have to be eighteen, legally. But most people wait until they're in their mid-twenties."

"But how long until a woman is considered a spinster?"

"We don't even use that word. If a woman doesn't marry, she doesn't marry."

"But what about children and a home and a husband?"

"You can have children without a husband, you know. In my world, it's common. You can't come with me, but if you did, you could have a child without marrying the father."

Such talk would have been cause for scandalized gasps among her friends, but Hazel did not laugh. For Miss Sanchez to even insinuate that she would do such a thing was offensive.

"I'll ask you not to mock me," Hazel said.

Miss Sanchez had a confused look. "I'm merely saying that women in my time don't always marry. And if they do, they can get divorced. So there are plenty of single mothers."

"Divorced?"

Miss Sanchez must have seen her shock, because her look became sympathetic.

"I know that in your time, it's a great scandal," Miss Sanchez said, getting up and coming to sit beside Hazel on the bed. "But in my time, people only stay married if they want to."

"But they took vows. Before God."

Miss Sanchez sighed, and Hazel felt more than ever

how different her world was from the future. Now playing in an orchestra with men and wearing trousers indeed sounded like childish delights.

"We're not so ... strict on things like that," said Miss Sanchez. "And not everyone believes in God, and everyone isn't Christian, even if they do."

"That doesn't bother me. I have friends who are Protestant, and we get on very well. Cassandra, my closest friend, is a Baptist, and Mr. Ross is a Methodist."

"Be that as it may, it's a very different world. But that's enough of that. Now, tell me about this Mr. Ross person."

"He's the son of an ink manufacturer, though he's running the business himself now. He'll own it entirely by summer."

"And what's he like?"

"We're good friends, and he's pleasant company. He's pleasant looking and has a kind heart."

"And you love him?"

Hazel sighed. That was the question. "I don't know. I know I could be happy with him, but I'm not sure if I'll accept his offer."

"And if you don't marry him, then you can go on playing and teaching music, correct?"

"If I like, yes. The Professor said I could stay here forever if I liked. I could be a happy spinster, maybe."

Miss Sanchez nodded, as if deciding something, and Hazel again felt much younger, like a child whose life was somehow being decided for her. She thought about mentioning Mr. Grey and his promised visit in a few days, but she didn't. A wedge had gone up between Miss Sanchez and herself, a split in their understanding of the world, and Hazel wasn't quite sure if she could breach it.

CHAPTER 16

January 5, 1864
Louisville, Kentucky

FROM HIS POSITION LEANING AGAINST the balcony railing of the Whitlock Hotel, Neil saw clearly that Louisville was a city at war. Kentucky was a border state, part of the Union, but historically a slave state. It had declared neutrality when the Confederate states seceded, but when the South had tried to claim it, Kentucky had asked the Union for help and had been under Union control since. As far as Neil knew, it would remain with the Union until the war ended.

Neil watched as four men, all in blue Union uniforms, patrolled below. People on the streets moved away from them as they approached. It was subtle, but the quick glances, the way people stiffened when they spotted the men, all told him that good guys or not, people did not like armed men walking the streets.

Elliot came out and leaned on the railing beside him. "I love this part. Just watching."

"They're at war."

"True, but this is still a beautiful city."

Neil glanced at him, and Elliot had a gentle smile as he looked down, like a benevolent spirit, watching over the people with a distant sort of affection.

A covered cart rattled past. "Munitions," said Elliot. "See the guards?" There were five men riding along, guarding the contents from all sides. "Ah, but this is a lovely city, so much history."

"Doesn't the war bother you?" said Neil.

"Of course. But I do love my job."

It was Neil's job now too. He had accepted Elliot's offer of employment with a group known as the Time Corps, and now they were heading to Memphis. The riverboat they were due to travel on would not leave until the next day, and Elliot's travel budget seemed to rival the one Mr. March had always provided for Neil. They were able to afford excellent rooms at the hotel and lavish cabins on the riverboat.

"Have you been to this time before?" asked Elliot.

"I was here a few years ago, before the war started. But I've never been to Louisville."

"Then you should see the city."

They took a walk, and Neil noticed that after they got away from the nicer area near the hotel, Elliot did not hesitate to go into the poorer neighborhoods, places where the gutters were filled with refuse and downtrodden people gave them wary looks, or hungry ones. Some were sizing them up.

Neil kept alert, ready for anyone who might decide to rob them, but he had no real fear. He was only of average size, but he was stronger, faster and more ruthless than all but the most skilled fighters. Though he was only twenty, he had enough experience to know how he held up in a fight. He wondered about Elliot. The older man had a jovial, carefree air about him, but Neil saw him taking in his surroundings, assessing. If Elliot knew him from the future, then he must know Neil was good in a fight. Was he counting on Neil to defend him, or could Elliot give as good as he got?

"The true heart of the city," Elliot said with a contented sigh. "You really get a flavor for how things are when you see how the poorest live." His tone was affectionate, which struck Neil as odd, considering the presence of a group of three young men watching them. Elliot gave them a quick look and said, "Sunset is not too far off, and we ought to be moving to another area of town."

They turned back and took a horse-drawn cab downtown. The homes grew nicer, the public buildings better maintained. They stopped at a restaurant where a short line wound out the door, but it appeared to be one of the nicer places in town and Neil was content to let Elliot take him wherever he pleased. A couple stood in front of them, and since Elliot seemed to be the sort of companion who was content with silence, Neil overheard their conversation.

"It's tonight, at the Branham house on Oak Street," said the man. "Many of the big decision makers will be there."

"But what if that abysmal Tooley woman is there?" said the woman who was presumably his wife. "I wouldn't want to be seen in the same room with her, the awful woman."

"Just listen to the music and look at the art. Make some polite comments. You won't have any difficulty. I need to talk to a few people, make some connections."

"Even so," she sighed, "I wish we didn't have to."

"Most of the city council will be there, Judge Abrams, and the governor even said he might come by. Also, two of the colonels from Virginia will be there."

"I detest war talk."

"I'm sorry, darling, but you knew you'd have to endure such things before you married me."

"Tell me about the art. That might not be so bad."

"There are some rarer pieces in the Branham collection. Rumor has it that Mrs. Branham will be unveiling a Rembrandt."

The couple was seated, and Neil did not have a chance to listen to the rest of the conversation.

"What do you say we drop by also?" said Neil to Elliot. "I'd love to see a Rembrandt."

"Not if all those movers and shakers are going to be there, we can't. Too much risk of us saying something wrong or disrupting an important conversation."

"I'll be as silent as the grave. They won't even notice I'm there. I can do that."

"I know you can. I just don't think it's wise."

"Do you know how much art was lost in the Civil War? Family collections were scattered. Some pieces were never seen again. Who knows what piece this is? And what if it gets burned or stolen or even painted over by some ignorant art student who can't afford fresh canvases?"

Elliot sighed. "Look, Neil, I know you love Rembrandt and Van Gogh and all the other Dutch guys ..."

"Not all of them," Neil said, defensive. "Only the good ones. And Rembrandt and Van Gogh are both brilliant, but are in different categories. Rembrandt had a way of capturing people, their life, their spirits shining out through their skin, their physical movement, all caught in an instant. And Van Gogh's rooms and landscapes are completely different. They live too, but in a different way." It was strange that his memory was so full of holes, and yet all of this was clear to him.

"Fine, if it'll keep you out of this art gathering thing, we'll take a steamship to Holland and ask Van Gogh to paint you something special."

"He's only ten years old right now," said Neil and then he caught the joking glint in Elliot's eye. "And I don't want to own the Rembrandt, only to see it."

Their meal of steak and butter beans arrived.

"It's too risky. Too many influential people will be there," said Elliot. "And that's all there is to it. We can't go."

Neil silently fumed. If anyone could be inconspicuous, it was he. He could get in, see the painting, and then get out. Simple. Did Elliot think he was an amateur?

They ate peach pie for dessert and after paying for their meal, they headed toward the nearest major street where they could find a cab to take them home.

"Have you seen the future of this world?" asked Neil. "Do you know who wins the Civil War?" He already knew the answer. The North would win, but he did not know if Elliot was aware of the fact.

"Yes, and it's the North," said Elliot.

"But if I go to that Rembrandt event, then that could be disrupted?"

"Doubtful. Time travel is not like it is in the movies from our time where you wink at a girl and she misses meeting her future husband and Einstein is never born. Or you squish a bug and the earth's climate gets changed. Things aren't so fragile as that, though some events are more fragile than others. It depends. But attending this social function is still risky. There is a chance you could affect some events. Like one of the colonels should talk to someone about a certain thing and then it gives them an idea about some strategy. If you're interrupting that, then a different battle might take place."

"And would that form an unstable time loop?" asked Neil. Elliot had spent most of the morning explaining how the Time Corps existed to repair time loops, straighten time lines and fix various mysterious things that could affect the proper flow of events.

Elliot gestured as if his hands were the two sides of a scale. "Maybe and maybe not."

"Setting aside the art party entirely, if you know that the war goes to the North, wouldn't it be better to speed it up on purpose? To try to intervene so fewer people die? It wouldn't affect the war overall."

"It's not so simple."

"But if you do nothing, it means more death. Seems simple enough to me."

"We can't spend our entire lives trying to fine-tune history. There are billions of people, and you could go a whole lifetime trying to tweak the timelines just so. We deal with the bigger issues."

Neil thought about the people he had killed. They were only individuals and were small and almost insignificant against the scope of all of human history. But they mattered to him.

They returned to the hotel, to their two adjoining rooms. Elliot went to bed and Neil stepped out onto the balcony. Cities were so much darker in this time, and the lights inside nearby buildings were barely visible while the stars were much brighter. Somewhere out there, the art party was being held, and he was missing it.

Well, this was a once in a lifetime opportunity, and he wasn't going to let it pass him by just because Elliot was overly cautious. His clothing wouldn't impress anyone, but he had passed through Hollywood parties and royal galas without being seen. A little party in wartime Kentucky would be nothing.

He slipped out the door, closing it silently, headed down to the street, hailed a cab and asked to be taken to Oak Street. Once there, he walked up the street until he found the most brightly lit house on the block where people moved in and out. He didn't want to go in the front door, and a few of the men were smoking in a side yard. It was nothing to slip around the other side of the house, into the large yard in back and then into the house.

As promised, a long room to one side held various paintings. A small knot of people stood off in one corner, crowded around a painting in a heavy gold frame. The Rembrandt.

He moved up behind the crowd, and though a man stepped backward onto his foot, he didn't move. The painting was one he had seen before in art books, but never in person. It was called *The Anatomy Lesson*. A group of men with pointed beards crowded around a table upon which lay a nearly nude male corpse. The man was stocky, and his chest was so large that he looked like he was taking a deep breath. Of course, he was dead, but the artist even made the dead look lively and interesting. A man in a black hat, not unlike a pilgrim hat, was cutting open the man's arm to show the bones inside.

Neil could not draw or paint. He couldn't play any instruments or write poetry. Elliot had been correct when he had said that Neil loved art and music and plays and opera, but never created anything himself. But Elliot did not know why. Neil could love things like this painting, the sculpture of a rounded miniature woman on the display table to the right, orchestras full of moaning cellos and drums that raced like heartbeats, but he could never create anything himself. Heaven knew he had tried over and over, failing each time. Like a machine, he could replicate the work of others, but what he created himself was as lifeless as the corpse on the table in the painting. It had the shape of life, but was colorless and cold, bereft of the breath that made the creations of others live.

A woman bumped into him, and he ignored her apology. "I'm sorry, but I'm not sure we've been introduced," she said, looking him up and down.

"I'm a guest of Miss Jones," said Neil. "I'm afraid I need to be getting back to her. If you will excuse me."

He left through the back doors and had reached the street in front of the house when he felt he was being watched.

Elliot. It was Elliot, leaning against a lamppost like a man in an old-fashioned movie, glaring at him from under his hat. Neil saw him wait a moment, push off from the lamppost and walk slowly to join him.

"Don't ever do that again," said Elliot. "A Time Corps agent can't simply do as he pleases. We have a job, and we do it."

"I didn't talk to anyone, I didn't prevent any conversations. I just looked at the painting and left, no harm done."

"Glad to hear it, but the issue is one of disobeying a direct order."

"Order? I don't take orders from you, Mr. Van Dorn."

"Don't call me that," said Elliot. "Look, I'm not trying to bust your ass. I'm just saying that we can't have a rogue time agent running around. I'm the one who is supposed to train you, and you have to do as I say."

"Like an apprentice?" said Neil, not bothering to disguise the resentment in his voice. Who the hell was this man, following him in the night as if he needed a babysitter? He had traveled through time many, many times and Elliot knew it. And yet, he was supposed to be some subservient student.

"Yeah, like an apprentice."

"I'm not your apprentice, Elliot. I'm your partner."

"Not yet, you're not. Not until you're trained. And doing this job with me is your first lesson."

"And what job is that? Where exactly are we taking this ship in a bottle? Why is it important?"

"I can't explain that, not entirely."

"Another of your time loops, right?"

"I'm not making things up to torture you. For any agent, their earliest times in the Corps are the most sensitive. Almost all the other agents already know who they are, so revealing anything important to them could be risky. Once you're trained up, you'll get the full briefing, just like the rest of us."

"Tell me now. If that little ship is something I need to know about, then I want to know. So tell me right now."

"God, you're a pain in the ass, do you know that?" Elliot said, and there was no laughter in his voice. "You are so difficult when you're young. You'll mellow a lot, I'll tell you that about your future. You're not a willful, thorny, sneaking pain in my ass then."

"I wouldn't have had to sneak if you weren't being unreasonable. You won't tell me why we're here, you give me no information about our job and expect me to obey you like you're my dad." He paused. "You're not, are you? My dad?"

"God I hope not."

Elliot hailed a cab and they climbed in.

"Look," Elliot said. "You're going to be a good agent. One of the best. But there are rules, and one of them is you have to listen to whoever is in charge of the mission. The Time Corps is not dictatorial and we don't expect mindless obedience. We value initiative and more than half our jobs don't work out according to plan. The ability to improvise can be key. But running off because you wanted to see a painting is just plain irresponsible."

Neil watched the city pass by out the window.

"The Time Corps is like a stabilizing force," Elliot continued. "We're like the stabilizing hand on the rudder of history." He sat back, satisfied with his analogy.

But Neil had heard that argument before. The hand of justice. The hand of stability. How different were they, really?

CHAPTER 17

January 6, 1864
New Orleans, Louisiana

H AZEL WAS SITTING IN THE library when she heard shouting from the backyard where the Professor and McCullen were running experiments. She threw her book down and rushed downstairs, wondering what horror awaited her. Perhaps the experiments with opening a door to the hub universe, the world that stood between their own and Miss Sanchez's world, had caused an accident like the one that had made the Professor's old laboratory vanish. Or they could have created an unstable time rip. Perhaps worst of all, they might have attracted the void wyrm. She had rarely seen the Professor frightened, but his look when he had described the creature to her was still vivid in her mind. If the thing scared him, she never wanted to encounter it herself.

Hazel threw open the back kitchen door, hoping she was ready to face whatever awaited her outside. Everything was calm. McCullen was telling Miss Sanchez something, and for some reason, she was smiling as if they were old friends. The Professor was off to one side, bouncing up and down on the balls of his feet. He stopped moving, got a startled look and hurried to the iron patio table to make some note in a little book.

"What is it? What happened?" Hazel demanded. They were all alive, smiling and happy, while she was scared out of her wits.

"They did it!" said Miss Sanchez. "The door, they opened the door to the other world! Right there." Miss Sanchez pointed to a spot of empty lawn. "They got the door to open, and the readings confirm that it's the world that September Wilde told the Professor about. They did it!"

"We all did it," said McCullen. "Do not discount your contribution, Miss Sanchez."

"He's just being nice," Miss Sanchez said to Hazel. "I didn't do much."

"Now, we'll have none of that," called the Professor as he continued making notes. "It was Miss Sanchez who came up with the Spaghetti Theory."

Mrs. Washington rushed through the kitchen, carrying a handful of spoons and a cloth, a terrified look on her face. She must have been polishing the silver. "What is going on out here?" she asked Hazel, stopping beside her.

"They opened a doorway into another world," said Hazel. "Nothing to worry about."

Mrs. Washington gave her a look as if to say that it was most definitely something to worry about. "As long as no one is getting killed or is disappearing. Now you, Miss Dubois, you shouldn't be getting involved in all this.

"I was reading in the library."

"You know what I'm talking about. If the Professor wants to risk his neck, that's his business. But you—just stay away from it. Promise me you'll look after yourself."

Hazel didn't answer, as she didn't want to make a promise to Mrs. Washington that she intended to break. The housekeeper touched her shoulder. "Try not to let them do anything foolish," she said before going back to her work.

Miss Sanchez helped McCullen with a small box with a twisted jumble of wires running to another box. Hazel went out to help them wind up the tangle.

"What is the Spaghetti Theory that the Professor mentioned?" she asked.

"Well," said Miss Sanchez, "you know how we perceive time as a straight line, one event after the other? As it turns out, time in each universe is like a strand of spaghetti. It's a line, but it can curve, touch itself and, most importantly, touch other spaghetti strands, other worlds. All of the worlds together are like a giant plate of spaghetti, each touching the others in various places. If you find the touch points, which are usually marked as synchronicities, then you can travel from one to the other. But the spaghetti strands move, so the touch points can change."

"Like a plate of worms," said Hazel.

"I suppose. But I like spaghetti better."

"And now," said the Professor, "we have some preliminary readings. Traveling is not safe yet, as we need to study it more, determine a few of the touch points between our strand and the other world's strand, and get time readings so we don't end up in prehistoric times or the distant future where we could be lost or arrested or who knows what?"

"How long will that take?" Hazel's birthday was only the day after tomorrow, and it was possible that when the Professor opened the time door, that it might be the method by which Neil Grey came to see her. It might also be her opportunity to go see the universe, or universes as the case may be.

"A few days, I'd say." The Professor glanced at McCullen for confirmation. He gave a nod. "Yes, a few days."

It was strange to see the Professor working so well with McCullen, and Hazel wondered what the two of them had been like together in prison in Ireland, or here in New Orleans after their escape. Perhaps the prospect of returning to his own time and world had given McCullen a chance to reform. Perhaps he no longer wished for power or war. But she doubted it. Her mother, God rest her soul, had not raised a fool. A scorpion's nature was to strike.

"Hazel, would you recalibrate the sensors to these settings?" The Professor handed her a slip of paper, grinning at her like a fool. He looked like he wanted to slap her on the back or muss up her hair like he had when she was younger. She couldn't help but smile back, so contagious was his enthusiasm.

"This is marvelous. It's all finally paid off," she said to him, low enough so as not to be overheard. "All the years, all that work. It paid off."

"That it has. That it has."

She gave him a quick hug and then recalibrated the sensors, wondering what time the new doorway would lead into, and how this other world would differ from her own. She wanted to go and see, especially if it was the future. She wanted to ride in an automobile, though the Professor had told her that it was a sickening experience. Apparently he had somehow managed to ride in one in 1961. More than that, she wanted to go on an airplane. Imagine, sailing through the sky, even above the clouds. Miss Sanchez talked about it like it was an ordinary experience, but how could anyone ever tire of such a thing?

But she was torn. On the one hand, leaving with the Professor, McCullen and Miss Sanchez would be a grand adventure, but she hated to leave Cassandra, Mrs. Washington and Mr. Ross behind. Mr. Ross was not her fiancé, not yet, but he was her dear friend, her beau, and he did not deserve abandonment.

On second thought, if they could travel through time, why not just return to the day they left? Was that too much to hope for? Could the Professor ever perfect the machine to have that degree of accuracy? When she was a child she would undoubtedly have thought so. Now, she wondered. The Professor and McCullen were brilliant, but not infallible. And if it hadn't been for September Wilde telling them that she and her siblings, whoever they were, would get rid of the void wyrm, then the doorway in Jackson Square would have remained and more people would have been killed. The two of them could not control their dangerous inventions.

Her own world here was safe, more or less. Marrying Mr. Ross was safe, but terrifying at the same time. Going with the Professor was both terrifying and unsafe. But it was so very, very appealing.

Time was running out. Her birthday was close, the prospect of the Professor opening a door they could travel though was a reality, and Mr. Ross awaited her answer.

CHAPTER 18

January 6, 1864
Cairo, Illinois

NEIL WALKED MORE THAN A block behind Elliot as he followed him through the streets of Cairo, Illinois. Elliot was unaware that he was being followed, or so Neil hoped. Whenever he had needed to stalk a target before, the person was unaware of his presence. Elliot, however, was presumably well aware of Neil's talents.

That morning, their riverboat had docked in Cairo, which, Neil had learned, was pronounced "kay-roh." It was still a day by riverboat to Memphis, where Elliot would deliver the Viking ship in a bottle to its mysterious recipient. Elliot had informed Neil that he had to meet with a fellow member of the Time Corps in Cairo, and that Neil should remain on the boat, or could sightsee. His choice.

The town was nestled on a point of land at the confluence of the Ohio and the Mississippi Rivers, where Illinois, Kentucky and Missouri met. It was not large enough to warrant much exploration, nor was Neil content to remain behind while Elliot had a clandestine meeting. So he had decided to follow him.

Neil slipped sideways to avoid being banged into by a large man carrying a box, and then resumed his pursuit. Elliot seemed to know where he was going, and opened the door to a candy shop with a window full of chocolates, lemon drops and colorful hard candies. The painted lettering on the window advertised "Sumptuous Sweets" and a cardboard sign informed him that fresh Brown Betty and apple trifles were available that day.

Now, what could Elliot want in a place like that? Well, everyone liked sweets. Perhaps he was getting some to bring to his colleague. Maybe a female colleague. Was that why he didn't want Neil to come along? Could it be something as innocent as a romantic liaison? No, he decided. If Elliot had some sort of office romance brewing, then with all of time available, Neil was sure they could get some time alone if they wished. Besides, Elliot could simply have told Neil he had a date, and that would have been that.

Neil waited on a far corner, where Elliot would not see him when he emerged from the candy shop. But he did not emerge.

Neil could have kicked himself when he understood that this place was the location of the meeting. For some reason, he had assumed it would take place in a fancy hotel restaurant or a seedy pub, perhaps at a person's house. But at a sweet shop? Why not?

It was no trouble to find the alleyway that ran behind the row of shops and to locate the door leading into the candy shop. It was unlocked, and Neil stepped inside, moving silently and with his practiced stealth. He did not go into the main shop or even peek around a corner. There was no way to know when someone might glance his way, so he leaned up against a door in the back hallway, presumably an office or storage room, ready to open it and hide inside.

Elliot was speaking. "I didn't even know what Brown Betty was until I started time traveling."

"You didn't need to time travel, just travel a little in your own country," said a woman.

"Well, I was living in a trailer on the beach in LA before

I joined the Time Corps, and I was too broke to even buy a Greyhound ticket. So travel was out of the question. But I had a lot of carnival desserts working at the boardwalk, that's for sure. Then I was indisposed for quite a while."

Neil hadn't known that Elliot was also from California. He hadn't bothered to ask, assuming that Elliot was as reluctant to discuss his origins as Neil was. The woman and Elliot talked back and forth about desserts, discussing Russian apricot cream delight and Asian sticky rice with mango until Neil wondered if he had wasted his time entirely.

"So, tell me about the new recruit," said the woman.

"He is surly and aloof and only follows orders when it suits him."

"That's our Neil, when he was young at least."

"Yeah, well, he'll be a hell of a lot more useful once he's trained up. He's the best strong-arm guy we have. Will have. You know what I mean," said Elliot.

"So why did you get him now? Why not wait until he's older?"

"Time was right, that's all. He was alone and with nowhere to go. It was the best time to recruit him, and we need him soon. There's a project being put together, and we need someone strong and fast. Someone who can handle himself in a fight."

"And he has other abilities we need," said the woman.

"I wouldn't be putting up with him if he didn't."

They went on to talk about other topics, and Neil was getting ready to leave when he heard Elliot say that he was going to visit the bookstore before he went back to the riverboat. Neil slipped out the back and headed back to the river.

He had the abilities the Time Corps needed. That was why Elliot had found him and offered him work. He couldn't say it was a shock. Why else would they need him? Certainly not for his sparkling personality and witty banter. He was useful to them, that was all. Like a hammer is useful for driving in nails. You don't love the hammer, you don't worry about it unless it breaks. It's a tool, a useful thing.

And that was what he was, a tool in Mr. March's hand, and now a tool in the hands of the Time Corps. Both wanted obedience. Both wanted him to use his skills to bring death to those they chose, or at least to fight for them, according to Elliot and the woman in the candy shop.

A small, grassy park ran along one side of the street, and he was tempted to stop and have a seat on the bench in the shade, to wait for Elliot and pretend he had heard nothing.

The woman had mentioned that this was how Neil was, when he was young. That meant that she knew him when he was older. Did that mean he was predestined to work for them forever? Or was that changeable? How much of his life was his own to determine? And how much was set before he ever had a chance to make a choice?

He kept walking, heading for the riverboat and the cabin he shared with Elliot, where their belongings were currently stored. Neil barely owned anything, just a few changes of clothing he had purchased at their last stop. Elliot had come with two wheeled trunks, one full of clothing and miscellaneous items. The other sat propped up in the corner on its end, and sometimes Elliot tossed his coat over it or set a book on top. He never opened it.

Neil boarded the riverboat and went to their cabin. The room was tiny, with two bunk beds, a small round table and two folding wooden chairs that were currently propped against the wall. Neil gingerly lowered the mysterious trunk onto the floor and opened it. Inside was a machine. The base of it was a thick wooden pedestal, like a box with a little door on one side. The side had a small panel with dials and knobs and at the top of the pedestal sat a paneled brass sphere.

This must be the time machine. Mr. March had never required such a thing, but Elliot was not the same type of being as Mr. March. Elliot was a regular, ordinary man. He was not especially strong or exceptionally talented, as far as Neil could tell, though he was intelligent. He liked to read. That they had in common.

Neil opened the little door on the side, and discovered a cloth bundle. He unwrapped it to find the Viking ship in a bottle. Rotating it, he studied the dragon-headed ship with its graceful curves and the red and white striped sail. What had Elliot said when he bought it in the thrift shop in Las Vegas? Monkeys. Perhaps he had been making an attempt at a joke.

He wrapped the ship and put it back inside its compartment, closed up the trunk and was about to tip it back into place when he stopped. This was an important moment. This was one of the moments, like the moment when he decided not to kill Trevor Grant in the robotics laboratory or like the moment when he decided not to work for Mr. March any more. This was a moment of choice.

He could stay, be obedient to Elliot and his Time Corps in the hope that they were one of the good guys. But really, who needed someone like him, an assassin, a murderer if he got right down to it, for good purposes? His skills were solely useful in spying or killing people. He was not a being made for peace, unless he took it upon himself to become one.

He was no pacifist, and he wouldn't hesitate to take down anyone who tried to harm him. But he wouldn't allow himself to become a tool for anyone again. He would not be used for the purposes of others. Mr. March had used him as a cat's paw, a thing to hurt others while March sat back, innocent of the wicked deeds, his own hands clean of their blood.

Well, those days were done. And so were his days of hoping that Elliot and the Time Corps would be any different. They had a job for him, did they? One that used his skills?

No. He would not help them. If the work was so noble and honorable, then why keep it a secret? All clues pointed in one direction. They wanted him to beat or kill people, and they would want him to do it without explanation.

So what if the woman in the shop knew him in the future? The future could be changed, and he would not be swayed by something that was only a possibility. He could make his own fate. He would steal the time machine.

He grabbed his heavy canvas bag and threw in the few items of clothing he owned. He still had the money from Mr. March, and he thumbed through it, seeing how much there was. Enough for a few weeks, if he was careful.

Then he had an idea. The little ship in a bottle was bound for Memphis, where Elliot was presumably going to sell it or deliver it to someone for one of his missions. If Neil took it, then Elliot might think that Neil intended to take it to Memphis to get the money himself. It would be a stupid plan, as Elliot had never told Neil exactly who wanted the thing or where they lived. But maybe Elliot underestimated him and would think him rash enough to do such a thing. If he did, it would send Elliot off of the trail, searching in Memphis. It was worth a shot.

Slinging his bag over his shoulder, he made sure the latches on the time machine's trunk were secure. He grabbed the leather strap and rolled the trunk out of the room, onto the ship's deck and down the gangplank. The machine was his freedom. It would let him travel to any world, once he learned how to use it. And once he could do that, Mr. March couldn't find him. No one would find him. He could be on his own, under no one's control and no one's authority. A free man.

He hired a trap to take him to the railroad station and then bought a ticket for the next train heading south. It was going to Nashville, but that would work well enough.

Anywhere away from the river would be best, even if it took him through war-torn areas. Now he was glad that he had never told Elliot about wanting to go to New Orleans to leave word with September Wilde. Elliot would have no idea where to find him.

The train arrived and Neil boarded, settling into his seat. The scenery didn't please him, and neither did the train car, however historical it might be. Perhaps things felt wrong because he had lost a bit of hope, the hope of working for a good organization, of having a place to belong, a group of people he could trust.

Elliot was not a bad man. He had been good company. He was one of the generally pleasant people in the world who smiled easily and laughed often. Neil would never be such a person. Maybe that was why he felt strange, because this companion had not been such a good friend after all.

The train rolled forward. It didn't matter if he felt strange inside. He was free now, free of false friends and free of the chains with which they wanted to bind him.

CHAPTER 19

January 7, 1864
New Orleans, Louisiana

"**Y**OU LOOK LIKE YOU'RE FIT to burst," said Seamus. Miss Sanchez walked down the street beside him with bright eyes and a bouncing step.

"Just looking forward to getting home," she said. "If we time it right, I can put my sister in touch with the doctor. And once that is done, and my nephew is all better, I will take you for burgers and frozen yogurt."

"It won't be long now, and you can you can make me the burgers and some of this frozen yogurt. Also, I would like to make a phone call."

"Really? Who would you call?"

"Oh, I don't know. I just want to try making a phone call."

Miss Sanchez laughed, and his spirits lifted with the sound. The poor woman had been through so much and now she would finally have a chance to get home. No wonder she was happy.

He was happy as well, more for her sake than his own. He had worked for so long to find a way to retrieve her from 1961 and get her home. Within the last few weeks, he had figured out a way to do both. Sure, he was saddled with McCullen, but his old partner's presence had proven almost pleasant. It had been like old times, more or less. There was the thrill of discovery, the shared struggle, and the companionship of an equal. McCullen would be going with them when they went to the hub world between this world and Miss Sanchez's. McCullen's home world was not this one, nor was it Miss Sanchez's world, but another one entirely. He wondered how many worlds there were and what surprises they held.

He sighed. "I feel guilty leaving Hazel behind. She'll not be pleased with me."

"I know," said Miss Sanchez. "She'll be upset with us both. But she'll be fine. Both of us met her in 1961, and she's healthy and happy."

"She dresses like a madwoman and drives like a demon from hell."

"Does she? I didn't think so."

"Her birthday is tomorrow, and I hate to miss it."

"We can leave the day after, if you want," said Miss Sanchez, but Seamus could tell it was hard for her to make the offer.

"No need for that. I know you want to be getting home. And her birthday is the day that Neil Grey is supposedly going to come visit her. If we took her with us, she wouldn't be here to meet him. It might be an event we can't mess about with for fear of creating an instability."

"You don't know that for certain. She could meet him on her birthday precisely because we take her with us."

Seamus sighed. He hated the idea of trying to match his actions to create the circumstances for some potential future to occur. He would simply do what he thought was best, and trust that it would all work out in the end. Any other way would drive him to madness.

"The fact that she's alive and well in a century means she chooses to be a time traveler," said Seamus. "That we know for sure."

"True," said Miss Sanchez. "We just don't know when she decides to do it. She could marry, live here and then travel later in life, or travel immediately. The important thing is that if we leave her here, she's financially independent and isn't forced into marriage. She has to make her own decision on it."

"Our Hazel is a headstrong thing and a right devil when she gets her mind set on something. So I'll not be the one telling her what to do. She's a grown woman now. Ah, here's the office."

He held the door open for her, and then followed Miss Sanchez into the solicitor's office.

"Mr. Connor," said the solicitor. "Back again so soon?"

"I need to modify my will again and make a few changes to the deed on my house."

Miss Sanchez sat by his side as he made his arrangements. The house, all his patents, equipment and fortune would be given to Miss Hazel Dubois upon her eighteenth birthday. He also stipulated that the patents and her house had to remain as her own, even if she married. He could do nothing about her money, as that would become her husband's, but his patents and the house could legally be kept separate. Any income from the patents would be her husband's too, and any husband was welcome to live in the house with her, but upon his death, the assets would revert to being hers. Whatever happened, he had to ensure that Hazel remained the owner into the 1960s.

The two of them stopped by the bank next and withdrew an enormous amount of money, and then exchanged all of it for gold.

When they returned home, McCullen was in the laboratory. He had packed up the few things he wanted into a leather case and the table he used near one window was as tidy as could be. His things might molder there for years, unless someone disturbed them, and Mrs. Washington wouldn't set foot in the laboratory, even if one area of it was clean.

If Seamus returned, it would be without McCullen. Seamus wondered. He had a life here, such as it was. He enjoyed working at Tulane University, but his true joy was in his own experiments. His family was in Ireland, but by necessity, they could never see him again. And when Hazel became a time traveler, he was sure to see her again as well. Perhaps he would never come back at all. Well, that was a decision for another day.

Mrs. Washington called them to supper but Seamus was too excited to eat, so he told McCullen and Miss Sanchez to go downstairs without him. He found a sheet of stationery, a pot of ink and a pen. He wrote out his resignation letter to Tulane and set it aside for Mrs. Washington to post later. Then he wrote a letter to Hazel, asking her to please send money to his family in Ireland. This time, he would not be back in a few days. If she thought it best, she could even tell them where he had gone, and that he was alive.

He touched the back end of the pen to his lower lip. Perhaps, at some point, he could even go visit them. So long as the authorities didn't know ahead of time, he would be safe. Well, for now, having Hazel send money to his mother was the best he could do. He asked her to watch over the time rips and to take good care of herself.

Most of the things he wrote, he had written before when he had gone to 1961. He wanted to write more, to tell Hazel something of value, something fatherly, but only practical things came to his mind. Renew the patents on time, pay the property tax, remember to keep the attic door closed or it would warp in the humidity. He could not put his heart on the paper, and had to trust that she knew that he loved her, that he wished her only good things, not the dangerous life he was about to undertake.

He sighed and read it over. It would have to do. He wished he could simply tell Hazel in person, but she would insist on coming. If she were a more malleable young woman, more obedient and docile, he would be able to manage her. But she wasn't, so he was forced to say good-bye in a letter. He folded the paper, sealed it and looked down at it. All their years together and it all came down to a slip of paper and some ink.

He left the note on the table beside her favorite reading chair in the library. She wouldn't find it until the next day as she usually spent time in the kitchen with Mrs. Washington after supper and then played violin in her room.

Seamus packed his things and confirmed and reconfirmed the coordinates, checked on the supply of gold which would serve as currency in any world, and then rushed to toss a few of his own belongings into a bag.

After supper, the three of them crept out of the house, bags in hand and rolling one trunk for Miss Sanchez's dresses, which took up more space than men's clothing, and another trunk with the time machine. The sound of Hazel's violin drifted down the stairs, hopefully muffling the rattling of the trunk wheels. Once on the street below, Seamus looked up. The gaslight gave Hazel's window a soft yellow glow. Mrs. Washington was probably in the kitchen or her own room.

They headed down the street until they found a trap they could hire, and rode to the riverfront. Seamus didn't think he would want to stay permanently in Miss Sanchez's world, in 2015. But if she could see her family any time she liked, she might like to come back with him, or go to Egypt or France or wherever they liked

Once they reached the banks of the Mississippi, they found a man with a rowboat and offered him an extravagant amount for it, payable immediately in gold. He took the payment gladly, eying the trio as if they might be criminals on the run.

"Let's load it up," said Seamus, and they filled the rowboat with their bags and trunks.

When Miss Sanchez had come to this world, she had been riding a bus in her world and there had been a horse-pulled omnibus in Seamus's world moving in the same location while Seamus was accidentally creating the conditions for a time rip with the equipment in his laboratory. There was no way to recreate events in reverse and get her home. McCullen had arrived from his world via a naturally occurring time rip, which never reoccurred, at least not in any predictable fashion.

The plan to get the two of them home was as simple as they could make it. Once they tore a hole from Seamus's world into the hub world, they would find themselves in 1864 once more.

From that world, they needed to get to McCullen's and Miss Sanchez's worlds. Unfortunately, a simple riverboat synchronicity would not work. Getting to the hub world was easy. Leaving might prove more difficult.

The synchronicities leading to both McCullen's world and Miss Sanchez's were earthquakes that would devastate Los Angeles. Miss Sanchez remembered both from history books, while McCullen only knew of the first one. One earthquake would be in 1864 and the other in 1958. They would use the earthquake synchronicities to move from 1864 to 1958, still in the hub world. Then they would hop to 1958 in McCullen's world. That was where they would part ways. And that was also the point where it would get tricky.

McCullen took the oars and rowed them out into the river, while Seamus set up the machine.

After they left McCullen, they would have to use the same synchronicity, the 1958 earthquake, to get from there to Miss Sanchez's world in 1958. Then, as Miss Sanchez had put it, they would "ride the noodle" along to 2015.

He knew things could go very wrong, which made him glad that Hazel would not be coming along. But nothing ventured, nothing gained. And if Miss Sanchez was willing to take the risk, then so was he.

They were at the center of the river now, and McCullen

pulled rhythmically at the oars. It was quiet out here, the water was dark and the city lights sparkled on the shore.

"Time to fire it up," Seamus said, and grinned at Miss Sanchez. "Isn't that how you say it in your time? Fire it up?"

She sighed in exasperation, and shook her head, but a moment later, she slipped her hand into his, and he reached forward and threw the switch.

CHAPTER 20

January 8, 1864
New Orleans, Louisiana

HAZEL BALLED UP THE PROFESSOR'S letter and threw it into the fireplace.

"Damn the man," she growled, forcing herself to keep her voice down so as not to disturb Mrs. Washington. She lit a match, threw it in and glared at the paper as it curled and blackened. "The filthy bastard." She added other curses, ones she had not uttered out loud in years. He had earned every one of them.

He had left without her. He and Miss Sanchez and even wicked old McCullen. The Professor had taken his worst enemy with him, but had left her behind.

This time, the letter held no indication that the Professor might come back in a month or would even try to return at all. He had left her money, his patents, the house, everything, but she didn't care. Did he think those things would matter to her? That they were important? He had assured her that she was not a burden on him, but when it came down to it, he gave her money and then off he went. It was wretched, to be paid off like an unwanted bastard child.

And it wasn't only the Professor. Miss Sanchez had also left her. She could have woken Hazel when they left, whenever that was, and taken her with them. Even if the Professor had objected, Miss Sanchez had never hesitated to disobey him when it suited her. Hazel thought back to her talk with Miss Sanchez, about the world of the future and how Hazel wouldn't be able to get along in it without seeming like a madwoman. This was from the woman who had shown up in the street wearing tight men's trousers and who hadn't known how to lace up a corset or put up her hair. Miss Sanchez had learned to live in their world, so why couldn't Hazel do the same in hers?

The entire thing was grossly unfair. Cruel even. The Professor had promised. He had promised not to leave her. Hadn't he? She couldn't remember if he had actually promised. It didn't matter. She was alone. Tears stung her eyes, tears of rage and pain. She stormed into the laboratory, not knowing what she was looking for or what she would do. She wanted to find something that mattered to the Professor and destroy it, to smash it to bits. Her vision blurred by tears, she surveyed the chaos of the room where she had spent so many childhood afternoons, sitting with the Professor, talking or listening to him rattle on about his findings. All around the room lay scattered ledgers and papers, half-finished mechanical pieces, rolls of tubing and wire, all of it abandoned.

She picked up a mechanical arm, most likely one of the limbs from an automaton at the cathedral. But she couldn't destroy it. It wasn't right, and it would be useless and futile. It wasn't as if the Professor would care if she burned the whole house to the ground. And even if she only destroyed things in the laboratory, it wouldn't make any difference anyway, as everything was already a mess. Everything except McCullen's table near the window. That was clean and orderly.

She drew closer, curious. She sorted through things. Perhaps he had left something, a clue, anything. But there was nothing useful. McCullen wasn't her friend anyway, but as lonely as she felt, she was willing to take any comfort she could find. She flipped through his papers, only pausing for a moment when she saw the name September Wilde. The paper was covered in equations, none of them decipherable to her.

Hazel had accompanied the Professor on visits to September Wilde before. The woman had been completely unhelpful in giving the Professor any useful information, and instead had offered them both pieces of molasses cake.

A fine birthday this was turning out to be. It was nearly noon, and Neil Grey still had not come to visit her. The Professor and Miss Sanchez had abandoned her, and Mr. Ross would surely come by, offering her a birthday gift and hoping she would accept his marriage offer.

She had to get out of the house if she wished to avoid Mr. Ross. It was cowardly, yes, but she only needed a little more time. If Neil Grey never came, or if he refused to take her with him, then she would marry Mr. Ross. But if she could leave, would she? Was her curiosity so strong that she would sacrifice a happy home, a pleasant marriage, money and security to satisfy it?

She grabbed her wrap, put on her bonnet and went to the kitchen to tell Mrs. Washington where she would be and to inform her that her employer was gone forever.

Mrs. Washington was having coffee, her feet propped up on a kitchen chair. When Hazel came in, she pulled her feet down.

"Put them up if you like. It doesn't bother me," said Hazel.

"It's just that they get tired," Mrs. Washington said by way of apology.

Hazel was about to take the chair across from her, but felt too restless. She needed to move or she would go mad.

"He's gone," she said. "The Professor is gone. He took Miss Sanchez and McCullen."

"Are they at his university laboratory?"

"No, they're gone completely, to another time. The machine worked."

Mrs. Washington got a strange look, but it was not one of either shock or disbelief. It was more like a bewildered sense of surprise. Hazel knew that the housekeeper had always known that the Professor had made a time rip, because Miss Sanchez had arrived. Through the years, Mrs. Washington had repeated her opinion that poor Miss Sanchez was an unfortunate woman who might have been touched in the head or had a bad family history. Hazel had never thought that Mrs. Washington truly believed it. She couldn't deny the evidence before her, that a woman from another time had come and gone, and that the Professor had made a time traveling machine.

"It's a cruel thing, to leave you on your birthday. I like the Professor. I truly do. But oftentimes he does things that aren't wise or considerate. It's a good thing he left you here though, instead of dragging you off. You're better off safe at home."

"But I'm not. I'm just as stuck here as ever." Hazel paced to the door and back. "I wanted to go see the future and other worlds. Just imagine it! And they left me behind. The Professor even left the house and everything else to me. He's never coming back, and I'm stranded here all alone."

"Now, you listen to me. This isn't like you. You are not an ungrateful girl. Lord knows you've been through enough to appreciate what you have. And that's what you need to do now. Be grateful for it."

"I'm going out for a bit," Hazel said. "I need to get outside and take some fresh air."

"You're pacing around this kitchen like a caged panther, or the Professor. You and he are more alike than you think."

"This moment would not be the finest time to tell me that. He's not my favorite individual at present."

"I'm simply saying that when you both get upset, you get restless. The two of you are kindred spirits, you are. Always wanting to run instead of walk."

"I'll be home before supper," Hazel grumbled.

"Before you go, there's a letter for you from the owner of the music shop you work for."

"Mr. Augustus?" Hazel found the envelope on the sideboard. Inside, a letter informed her that he would be closing the shop for a few months. He was going on an extended visit to see his siblings. Now, that was odd. The shop was not doing well, and for him to close it would perhaps lead to its bankruptcy. He would only do this for the direst of reasons.

And there was another strange thing. Mr. Augustus knew that she could run the shop. She knew how everything operated, could place orders, repair most broken instruments herself and was trustworthy. So why would he rather risk the ruin of his business than ask her? She would have done the favor for him gladly.

At the bottom of the note, after his signature, was a postscript. It was a series of numbers with dashes breaking them into groups. Perhaps he had installed one of those combination locks on the shop door, and her old key would not work. Did he want her to go look in on the shop? If so, why hadn't he asked her? It was just another in a frustrating series of events.

She said good-bye to Mrs. Washington and walked down the street, her anger giving her speed. She had nowhere to go, but moving felt good. When she grew tired, she thought of looking in on Mr. Augustus's shop. She waved down a trap, but a second before she gave him the address, she changed her mind. She didn't remember September Wilde's exact address, but she knew the street and would recognize the house. She told the driver to take her there.

As she passed through the streets of New Orleans, she thought of the time she had spent as a child of the streets, dressing as a boy and living off the coins she earned playing her violin. She had neither confided in nor trusted anyone. Certainly, she had liked the Professor, one of the few adults who regularly gave her work and paid her well. But she was alone then, seeing the world as a hostile and cruel place and people as untrustworthy.

Perhaps her view of the world had been clearer then. There were no illusions then, no silly hopes. She was self-sufficient, strong and independent. Now, she had become soft, needing others. Imagine, being sad because someone who wasn't even family had left her. It was foolish and weak.

She paid the driver and walked the few blocks to Miss Wilde's house. Mrs. Washington had told her years ago that Miss Wilde held a bit of notoriety for choosing to live in a white neighborhood. Strangely, few people minded, and whenever a group of citizens, or rarer still, the police, paid a visit to her, they always left with baked goods and smiles on their faces. And so Miss Wilde stayed, living in her little house, unmolested.

Hazel knocked on the door, shifting her weight from one foot to the other when no one answered. She knocked again and was about to leave, angry that she would have to walk a few blocks to find another trap, when the door opened.

The man standing there was known to her, but he was young, far too young. When she had seen him last, he had been in his forties. And now, he was only a few years older than she was.

"Mr. Grey?" she said. "It's you! You're here. Oh but this is a surprise! You did come on my birthday!"

"Do I know you?" He looked like he was about to close the door.

"It's me. Hazel. You haven't seen me since I was eleven." She sighed. "And you were older then, so you won't remember. But you did meet me and told me you'd see me again on my birthday."

"And it's your birthday today?"

"It is. I came to see Miss Wilde. I didn't know you'd

be here." She wanted to jump up and down and do a little dance, but Mr. Grey was looking at her like she was somehow dangerous. Well, she must look a little wild around the eyes and she was smiling too broadly. She composed her features and waited for him to invite her inside. It was impolite to leave a lady standing on the doorstep.

"May I come in?" she finally asked.

"You may. No one else is home. Miss Wilde left this morning."

He backed up from the door and she entered, pushing the door closed behind her. A white cat sat halfway up the stairs, watching her. It licked its paw and swiped circles over its face.

Mr. Grey looked uncertain, as if deciding if he should let her stay and talk or ask her to leave. "I was making a sandwich when you came."

"Don't let me interrupt," she said and followed him to the kitchen. He hadn't even offered her a drink or a seat. She tried to remember what Miss Sanchez had said, that manners were different in her time.

"Will Miss Wilde be back later?" she asked.

"She said she had to go see her brother in town at his shop. Then they're going to leave the city for a few months. So no, she won't."

That was the second time she had heard of someone leaving the city. "That's odd. I know someone else who is leaving for a few months. Mr. Augustus, the owner of a music shop I work for."

"That's him. She said her brother, Mr. Augustus, owned a music shop."

"That doesn't make any sense. Miss Wilde is black and Mr. Augustus is white."

"Do you mean they can't be brother and sister?" he asked, looking up.

"It's possible," she said, but she felt her cheeks grow

warm. It was certainly possible that they shared a white father who was married to Mr. Augustus's mother but who had fathered a child with a black maid. The house was modest, but it appeared that Miss Wilde did not live in poverty, so perhaps the father had seen to her upkeep. Or her mother had been a kept woman and she had provided for her daughter. It was not unheard of, but for Hazel to speak of it was unseemly.

Mr. Grey set two roast beef sandwiches on the kitchen table and scooted in his chair. Hazel thanked him, noting that he wasn't completely devoid of manners, and sat opposite him as he ate in silence. He wasn't watching her directly, but she knew he was studying her, probably trying to understand how he would meet her in his future and why she would have expected him today.

"Do you have a time machine?" she asked.

He almost choked. "What?"

"A time machine. You had to get here somehow. I know you were born in the future, sometime around Miss Sanchez's time. And her time was 2015."

"Who is Miss Sanchez?"

"Another time traveler."

"And what else do you know about me?"

He was wary now, and she didn't want to make him uneasy. Of course he would be cautious around someone who already knew so many things about him when he knew nothing about her at all.

"Only that you work for a group of time travelers, that you have a time machine that the Professor made. Last time we met, you knew more about me than I knew about you."

"And what did I know about you?"

"You didn't tell me much, but you knew my name, my real name. When we met, I was a child and I went by the name of Henry and dressed as a boy. You also knew I played violin and you bought me a beautiful instrument. I have it still."

He seemed to be thinking this over. "Can you play well?"

She wondered what she should say. On the one hand, she could be properly modest, but she got the sense that Mr. Grey was looking for information, not just making conversation.

"Yes, I'm a good player." She didn't elaborate or tell him how she had been the best player in her class, nor how Mr. Augustus had asked her, at age eleven, to represent his shop even though he had not taught her to play. She was one of the finest players in the area, but she couldn't tell him that.

"Do you play concerts?" he asked.

"Me? I'm a woman. Playing piano in the drawing room is proper in this time. Standing on a stage playing violin is not."

"Oh, I see," he said. He seemed to be adding it to the catalog of information in his head. To be a time traveler must require that he remember so many details from so many times. "So women aren't supposed to play violin, right?"

"It's allowed, but most people approve of piano or harp or other feminine instruments more, but rarely on stage."

"The violin seems pretty feminine to me," he said, watching her. "The body of it is curved like a woman. It has hips and a waist and it sings with a soprano's voice."

She felt herself blush again and wished Mr. Grey wouldn't say such things. They were completely improper. She tried to remember that Miss Sanchez and Mr. Grey's times were barbaric and strange. Or perhaps he was trying to goad her, to tease her so he wouldn't be the only one who felt uneasy and off guard.

Mr. Grey continued. "I also heard that people in this time think the violin is the devil's instrument, because it sounds like a screaming demon. It possesses men's souls."

He looked dead serious, as if he was giving her a dire warning. She chortled and then burst out laughing. "We're not all mad, superstitious old women here. We have some common sense. It's an instrument, nothing more."

His mouth turned up at the corners, just a fraction, as if he were about to smile. But he continued to eat, and she got the odd sensation that she had just passed some sort of test.

"Do people in your time think the violin is the devil's instrument or some sort of feminine homunculus?" she asked.

"No. I was just asking to see what you thought. That and I love music."

"Do you? I teach people to play, if you'd like to learn."

"No, that's all right. I'm not very talented musically."

"I teach all sorts of people, musical or not. Every person alive has some music in them. That's what I say and I firmly believe it."

The white cat strolled into the room and leaped up on the windowsill. Its ear flicked once, twice, and then it closed its eyes.

A touch of humor crossed Neil's face, and at that moment, she realized what a grim person he was compared to other young men his age. When he was older, he was serious, yes. But at this age, he should have been more animated, more lively.

"So according to you," he said, "we're going to be friends in my future and your past?"

"Both our futures."

"Well then, it appears we have no choice in the matter." The way he said it was half bitter, half humorous. It bothered Hazel, because she knew exactly what he meant.

"It's not as if anyone is forcing us," she said. "We can do as we please. We can part ways, say our pleasantries, and I can go back home and play sad pieces on my violin. Then, you can head off to wherever you're off to."

He seemed to relax a little at that. "You really can play?"

"I'm not inventing stories, if that's what you mean. Would you like me to prove it to you?"

"You would play for me?" he said it as if she was granting him some kind of sacred gift. He looked hesitant, expectant, and also like he was preparing for disappointment.

"Certainly, if you like. I have to return home and fetch my violin though."

"I'll be here all day. I was planning on leaving tomorrow."

She set her plate near the sink and the cat cracked its eyes open enough to look at her, then resumed its nap.

"How do I know you'll be here when I get back?" she said. Her voice came out softer and more childlike than she had intended. Mr. Grey could leave, and his promise to see her on her birthday would be fulfilled. He had never promised to take her into the future.

"I'll be here. Promise."

She looked at him, assessing if he was telling the truth, but she simply didn't know him well enough to be sure.

"You don't believe me," he said. "And really, you shouldn't. How can you really trust anyone? You're smarter not to."

"That's terribly cynical. And you promised to see me on my birthday, and you have."

"If it's in my future, it was simply me stating what had already happened. I didn't intentionally fulfill a promise. And yes, it's cynical. I don't make apologies for that."

"I think you're more optimistic when you're older."

"So I've heard. Now, are you going to go get your violin? Or do I need to take a stroll downtown and see what's happening in the jazz clubs?"

"What is jazz?"

"Another anachronism, that's what. It's music, a type of music. And New Orleans is, will be, famous for it."

"A new type of music?"

"Yeah, and I'll tell you all about it when you come back with your violin."

"Do you promise, do you swear on your mother's grave, to be here when I get back?" she said.

146

"Jeez, you are distrustful, aren't you?"

"The last person I trusted ran off last night into another time."

"Who was that?"

"The Professor."

"What's his name?" He looked wary.

"Seamus Connor."

He relaxed. "Fine. There are a few time travelers I'd rather not cross paths with, that's all. I don't know him."

"Well, you will. But wait here, and I'll return with my violin."

She left him sitting in the kitchen, wondering if he would be there when she returned. She was a fool to trust him, so she decided to pretend that he wouldn't be there when she got back. The whole thing would cost her nothing but a cab fare. She retrieved her violin and returned to Miss Wilde's house.

After she knocked on the door, she turned toward the street, ready to leave. The door opened and Mr. Grey invited her inside.

"You said it was your birthday, right?" he said.

"Yes."

"Then Happy Birthday."

He handed her a little glass bottle with a tiny dragon-headed ship inside.

CHAPTER 21

March 21, 1864
New Orleans, Louisiana
Hub world

"DID IT WORK?" ASKED MISS Sanchez. "I can't tell if it worked." She craned her neck to look onshore. A moment later she groaned and put her hand to her head, presumably from dizziness.

Seamus felt ill as well, and he studied the area along the riverbank, but everything looked just as it had in his own time. Horse-drawn carriages rattled along the riverfront and women with bell-shaped skirts strolled with men in bowlers and top hats.

"We need readings," said McCullen. "I'll take us to shore."

While McCullen rowed them ashore, Seamus put away the time machine and retrieved the portable sensor used for readings. His nausea wasn't as bad this time around. When they touched the shore and he leapt out to pull the boat to shore, he saw that McCullen and Miss Sanchez did not feel well at all. He took readings.

"It's most definitely another world," he said, confirming the readings while McCullen helped Miss Sanchez out of the boat and removed their belongings. "And it appears to be March. I'm thinking about the second or third week."

They rolled the time machine and their trunks onto the sidewalk where they bumped along the wooden planks. Stopping by a newsstand, Seamus was pleased to learn that it was March twenty-first, that there was a Civil War in this world and that the president was named Joshua Lincoln.

"Lincoln lived in this world. Not Jacob Lincoln from my world, but a Lincoln," said Miss Sanchez.

"Interesting," said the Professor. In his world, Ezekiel Lincoln had been assassinated when he was still a senator. Breckinridge was now president. The man beside him, McCullen, had been responsible, at least partly. His krewe had arranged the killing for political reasons. Seamus didn't think McCullen was aware that he possessed this information.

"McCullen," Seamus said, "who was president during the Civil War in your world?"

"Obadiah Lincoln. I would be interested in seeing a photograph of this Joshua Lincoln to see if they are the same man."

"Their feet are like mine," said Miss Sanchez softly.

"Never mind that," said Seamus. "Look what they've done to the cathedral."

Saint Louis Cathedral stood at the back of Jackson Square, and though it was still bright white with three steeples rising into the air, it was also changed. Instead of a cross at the tip of the steeple, there was the figure of a leaping horse.

"What have they done to it? They've desecrated it," said Seamus.

"No, Seamus," said McCullen. "It's more like my world. The Christ religion existed, but it didn't spread so widely in Europe in my world. I was visiting a temple of Epona, the horse goddess, in Ireland when I came through to your world. This may also be one of her temples."

"Let's find the train station," said Miss Sanchez. "We need to get going."

"The earthquake synchronicity isn't until September,"

Seamus said. "We intentionally gave ourselves plenty of time to get to Los Angeles."

"The city will be damaged," said McCullen. "The earthquake will rival the one later in San Francisco, though Los Angeles is more sparsely populated, if I remember correctly. Terrible destruction."

"Cheery," muttered Miss Sanchez. Without waiting for the men, she set off down the street and Seamus had to hurry to keep up, burdened by the bags and the wheeled trunk as he was. McCullen wheeled the other trunk, and Miss Sanchez carried two bulky bags. She paused now and again as nausea or dizziness overcame her, and he and McCullen did the same. Seamus hoped Hazel was right, that this sickness would get easier with time. Otherwise, frequent travel would be a miserable experience.

"We need to get money," said McCullen. "Give me some of the gold."

Seamus hesitated, but then dug out a ring and gave it to McCullen who then set off to ask where he could trade gold for money.

"Take this." Seamus gave Miss Sanchez a gold necklace. "You might want to hide it so you don't tempt any thieves."

"Thanks." She turned away from the street and discreetly triple looped it around her ankle and fastened it.

"Six more months until I'm home," she sighed with a little smile of longing.

That brought Seamus a twinge of pain, like a tiny cut. Naturally, she wanted to return home to her own time. And he would do everything within his power to get her there. But once there, then what? Would she want to part ways, or would she, perhaps, wish to see what else was out in the vast set of universes? There was no sense in asking her now, as her heart was set on one goal and one goal only. But once that goal was attained, perhaps she would consider his offer.

McCullen returned and split the money three ways.

"The exchange rate isn't bad. The people on the street back there must think I'm mad, but I asked the prices of a few things, and they're comparable to what things cost in our world. No need for the two of us to hire ourselves out as ditchdiggers to earn our wage."

McCullen smiled at the jest, but Seamus didn't find humor in it. He and McCullen had worked together doing grimy, miserable work at Mountjoy Prison, and later they worked on the machinery together. He didn't care to rethink the memory. He pulled out a gold watch and gave it to McCullen.

"If we get separated, you'll need the money," he said and turned away before McCullen could thank him. They found the train station and Seamus inquired at the window about a train through Houston. It was the most direct route to go west.

"I'm sorry," said the man behind the counter. "There's still a Union blockade. No trains in or out."

Texas was a Confederate state and if it was supplying the southern troops, then a Union blockade made sense. It made their plans more difficult, however.

"But if you are interested," said the man, "you can go north through Arkansas and then west, through Indian Territory. Next train isn't until day after tomorrow. Leaves at quarter after eleven in the morning."

"That will do. Three tickets, then," said Seamus, and paid him. McCullen walked off to talk with some of the other people at the train station.

"What are we going to do for two days?" sighed Miss Sanchez. She looked off down the train tracks.

"We can get rooms in a hotel. And McCullen and I can start time mapping this world. A small delay is not necessarily a bad thing. I can take readings in the same locations in town here as I did at home."

"That will be useful, I suppose. And I should probably learn more about how the machine works and how to operate it. Just in case something happens."

"That's an excellent plan."

He thought of Hazel, and how he had taught her to close the time rips. He had left the equipment there for her, and he hoped she would continue the work. He had also taught her as much as she was willing to learn about how the time machine worked. She understood it as well as she could. She didn't have his head for numbers, but few people did. Even McCullen occasionally had difficulty keeping up. It was as if the numbers were alive and moved themselves into position on their own inside his mind. He knew his own brain was doing the work, but it sometimes felt as if an invisible hand were rearranging things, allowing him to see patterns that others missed. It was useful, exceedingly useful. It allowed him to win hand after hand of cards on the riverboats and to create useful inventions.

By inheriting, now Hazel would reap the benefits of his ability. He had spent years now trying to correct his mistake in creating the time rip through which Miss Sanchez had come. And once he atoned for his deed and got her back home, he might still return to his home. But no. He understood his own nature well enough to know that if he could explore something new, solve an equation, turn a dial and step into a new place, he would take that chance.

Miss Sanchez was not like this. She wanted to get home, and that was that. Though she was concerned by what was history to her, events mattered less to her than people did. He remembered how much interest she had taken in Hazel when she was a child, and how she had insisted on helping at the hospital after an explosion had injured a number of people. She had been training to be a doctor when she came into his world and she wanted to cure disease, help the sick and heal people. Like McCullen and himself, she was tireless and relentless, in her own way.

McCullen returned. "I asked someone, and there's a hotel up this street that will do." They headed up the street, and McCullen paused to buy a copy of the *Picayune*, the *Louisiana Courier* and a copy of *Harper's Weekly*. When they got to the hotel, they paid for two rooms, one for Miss Sanchez and the other for Seamus and McCullen.

While Miss Sanchez settled into her room, Seamus watched as McCullen went through both of the newspapers, page by page.

"There!" he pointed.

"Who is that?"

"Joshua Lincoln, the president in this world. He's not the same man as my Obadiah Lincoln."

"I wish I had seen a daguerreotype of Ezekiel Lincoln in my world. But he was just a senator from Illinois."

"You knew of him?" asked McCullen.

"I only heard of him." Seamus had the strong feeling that he should drop the subject. He wondered if McCullen had seen an image of Senator Ezekiel Lincoln before he and his krewe had arranged his murder. But if he had, then McCullen would have already known that Seamus's world's Lincoln and the Lincoln from McCullen's world were two different men.

That meant that McCullen had arranged the killing of Senator Lincoln, sight unseen. It was inhuman. He had not only failed to look the man in the eye, but had not even seen a picture of his face.

McCullen had other blood on his hands. He had also arranged the murder of President Elect Buchanan, which had led to Breckinridge becoming president. If a Lincoln, by whatever first name, was president in McCullen's world, Miss Sanchez's world and this one, did that mean that it was somehow foreordained? Were the events of time, perhaps, more set than he had thought?

"Do you know what this means?" said McCullen. "I had wondered, when I first came through the time rip into your world, if each person was truly unique."

"We won't be meeting our doubles then?"

"No. And that's a relief," said McCullen. "Two of you would be too many."

"You're too kind."

"Although two Miss Sanchezes might not be such a bad thing."

"You leave her alone."

"Yes, yes. I see how you look at her. Poor lad. You want to please her by taking her home, and all she wants is to leave and be rid of you. You've given years of your life and even left your little Hazel behind, all for a woman who barely gives you a second glance."

"It's my fault she got pulled from her world, and it's my duty to get her back." Seamus started unpacking his things.

"Your duty, you say? Then I ask you this. When do you get to stop doing your duty and start doing what you want? And secondly, what, exactly, is it that you want?"

CHAPTER 22

January 8, 1864
New Orleans, Louisiana
Hazel and Seamus's World

NEIL DIDN'T LOOK AT HAZEL while she played, not at her face anyway. He watched her hands, the swift presses of her fingers against the strings on the neck of the violin, the slight sway of her upper body as she played, but he didn't look directly at her face. It would have been invasive, like watching her bathe. Too personal. Too intimate.

The white cat jumped onto the living room chair across from him. The creature had never approached either of them for petting, but seemed to want to be in the same room with them.

Neil closed his eyes. Hazel was playing a Baroque piece, at his request. It was Vivaldi's "La Tempesta di Mare," an energetic piece which had not been created as a piece for a single violin, but the way she played it made him think it was improved by the reduction. The piece went on, then slowed, and he felt the movement of the sea, and more, of the air and the earth beneath the sea.

This girl, this very strange girl, played in a way that felt like her fingers were twining up inside his stomach, around his lungs and heart. The sound coming from the instrument was alive, and he saw how the ignorant could say it sang with a demon's voice. But he knew that it was a sublime thing, not of good or evil, heaven or hell. It was simply and utterly itself. And in that wholeness, that integrity, it was a living spirit.

The final notes brought the piece to a close, but he did not open his eyes. For one, they were moist, and he would not let Hazel see that he was such a strange person to be so moved by some music. And for another, he didn't want to look upon her face and see the features, the freckled nose, the brown eyes that hid behind them the being who could bring the magic from the instrument. That was like looking at the velvet box instead of the diamond inside it.

"Thank you," he said after a pause, wondering by her silence if she thought he might have fallen asleep.

"What else would you like to hear? Perhaps Bach or Mozart?" Her voice was soft and he liked the gentle sound of her Southern accent.

No, not Mozart, he thought. Nothing so mad and beautiful or he might break somehow. There was a fragile thing inside him, and listening to her play poked at it, like moving a log on a dying fire. It might erupt in flame. But he did not want her to stop.

"Surprise me," he said.

And she did, gently. She played a piece he did not know, a slow, simple piece, almost like something a child would play when he or she was first learning. Only it was far too sad and full of darkness to be from the world of childhood. Or maybe it wasn't. He did not remember his own childhood except in bits and pieces. Perhaps it had been painful, and his own mind kept him from remembering it.

Then Hazel played a piece by Bach, and his mind quieted, and then she played Mozart, saving the best for last. When she was done, he stayed motionless and heard her put away the violin and bow and snap the case shut. She did not disturb him, for which he was more grateful than he could say.

The white cat still sat on the chair, napping. He wished

he could stay there, perhaps fall asleep. He so rarely slept. But the world required his return.

Hazel Dubois was this girl's name. He thought of the man on the train he had killed, Andrew Dubois, but it was a common name among the descendents of French immigrants. There were thousands of people named Dubois in the United States. There was no need to consider it anything but a coincidence.

He found Hazel in the kitchen examining the little ship in a bottle.

"Do you see anything weird in there?" he asked. Perhaps she would know something that would give him a clue as to why Elliot had valued it.

"No. I was just wondering why you gave it to me."

"It was all I had. And it was your birthday. I know it's kind of a strange gift."

"It is, but I still like it. You'll have to tell me when your birthday is, so I can return the favor," she said.

"I don't know my birthday. I grew up in the 1970s and 80s. That's all I know."

"No parents then?"

"Not that I remember."

"Were you a baby when they died?"

"I don't know," he said.

"Well, who raised you?"

"I was raised by a series of foster parents."

"And then you became a time traveler?"

He didn't want to tell her about Mr. March and his life working for him. "Yeah."

Hazel waited for him to continue. But there was nothing else he wanted to tell her. What could he say? He was an assassin and a thief. Hazel seemed like a nice girl, sweet but damaged by whatever past betrayals that had befallen her. He didn't want her to dislike or distrust him. Why, he couldn't say.

"Will you take me with you?" she asked, still looking at the ship.

"What do you mean?" He hadn't told her that he was on the run and she had no idea where he was headed.

"When you leave this time. Will you take me along?"

"No. Of course not. You belong here. This is your time."

"But why? What's so terrible about the future that I can't see it?"

"It's nothing terrible. Only ... I just don't need a kid tagging along."

"A kid? You're calling me a goat?" She seemed half offended and half bewildered.

"A child."

"I'm not a child! For one, I'm a property owner with my own money. I am an independent woman."

"Then why leave?"

She sighed and looked out the kitchen window. "I'm curious, I suppose. When Miss Sanchez came, and then when you came, it opened up a window of possibilities. It's your fault, you know. You said you'd be back on my birthday, and just the possibility of seeing other times made me restless. If you had just gone and said you'd never see me again, I think perhaps I could have settled for an ordinary life. But now, an ordinary life isn't enough."

Her expression was so full of sadness. But she could be as sad as she liked, he wasn't going to take her with him.

"I can't take you. It's too dangerous."

"Because of the void wyrm?"

"The what?"

"Perhaps you have a different name for it. It's this monstrous thing that lives between worlds. And it'll eat you."

"Sounds like a children's story."

"It's not. The Professor saw one and he told September Wilde about it. She was going to talk to her brothers and sisters and find a way to get rid of it. The monster is near a time rip in Jackson Square and it has eaten a few people."

"It eats time travelers?" he said, a little incredulous.

But if that was the case, then why had Mr. March never encountered it? Or had he, and he had never told Neil? Perhaps they had not seen it because every time Mr. March had taken Neil through time, he had not used a machine.

"It seems to eat anyone," she said. "But making time rips with the machine seems to draw it."

"Then coming with me is even more dangerous than I thought. So no, you still cannot come with me."

"Tell me when you'll be headed next. Twentieth century? Twenty-first?"

"I don't know."

"Don't you have a job to do? Before, you had a mission and once you were done, you left."

"No mission. No job."

Her mouth opened slightly in shock. "You haven't joined that time traveler group yet, have you? When I was a little girl, there were other travelers, like September Wilde. So I assumed you were working with her like last time. But you're not. That's why you're here with no job and why you're so young. That's why you don't know anything. I think you're lost."

"I am not lost. I've traveled all over time, just not with this particular machine. But since you know so much, why don't you tell me how to operate it?"

She got a smug look. "No."

"Why not?"

"I won't help you out of any goodness in my heart, I'll tell you that. But I'll strike a bargain with you. I have a letter. At first, I didn't understand why Mr. Augustus sent me this series of numbers as a postscript, but I think I know what they are now. They match the pattern of coordinates that the Professor used for his machine. It didn't make any sense for Mr. Augustus to use those numbers, but if he's related to September Wilde, then that changes everything. He'd know about the machines and how they operate. The Professor said there is a world from which it's easy to travel to other worlds. He called it a hub world. You get to that world, and you can go anywhere. There's no guarantee, but Mr. Augustus and I have been friends for years, and he wouldn't give me coordinates that were dangerous. I'll share the coordinates with you, but you have to take me with you."

A hub world? Neil considered it. Mr. March might have a much more difficult time finding him if he could get to this hub world and then go somewhere from there. And as it was, he was stranded in this time unless he learned how to operate the machine. Arbitrarily turning knobs and randomly picking coordinates could only lead to disaster, or to this void wyrm.

And perhaps Hazel would not be such bad company. She seemed clever and intelligent and she could play violin for him, though a large part of him was wary of hearing her play again. He did not want to like her too much and later be betrayed by her. He didn't want to be entangled with her emotionally at all. What sort of man was he? Was he liable to fall for this sylph of a girl who was now sitting in her old-fashioned green dress with a look of smug satisfaction? Or did he prefer another type of woman? It was another thing about himself that he did not know.

He did not need to worry about that right now though. If Mr. March found him, nothing else would matter.

"Fine. It's a deal," he said.

CHAPTER 23

January 8, 1864
New Orleans, Louisiana
Hazel and Seamus's World

HAZEL COULDN'T BELIEVE HER LUCK. Convincing Mr. Grey to take her along had not been too difficult. Compared with arguing a point with the Professor, who could be maddeningly stubborn, it had been rather simple. And what a stroke of luck that Mr. Grey had no idea how to operate the machine and needed her coordinates. The idea bothered her though. For one, how had he gotten to her time if he didn't know how to use the machine? Second, once they traveled using the coordinates Mr. Augustus had given her, how would they get from the hub world to other worlds? And lastly, why would Mr. Augustus give her coordinates anyway? If he and Miss Wilde could close time rips and eliminate void wyrms, then they were experienced time travelers. But why help Hazel in this way?

The Professor had left some equipment behind in the laboratory, including some of the older machines that took readings from the time rips. She knew how to use those and perhaps Mr. Grey knew more than he was letting on. She hoped so.

In the laboratory, she packed up as much of the Professor's abandoned equipment as she thought she could use and then went to her room. She tossed some clothing, a few books and an extra pair of shoes into a bag. Then she picked up the little toy jackal from its place. It was a silly, sentimental thing, but she felt like she didn't want to leave it behind. Mr. Grey already knew that he had given her the violin in her past, his future. So knowing the same thing about the toy jackal could do no further harm. She dropped it into her handbag, where it rested beside the tiny ship in a bottle.

Her trip to the bank and the solicitor's office dragged on, but within a few hours, she had exchanged a large sum of money for gold, just as the Professor had told her he was going to do. She had also ensured that Mrs. Washington was financially well-off, that the house would be maintained, that the Professor's family in Ireland would receive a generous yearly amount and that all her patents and money would be held for her in perpetuity. One day, she hoped to come back.

For now, her choice was made. And it had been so easy. Mr. Grey had come, and now she could travel. A little voice reminded her that if something seemed impossibly good, something bad was lying in wait. But she was leaving behind a life here, friends and a potential fiancé, security and relative safety. That was a sacrifice, was it not?

Now, she had to write letters, one to Mrs. Washington, one to Cassandra and one to Mr. Ross. Part of her wanted to run away with Mr. Grey, hoping that she would return some day to explain everything to Mr. Ross. But she couldn't do that. Even the Professor, with whom she was still furious, had left a letter each time he had left.

Guilt plagued her as she sat down at her writing desk. Mr. Ross, Cassandra and Mrs. Washington deserved better than a letter. The Professor's letters had caused her so much pain, and now she was about to inflict that pain on others. There was no way around it though. How could she explain to Mr. Ross or Cassandra that she was about to embark on an expedition through time? They would think her mad. And Mrs. Washington would forbid it. Though both of them knew she had no real authority over Hazel, she would do everything within her power to protect her. Worse yet, she might cry or beg Hazel to stay.

She sighed and pulled out a sheet of paper, a pen and ink. First, she wrote to Mrs. Washington, informing her about the money waiting for her and how she could live in the house as long as she liked. If she did not want to stay there and preferred to retire or move in with her daughter, then Hazel had arranged for the solicitor to hire an outside agency to maintain the building. She paused, then told Mrs. Washington that she loved her and was thankful for all the trouble she had gone through in bringing her up.

She stopped and thought of how good a soul Mrs. Washington was. She had given extra money and food to a hungry child, and then had been the only feminine influence in Hazel's life since her mother had died. If only for the sake of seeing her again, Hazel would come back to this time. This was not good-bye, but only a temporary parting.

Writing to Cassandra was easier, in a way. She hated to lie, but she couldn't exactly tell her that she was going to travel into another world with a strange man she barely knew. She decided to tell a modified version, that she was going to travel for a few years to further her education. That was true, as far as it went. She told Cassandra that she was not accepting Mr. Ross's offer of marriage and that Cassandra might be a good friend to Mr. Ross if he was disappointed that Hazel had left the city. She didn't feel the need to say anything more, as Cassandra would be happy to solidify her acquaintance with Mr. Ross. While Hazel had been courted by him, Cassandra would never have betrayed her, but now, she was freed of any such constraint.

She took out a third piece of paper and wrote to Mr. Ross. She told him how she would be traveling and also wrote that Mr. Ross should not wait for her, but should find another young woman who would make a good wife. She said she cared for him deeply, but she was not the woman he should marry.

All of that was true. She wished she could be a sweet little wife who would be content sewing and cooking, but her years of waiting to see other worlds had ruined that for her. She would never be happy until she saw other times and other worlds. And if she stayed and married Mr. Ross, she would secretly resent him for confining her. It would be unfair to him. She dipped her pen and wished him good fortune and assured him that he was the sort of man many young women would be eager to marry. She hoped he would not resent, or worse, hate her.

She sealed all three letters, set Mrs. Washington's on the kitchen table and left a note asking Mrs. Washington to post Mr. Ross's and Cassandra's in the morning. Then, she gathered her bags and the trunk with the Professor's equipment and went to meet Mr. Grey.

He was at September Wilde's house, making a stack of sandwiches and wrapping them in paper.

"Never know how things will go. Better safe than sorry," he said.

"I need to leave a note for Miss Wilde," she said. "Do you know where I can find some writing paper?" She should have written the letter at her house, but had not thought of it until now. How foolish to think of her own feelings and not the safety of the entire world.

"There's a desk in the front room."

Hazel left, the white cat trailing behind her. She located the desk and wrote out a note for Miss Wilde, telling her the location of the time rips that needed to be monitored and closed. If the woman could manage the void wyrm, she could manage a few little time rips. It would be a month or two before they needed to be dealt with anyway, and Miss Wilde would hopefully be home by then. They were no longer Hazel's responsibility.

"Are you just going to sit there and watch me?" Hazel asked the cat. The animal sat, staring at her and curled its tail around its feet. "It isn't as if I am going to steal anything."

She let the ink dry, folded the note in half and wrote Miss Wilde's name on the outside. Then she placed it on the kitchen table.

"That's the last of the business I needed to take care of," she said. "I'm ready."

"I have the machine in the other room. Do you have the coordinates?"

"I do, but we certainly can't use it here. We need a synchronicity."

At Mr. Grey's questioning look, Hazel sighed and explained the conditions necessary to use the machine.

"How did you get here, anyway?" she asked.

"I stole the machine," he said, looking her straight in the eye, as if daring her to condemn him.

"You didn't steal it from the Professor, did you?"

"No. From someone else. Someone who wanted to use my abilities for themselves."

"Abilities?"

"Look, Hazel, you seem like a nice person. But you ought to know that I'm not such great company for you. I stole the time machine, and the person I took it from is probably trying to hunt me down as we speak. And he's not the only one. I used to work for someone else before that, and he's going to be looking for me too. You're not safe with me."

"Who are these people?"

"I doubt you've heard of them. One is Mr. March and the other is a man named Elliot Van Dorn."

"And what are these abilities you have?"

"For one, I can move quietly and people don't notice me."

He had seemed quite noticeable to her, but she would never tell him so.

He continued. "I can sneak up on people and I'm good at fighting."

"These people, March and Van Dorn, wanted you to fight for them?"

"Something like that. They needed me to do jobs for them, and I refused."

"And then you stole a time machine."

"Yep."

"Why are you telling me this?"

"Because you shouldn't come with me. It's dangerous, and you're better off here. I can take the coordinates and leave and you'll be safe and sound."

"No, I'm not staying. You know your past, but I know your future, at least a little part of it. And you're good, very good. You help people."

"I've killed people." He didn't look away when he said it, but his expression was unreadable. "Lots of people. I'm not a good companion for you."

"You don't seem pleased with yourself about it."

"I'm not. Mr. March convinced me that they were bad people, murderers. They were people who had evaded the law, and I killed them to keep them from harming others, not for vengeance. It was only after I did some investigation on my own that I learned that they may have been innocent."

"So you ran away because he wanted you to kill more people who might have been innocent?"

Mr. Grey nodded.

"And now you think you're dangerous to me?"

"Not because I'd hurt you. I wouldn't do that. But because I have enemies."

"I've heard it said that the quality of a man can be known by his enemies. These men don't seem like good people."

"That's all very nice, but if you want to come with me, then you need to know that you're putting yourself in danger."

"Is that why you're so eager to leave this time?"

"Precisely. The farther I get from here, the harder I am to find. Simple as that."

"So there's no telling where we might end up?" She smiled.

"None."

She picked up her bag. "Then let's go."

Hazel knew that the Mississippi was where the Professor would have gone to create a synchronicity. It was the safest place, as he could wait until there was an empty area and then row back and forth with his machinery, creating the opportunity for a time rip until a synchronicity occurred. A man eating his lunch on shore told them that a friend of his had sold a rowboat to two men and a woman the day before.

"Got a good price for it too," he added.

"How much do you want for yours?" asked Mr. Grey, and after a short period of haggling, Hazel and Mr. Grey were rowing out into the wide, brown Mississippi River.

Hazel opened the trunk containing the time machine.

"It looks almost identical to the one the Professor has," she said.

"It might be the same one, just a future version."

"It would be even better if he had made a number of them."

"The more there are, the more people who will be using them. That might not be such a good thing."

Hazel couldn't argue with that. She set the coordinates to match those on the paper Mr. Augustus had left for her, sliding the panels on the globe to the corresponding locations.

"Please take us downriver, if you would be so kind," she said.

Mr. Grey set to the oars, rowing strong and steady. Twenty minutes passed, and still he rowed. The machine was on and functional, presumably ripping a hole in time to another world, but the air wasn't shimmering as it should. She checked the coordinates and the settings, verifying that the machine was operational. Mr. Grey did not appear at all tired, and Hazel couldn't help but think that any other person would have been sweaty and exhausted by such exertion. Perhaps strength and endurance were two of the abilities for which Mr. March and Mr. Van Dorn had wanted him. A tireless, strong man who was stealthy and good in a fight might be a useful person to have around. Well, he was traveling with her now, and if they were to be friends, then those abilities might become useful.

Hazel was about to tell Mr. Grey that they should head upriver and try there when she caught a slight movement from the corner of her eye. The air had quivered, she was sure of it. Then it moved again, and shimmered.

"Keep rowing!" she cried, and Mr. Grey did.

The shimmer enveloped them, and a moment later, Hazel caught sight of the prow of a small ship from the other world. She didn't want the ship to slip through into her own world, so she flipped the machine off as soon as their rowboat was through the doorway, heaving a sigh of relief when the shimmer vanished, leaving them floating in the water as the other ship passed by.

"Well?" said Mr. Grey. "Are we here?"

Hazel felt sick to her stomach, and the boat seemed to be moving too much, making her dizzy. Something bumped where her handbag hung against her hip.

"I'll have to take readings. Take us to shore," she said. She closed her eyes, hoping the sensation of dizziness would fade, but the rocking of the boat made her feel even worse.

"Are you all right?" Mr. Grey asked.

"I just feel a little sick."

Again, there was a feeling against her hip, as if something was moving inside her handbag. She pulled it away from her body, and the thing twitched. She opened the bag and pulled out the little jackal, staring into space with its little glittering green eyes. When it had possessed its original power source, it had been able to move. But the Professor had long ago taken the tiny engine out, so it couldn't be the mechanical toy causing the bag to move. The handbag twitched again and she caught sight of movement. It was from the ship in a bottle. She pulled it out.

The little ship was crawling with tiny monkeys. They hung from the mast, scampered over the deck and even crawled in the bottom of the bottle. A number of them pushed at the cork that sealed the bottle. Back and forth they went as a group, creating enough momentum to make the bottle bump each time they rammed the cork.

"What is it?" asked Mr. Grey.

"Monkeys. Look. I think they want out."

That was the moment that the little ship inside seemed to fold, like a cloth or a piece of paper, and vanished. One of the monkeys wore a tiny vest and he put something into his pocket and then appeared to be shouting at the other monkeys. Then he turned to Hazel and she gasped. He was looking straight at her, pointing a tiny black finger at her, and then at the cork.

"He's telling me he wants out," she said. Part of her wanted to drop the bottle or toss it into the water. But the little monkeys were alive, frightening and strange as they were.

Mr. Grey took the bottle and turned it this way and that, careful not to move it too quickly, lest the monkeys get injured. "We should wait until we're on shore."

Hazel held up a finger to tell the monkey to wait a minute, and he folded his arms and watched her. Once on shore, she knelt down in the sand, set the bottle down and pried out the cork which came loose with a little pop.

A clot of capuchin monkeys clung to the cork and once free of the bottle, they grew to full size within moments. They crawled over one another and then dashed away from the bottle. More and more monkeys poured out, and Hazel felt Mr. Grey pull her arm to get her away from the tumbling mass of fur, arms, legs and tails. There were perhaps fifty or sixty of them, some screaming, some silent, all moving and forming a group about fifteen feet away. Once there, they turned back, as if expecting something.

Last of all came the monkey in the vest. He jumped from the bottle's neck and grew to full size. Like the others, his arms and chest were white and white fur surrounded his face. The remainder of his body was soft black, including a little cap of black on the top of his head. The skin of his face was light pink, though some of the other monkeys had lighter or darker faces. His black eyes were steady and intelligent and his expression was serious. He took a look around and brushed himself off.

"That was inconvenient," he said. His voice was high and inhuman, but his speech was clear. "May I ask your name?"

"Hazel," she said, taking a wary step back from the animal. She almost lost her footing, since the world chose that moment to lurch and she again felt like vomiting. "Hazel Dubois," she forced herself to say, swallowing hard.

"For formality's sake, I must ask, are you the owner of the ship?"

"Do you mean the one that was in the bottle?"

"That is the one," said the monkey.

"I owned the ship in the bottle, yes."

"And it was gifted to you by this man after he stole it from another man who purchased it."

"I don't know," said Hazel, looking inquiringly at Mr. Grey.

"Yeah," said Mr. Grey. "I got it from a man who bought it in a thrift shop."

"Stole it," said the monkey.

"Fine, I stole it," Mr. Grey said.

Hazel looked at him in shock. So, her birthday gift had been stolen!

"Well then," said the monkey. "Everything seems to be in order. On behalf of the dragon who is Skidbladnir, I deem your claim, Miss Dubois, to be legitimate."

"What claim is that?"

"The claim of ownership of the ship Skidbladnir."

"What's that about a dragon?"

"She's the ship but also the dragon. And she is yours."

"I don't understand. I already owned that little ship."

"You held it, and now that we are all free, we are yours."

"I don't—"

Mr. Grey touched her arm and spoke quietly into her ear. "The ship and crew were trapped. You freed them. Like in the children's stories, they're now in your debt."

"But what's this about a dragon?"

"The ship had a dragon's head, remember?" he said.

Hazel considered this. The little monkey was looking up at her, earnest and expectant, his little hands clasped together, his long tail curled up behind him. The other monkeys watched from a distance.

"Where is this ship?" she asked.

"It is here." The monkey handed her a folded brown cloth from his vest pocket. Hazel hesitated, fearful of touching the creature's black clawed hand. She forced herself to take it.

"And who are you?" she asked.

He gave a little bow. "I am Mr. Escobar, your first mate, if you'll have me."

"I will, thank you. And what about them?" She looked over to the crowd of monkeys who were watching them.

"The rest of the crew."

"And why did all of you come to life when we came into this world? Why was the ship just a little model before that?"

"The ship was taken and put into the bottle, and us with her. The ship is very old, though we did not crew her when she was young. She is also very valuable. We were

171

trapped with her, and when we were taken to another world, no one could see any of the crew, though the ship was still visible."

"Elliot Van Dorn saw the monkeys," muttered Mr. Grey. Hazel turned to ask him about it, but he shook his head to indicate that they could talk later.

"Tell me more about this ship," she said to Mr. Escobar.

"Gladly, Captain. Although I might point out that your crew is attracting some attention."

Passersby were slowing to get a better look, some of them stopping. A few people gathered and were casting dark and suspicious looks at the monkeys, then at her and Mr. Grey.

"We should get out of sight," said Hazel. "But where should we go?" She looked up the riverbank, at the city of New Orleans, which looked almost identical to the city in her own world. There would be nowhere to hide a troop of monkeys.

"Can we take the ship?" asked Mr. Grey. He addressed Mr. Escobar. "If Hazel unfolds the cloth, the ship will come out of it, right?"

"The cloth is the ship. It folds and unfolds. And yes, if you unfold it, then it will become the ship."

"And we can take it, go anywhere?" Mr. Grey asked, and Hazel heard the hopeful note in his tone. For his sake, she was pleased to have the ship, if that was what it truly was. At the thought of a real a ship, an actual, foldable ship, a thrill went through her.

"Anywhere on water," said Mr. Escobar. "And, as you can see, it can be folded to carry across land."

"Very handy," said Mr. Grey.

"Won't having a dragon-headed ship in the middle of the river bring attention?" said Hazel. "We'll look like pirates. Someone might send a boat out to try and stop us."

"If they come, we'll outrun them," Mr. Escobar said simply.

Hazel exchanged a glance with Mr. Grey, who gave a little shrug.

"I think we should do this soon," said Mr. Escobar, assessing the people on shore.

Hazel examined the piece of folded brown cloth. "What should I do with it?"

"I would unfold it over the water."

Hazel held the cloth a few inches above the muddy brown Mississippi water.

"When it starts to grow, I would recommend jumping on quickly," said Mr. Escobar. "Unless you are very talented, for a human, at climbing."

"Ready?" Hazel asked Mr. Grey who moved up beside her. She unfolded the cloth once, twice, and before she could do anything more, the thing unfolded itself into a small ship, larger than it had been in the little bottle, but not by much. Then it began to expand.

The body of the ship was made up of long, horizontal overlapping planks gracefully curving outward as it grew. The ship was long and shallow, though not flat-bottomed, and the keel came to a tapered point that ran along its underside. It settled into the water, floating high but sinking as it grew larger.

The prow arched into a dragon's neck and head, its mouth open and its wooden eyes staring into the far distance. The front most point on the ship was below the dragon's chin, where its chest would be, and was reinforced with vertical metal bands, each carved with artistic representations of vines. These matched the carved metal edging that ran around the gunwale. At the back, the stern curled into a rounded crook, not unlike the tails of the monkeys. An unlit metal lantern swung from the tip. The sides of the ship were armored with a row of round metal shields, each with a wicked spike protruding from its center.

Hazel took in all of this in moments, for Skidbladnir

grew quickly, taking only to the count of three to be the size of the rowboat. Mr. Grey and Hazel scrambled up into it, sitting on either end so as not to cause the vessel to capsize. Plank benches filled the interior of the ship, each with an oar waiting in the oarlock. There must have been forty seats, though they were now still too small for adults. The great mast in the center grew taller, and the red and white square sail snapped taut as it filled with wind.

The ship grew further, and with a series of sharp yips from Mr. Escobar, the monkeys on shore leapt onto the ship, scrambling over its sides and taking places at the oars or climbing up the rigging. One burly monkey took a place at the stern, on the starboard side, and took hold of the tapered end of a long, flat rudder that lay in the water. Two monkeys lowered the gangplank and the last few crewmembers who had remained on shore pulled Neil and Hazel's luggage onto the ship.

Skidbladnir's deck was long and flat, with an aisle between the rows of benches where monkeys now sat, clutching long, thin oars. How they would manage to row was still a mystery, but then, here Hazel was, on a Viking ship from a bottle, crewed by talking monkeys.

"Not bad as far as birthday presents go," said Mr. Grey beside her.

"One of the better ones I've received, even if it was stolen."

The crew pulled up the gangplank while others carried the luggage to the stern of the ship, where Hazel now noted two large trapdoors, hinged on the outer edges and set with round metal rings. The monkeys swung the doors open to reveal a set of steps and their belongings vanished down into the dark.

"We have an area below deck for cargo, and your quarters are there also," said Mr. Escobar. "The original ship was simply a longship and had no area below. The crew slept out on deck. But over the centuries, modifications have been made."

It must have been quite a modification, because physically, there could not be much room for any sort of quarters below the deck. The ship was simply too shallow. Hazel was about to ask for specifics, including who had made these modifications, but Mr. Grey touched her arm and pointed out the crowd gathered at the shore. A police officer joined them and called out, then strode toward them.

"We'd better go," said Mr. Grey.

"Where to?" asked Mr. Escobar.

"I'm not sure," she said. "But first off, let's get out into open water."

Mr. Escobar shouted instructions, this time in English, and some monkeys adjusted the sail, while others took to the oars. The ship moved, slowly at first but quickly gaining speed. It felt like it was skimming over the water, almost flying. The rowing monkeys were hard at work, and they seemed to generate plenty of power, their oars dipping and pushing through the water, dipping again. One monkey sat on a barrel at the front, facing the rowers, and sang a rhythmic song in a high, accented voice.

Hazel felt dizzy again, and she placed her hand on the dark wooden railing to steady herself. The wind blew strong on her cheeks and her skirts billowed around her legs. They sailed down the river, toward the Gulf of Mexico, the land flying by at incredible speed. Once in open water, they could go anywhere, perhaps to the Caribbean or to South America. The men hunting Mr. Grey would never find them, and perhaps she would find the Professor and Miss Sanchez.

Anything was possible.

CHAPTER 24

March 23, 1864
Camden, Arkansas
Hub World

SEAMUS PULLED OUT HIS POCKET watch and snapped it open. It was nearly suppertime, and the train had been stopped for two hours in some empty place in southern Arkansas. The latest report from the porters was that a battle had taken place somewhere near Camden, and with wounded Confederate soldiers and attacking Union troops still in the area, it was unsafe to travel farther. So they waited.

Miss Sanchez sat beside him, reading a magazine with McCullen across from him, reading the day's newspaper. McCullen had taken to this world like a researcher, trying to discover the differences between it and Seamus's world, as well as McCullen's own. Occasionally he would lower his paper and inform Seamus and Miss Sanchez of a political or social disparity or some little detail that he thought might be useful for them to know. So far, the only useful thing Seamus knew for sure was not to remove his shoes where anyone could see.

"I need to stretch my legs," said Miss Sanchez. But no sooner had she closed her magazine than a porter appeared at the end of the car.

"I have good news. We will be resuming our trip shortly," he announced. "Although we will be stopping in Camden for the night."

A groan went up among the passengers, who were already hours delayed and were irritated with any further bad news. They had planned on getting through Camden hours ago and arriving in Little Rock a few hours later. Now, they were trapped and there was nothing anyone could do about it.

The train eventually rolled forward and picked up speed. Twenty minutes later, it came to a stop in the town of Camden. Calling Camden a town was being generous, Seamus thought. The train station was simply an uncovered platform. A short main street ran past it and between a few buildings, including a general store, a post office and some small shops. A few houses were clustered behind the shops, and he saw other buildings, farmhouses, silos and barns, farther out.

"Lucky it's a sleeper car, or we'd be hard pressed to locate a hotel," said McCullen.

"I need to move. I'm going to take a walk," said Seamus. He was restless and felt like a caged animal, stuck in his seat for so many hours. "Care to join me?" he asked Miss Sanchez. McCullen was looking out the window, studying the town in his strange way, and Seamus didn't care if he was insulted at not being invited.

They left the train and Miss Sanchez walked with him to the end of the main street. They took their time, unwilling to return to the train too quickly. They reached the end and were about to turn back when they caught sight of a row of carts approaching.

"Wounded soldiers," said Seamus. "If there was a battle, this is the closest town."

"But they don't even have a hospital here. Where will they take them?"

"Some of them will be transported by train to Little Rock, or perhaps Monroe or Shreveport. Those who can be transported, that is."

"And those who can't?"

"Unless my guess is wrong, there will be a field hospital."

"Then that's where I should be."

Miss Sanchez was studying to become a doctor before she came through the time rip, and though she was the wrong sex in this era, Seamus knew that she would not be deterred from the duties of her profession.

"It'll be little more than a tent, nothing like what you're used to," he said. He knew it would not make any difference, but felt like he should at least warn her. A field hospital would not be like the large New Orleans hospital she had seen six years ago.

"I spent time in one of this era's hospitals before, and I helped then," she said. "With the wounded is where I ought to be. I'm no help sitting on the train, waiting."

She brushed past him and approached the men walking at the front of the row of carts. They appeared relatively healthy, albeit a little thin and sunken-eyed. Some of them wore ordinary clothes, and the few gray Confederate uniforms in the group were shabby.

Seamus followed her, not because he had any business being near the wounded, but because it was ungentlemanly to allow a woman to try to negotiate with a band of soldiers. And negotiate she would. He knew well enough how once Miss Sanchez had an idea in her head, especially involving medicine, nothing would stop her. These may be Southern soldiers, fighting for the side she opposed, but wounded were wounded, and Seamus knew that she would not be at peace while there were people to be treated.

"Excuse me, but are you taking these men to another city?" Miss Sanchez asked the soldier in front with a bushy moustache and wild, unkempt auburn hair.

"That's right, ma'am. They've cleared a car for them, and they'll be taken down to a hospital in Monroe."

"What about the others? Are there other wounded?"

"Yes, ma'am. Back at camp."

"And is that down this road?"

"It is, two miles down, but don't you think of going that way. It's rough, terribly rough."

"Is there still fighting?"

"No, ma'am. But the wounded are suffering."

"I'm a nurse, a highly trained one. I can help the doctors you have."

The soldier glanced at her dress, which was a typical style for an upper middle class woman with flounces and a bell-shaped skirt, not an aproned nurse's uniform.

"I don't mean any disrespect, ma'am. But it's not small wounds back there. Those are the men who couldn't come, not even in a cart."

"All the more reason for me to go."

The soldier hesitated, as if he wished to say more, but contradicting a lady didn't seem to be in his makeup. Already, Miss Sanchez was checking a man in the nearest cart, moving on and speaking with others, checking bandages and giving advice. She had medical knowledge from the future, of germs and vaccines that went into a person's blood through a tiny needle. She knew of reasons to keep surgical instruments clean, very clean, to keep infections from spreading. Seamus believed her strange claims because he knew her. But she would not have such an easy time with any medical personnel at the camp.

He trailed behind her as she talked to the soldiers, making her way farther and farther along the road until the parade trickled out and the men were all in town, headed for the railway station.

When the last soldier had passed, Miss Sanchez turned to Seamus. "You don't have to come. I believe what the man said. There will be open wounds, amputations, death." Her expression was anxious and he knew that she would screw her courage up to venture into the camp hospital. She would not forgive herself if she quailed in the face of such suffering.

"I've seen people starve to death, lass. And I've seen

them bloodied by gunshot wounds. I've been in an Irish prison, with men dying and lying in their own filth. I'll join you."

"It's only for one day," she said. "We'll leave in the morning." She looked out toward the train station, the last rays of evening light illuminating her face and her too-light eyes, making them shine golden topaz.

Two weeks later, they were still stranded. All of the ways in or out of the area were embroiled in battles, and they were fortunate that Camden was not strategic enough for the Union to want to occupy. All of the horses in the town were either hired out already or confiscated by soldiers. Along with the rest of the train passengers, they could go nowhere.

The last of the surviving soldiers in the medical field tent were ready to be transported to Monroe, though they had to wait until the way was safe. Most of the men had perished. The lucky ones had died quickly of their injuries, although some lingered in pain as they slowly bled to death from punctured organs or other interior wounds. Some burned with fever, lost in delirium for days before dying. Others perished later from infection, though Miss Sanchez had done everything she could to sterilize the instruments with boiling water and as much whiskey and scotch as Seamus could procure from the town.

Seamus could do nothing but comfort the dying. Some men asked him to write letters, and he had sat beside them, writing by lamplight. Others had asked him to read to them, some from the Bible, and others from a book of old children's tales that one of the younger deceased soldiers, a boy of fourteen, had carried in his pack.

After supper, Seamus trudged back to the tent he shared with McCullen. Lacking a hotel, the three of them had, by necessity, been forced to stay in the military tents.

There were two other female nurses, so Miss Sanchez was given a cot and a blanket in the women's tent. Seamus and McCullen had to share a tent with crates of supplies, but it was better than being woken by the tormented moans and cries of the wounded and the dying. McCullen, who had seen both moldy prison cells and luxurious New Orleans parlors, had not uttered a word of complaint. But he had also not offered to help in any medical duties.

Now he was studying a map, tracing routes from their location in Arkansas to Los Angeles.

"I think I can get through the lines on foot," said McCullen. "I'll take the machine and wait in California, and you can join me once you can safely travel."

"Not on your life. We stay together. No negotiations." Seamus was in no mood to play games with McCullen. He was wary of the notion that the man had changed, however much he wished it to be so. What little trust existed between them was due to their mutual need of each other's expertise. He wished it could be otherwise, but the leopard did not change his spots.

McCullen sighed. "The earthquake is in September, so we have a little under six months. That's more than enough time, if we can leave soon."

To the North, Union soldiers had destroyed a section of track between Camden and Little Rock, cutting off Confederate supply lines to the northern part of the state. Crews were laboring to repair the damage, but Seamus knew it would take time. Rumor had it that tracks to the south were also destroyed. A pair of sisters who had been with them on the train had told him that they might be able to travel west to Texarkana, on the Texas border, and then get another train west. Seamus hoped so.

"I still don't understand Miss Sanchez," said McCullen. "She doesn't want the South to win, and yet she aids their soldiers."

"She doesn't care which side they're on. A medic is a medic, she says."

"Well, if she's treating them, then they're getting the best care possible."

Seamus felt a flush of pride at McCullen's acknowledgment of Miss Sanchez's capabilities. He was proud of her as well. He had seen the same horrors she had, and understood that unlike the other nurses, Miss Sanchez knew that many of the wounds were treatable with her time's equipment and expertise. In her time, they had anesthesia, which was even more effective than either chloroform or ether. Here, Miss Sanchez assisted in amputations, and after the first one, Seamus found her white-lipped and shaking behind her tent. He had tried to speak to her, but she shook her head sharply, straightened her apron and went back in.

She worked herself to exhaustion, barely ate and as the days wore on, she developed the haunted look of a person who had reached the point of hopelessness. And yet, she did not give up, but worked to treat each man, even the hopeless cases, until they either died or left the hospital tent to be quartered in the barns or homes of local residents.

Though Seamus didn't have the skill to treat the sick, he had begun to form an idea while watching some of the men recover from amputations.

"There's something we can do while we're trapped here. With some spare mechanical parts, I think I can put together a false leg. It would have a weight-bearing joint with a spring-loaded knee so it would snap straight when the man moved his leg forward. Then there's a wide, flat foot and a soft pad for the stump to rest in."

"I take it you've made a drawing or two?"

"I have."

CHAPTER 25

June 27, 1864
Long Island, New York
Hub world

N EIL STEPPED OUT OF THE way as the bosun passed, carrying a heavy coil of rope. He was a stout monkey with scarred paws and a perpetual sour attitude, but along with Mr. Escobar and Hazel, he kept the crew functioning. On deck, Hazel spoke with Mr. Escobar about taking on rations in Charleston. She shielded her eyes from the sun with her hand, squinting out over the sea.

Neil thought it had been a glorious four months, the two of them and the crew of monkeys, sailing out on the open water. After a few days at sea, Hazel had insisted on returning to New Orleans, docking far outside the city where no one would notice the ship. She and Neil had asked around, trying to find any indication of where the Professor, Miss Sanchez and Mr. McCullen had gone. They had no luck, and eventually Hazel was forced to conclude that they were either already in another world, one where she could not follow, or they were in this one, but she had no way to locate them.

After New Orleans, they sailed to Key West, around the tip of Florida and up the coast. There was money to be made in carrying cargo, both from south to north and back again. The Confederacy was falling, and Southerners paid handsomely for someone to reliably transport

Grandmother's silver or Pa's gun collection north, or occasionally, to Cuba or the Bahamas. The families would find their own transport, as Hazel did not allow people to travel with them.

She made one exception, and that was in the case of escaped slaves. After helping a family of two sisters and one of their sons to freedom, word had spread, but only among those who assisted in such things. The term "Underground Railroad" was not used openly, of course, but Neil had informed Hazel that it was the term that would be written in the history books.

Neil and Hazel had a partnership, and it worked well. She managed the ship, a task she had taken to quickly. She studied maps and learned to use the ancient Viking navigational device, a wooden disk the size of a dinner plate with curved lines carved into its face and zigzags around its perimeter.

Neil's job was to make arrangements on land. His ability to read people and to go unnoticed made him ideal for a career in smuggling, and they charged wealthy people exorbitant amounts to transport their goods north. On the trips back south, they brought whiskey, bolts of fancy cloth, lace and ribbons and expensive tea, things that would sell well in the war-ravaged cities. They could have made more money smuggling weapons and ammunition to the Confederacy, but neither of them were willing to do it. Hazel refused on principle, citing Miss Sanchez's and Mrs. Washington's influence on her and the common humanity of all men. Neil, although in agreement, hated to be an instrument of death, even a remote one.

Even with that in mind, he taught Hazel to shoot, using the various weapons that passed through their hands. She was a surprisingly good shot, not as accurate as Neil was, but then he would have been astonished if she had been.

The monkeys, as it turned out, all spoke English, although with an accent. Most of them were from an island off of Panama and had learned both English and Spanish. They were paid for their services by their former captain, who had been killed. By their own calculations, they still had over a year remaining on their current contract, attached to the ship, and not to the individual who owned or captained her. Being imprisoned in the glass bottle for over a century meant that their kin would be dead and gone and Neil had seen some of the younger monkeys being comforted by older ones when they had learned of it.

At the end of their contract, Hazel would provide them with a share of the money, and take them home to Panama, since this was their home world. Some would probably choose to leave them and some new recruits would join them. The ship had operated in that way for a few hundred years, passing through various hands. And before the discovery of the New World, it had been a battleship. Mr. Escobar didn't know much about those times, but he said that the ship missed her past.

Neil kept busy, learning from the crew how to tie knots while the bosun, Mr. De Leon, taught him to manage parts of the crew. The grizzled old timer had informed him that he would be retiring after this voyage, and Neil thought the bosun's job wasn't such bad work. There was the sea air, sunshine and best of all, the feeling of being free, able to make his destiny. Sure, it was dangerous, but little he had done in his life up to that point was not.

They arrived at Nicoll Bay near midnight. It was an almost uninhabited place on the southern edge of Long Island. Ideally, they would have made port a few miles away from a city with a higher population, giving them more opportunities to purchase quality goods to take south. But one of the escaped slaves they had helped, the sister named Celia, had asked that they return to Nicoll Bay. They sailed up the inlet which curved inland, taking advantage of Skidbladnir's ability to travel up shallow waterways, and then docked at a pier. Two fishing boats rose and fell with the gentle movement of the water, bumping against the pier's pilings. On shore stood a wood-framed house, modest and rough, with a few flowers growing in pots near the front door. A single light glowed in the window. Other similar houses were nearby, all of them dark.

Hazel leapt from the ship to the pier, nimble as a cat, her long brown braid flying out behind her. She had long ago forsaken the skirts that women of this time wore, preferring pants tucked into soft leather boots. A wide belt cinched the pants in tight around her narrow waist, and the vest she wore over a men's white cotton shirt was often unbuttoned and hanging loose. She had mentioned that though this clothing was more efficient and comfortable, she thought she looked too masculine. But that was only by the standards of this time, Neil thought. In his opinion, she looked every inch the female, especially now when she looked over her shoulder at him and crooked her finger playfully.

He jumped out behind her, scanning the area to make sure that no people were around to see the strange Viking ship full of monkeys. Celia would have made sure they'd be alone, he was certain. Like all of their passengers, Celia had been shocked by the monkeys. Though this was their home world, creatures like them were rare, and ships like Skidbladnir were rarer still. But a trip to freedom was a trip to freedom, and any revelations about the ship to outsiders would have been written off as a tall tale or the ravings of a delusional mind.

The door to the lit cottage opened and Celia hurried down the pier. She took Hazel's hands in hers. "You can't stay long. Another ship is going to be coming in any minute. But I got word to my Alma."

Alma was her daughter, aged twenty-two, who was still a slave in South Carolina. Celia's dearest wish was to get her free as well. Neil had explained to her that the South would lose the war and Alma would be freed eventually, but Celia was undeterred and had insisted that they return to her at Nicoll Bay. He didn't blame her.

"There's a conductor who will take her," said Celia. "But she needs a way to get from Savannah to here. Can you bring her?"

"How long until she'll be in Savannah?" asked Hazel.

"Next new moon, when it's dark. That's in three weeks."

"We can make it to Savannah by then. Yes, we can do it," said Hazel.

"It won't be as easy as with Lucy and me. Our master wasn't too hard to escape from. He wasn't friends with the local lawmen, so they didn't hunt for us too hard. Alma's owner has many, many slaves and he's had two of them whipped to death who tried to run away."

"We'll get her," said Neil.

"You haven't even named a price," said Celia.

Neil glanced at Hazel who was studying the outside of Celia's house. "What goods do you have?"

He knew that they had enough money from their last trip carrying valuables to Richmond. They could easily take on one woman on their way back from their next trip. But Celia would not appreciate being a charity case. While on board, she and her sister had insisted on working, finding occupation cooking and mending, though the monkeys didn't always like what was prepared and only a few of them wore clothing. If he and Hazel helped Celia's daughter for nothing, it would create an obligation in her mind, and Neil knew that Celia was a woman who did not like owing anyone.

Neil took a stroll along around the side of the house as Hazel and Celia negotiated their price. Against the wall stood a few small crates of supplies like hard tack, dried jerky, and one medium crate full of fruit, both dried and fresh. The monkeys would adore the fruit. It must have taken Celia some doing to collect so much of it.

A price agreed upon, the monkeys came on shore to

load the crates while Hazel went into Celia's house to collect whatever small amount of money she had agreed to take. Later, Celia waved to them from the pier as they sailed out to sea. Once they were near a reef, they dropped anchor for the night.

A few low-ceilinged rooms were below deck, most of them used for cargo and one at the front for the few monkeys who did not like to sleep up in the rigging. At the stern of the ship was the captain's quarters, which Neil shared with Hazel. She insisted on hanging a thick red and gold Chinese rug to bisect the space and called the two sides separate rooms. It was improper for an unmarried couple to share a room, and though Neil thought it was silly, he knew that Hazel did not. Each of them had a hammock, a trunk of their own things and a shelf with a brass railing around it to keep the items from falling off. Hazel's shelf held a little black jackal toy and a few shells and oddments she liked. Neil's held only books, which Hazel often borrowed.

He changed into his nightshirt and climbed into his hammock which swayed with the movement of the ship. Three rows of square glass panes, half of which were in Neil's room, gave a view behind the ship. From outside the ship, one could not see the window. It was one of many strange things about the ship.

He watched the water glittering outside in the moonlight. He probably wouldn't sleep much, and would spend most of the night reading, but for now, he was content to just relax. Hazel moved about in her room, and he heard the snick of the latch on her violin case. She no longer bothered to ask if it would bother him to play, because his answer was always the same.

She tuned the violin for a minute and then played, and Neil closed his eyes, the sound of the violin mingling with the gentle low creaking of the hammock's fastenings and the groan of the ship's boards. After she played, Hazel turned off her lamp. Neil picked up a book. This ship could have been his, if he hadn't given it to Hazel when it was still in the bottle. He would have been captain. The thought had its appeal, that was for certain, but in the end, he supposed it was for the best. Hazel loved the ship and their life at sea, and he wondered how long he would stay with her. He would like to stay a long time, maybe forever, but if Mr. March appeared to be on his trail, he would have to abandon her for her own safety. He would be a hunted man for the rest of his life.

The Chinese carpet moved aside.

"Are you awake?" she asked. She was in her nightdress and her long brown hair was loose over her shoulders.

"Yeah."

"Can I talk to you?"

He sat up. Hazel was still on her side of the curtain and she would not step onto his side. She wanted him to walk out on deck, or go into the cargo hold, but one was far more pleasant than the other, especially on a summer night such as this.

"Sure," he said and threw on his coat over his nightshirt. He didn't bother with shoes. Hazel didn't either, but he had learned not to stare at her hairless apelike feet. She was so sprightly and petite, and the feet were out of place on her body. But then, to her, his must seem deformed.

They walked down the deck, toward the prow where the dragon head watched the sea in its silent vigil. The monkeys were all wrapped up in the rigging, some snuggled in groups and others by themselves. Slumbering and nonverbal, they were adorable, their little faces serene and sweet. He knew better than to try to pet one.

Once at the foremost point of the deck, far from any monkeys, Hazel leaned on the railing and looked down into the water.

"I want to find the Professor," she said. "I don't know how, but I want to try."

"That's assuming they're still in this world at all."

She sighed. "I wish the Professor had left more information. All I have to go on are guesses."

He leaned over beside her, their shoulders touching. The water sloshed against the side of the ship and a cold breeze blew in, making her shiver. Neil was not affected by it. Hazel leaned against him, just a little, and the wind caught her hair and blew a few strands across his face. He did not brush them away.

"Your guesses tend to be pretty good," he said. "Remember Norfolk?"

They had barely missed being boarded off the coast of Virginia, and it was only Hazel's gut instinct that had led them to flee just before being caught. She shook her head and smiled. "That was dumb luck."

"It still saved us."

"We're developing a reputation," she said. "People are noticing us. A few people have seen the ship, and we've had a few too many tight scrapes."

"Goes with the territory."

"You don't mind it?"

"Sailing the seas, wind in my face, doing as I please, getting out of scrapes alongside my best friend? I don't mind it, no."

He saw her smile in the dark and he moved his hand to take hers, but she moved it away, just a few inches. It was a tiny rejection, and it hurt.

"Do you know what bothers me, a little?" she said. "I barely miss home. I miss Mrs. Washington. And I miss my friend Cassandra. But I barely miss Mr. Ross. We were good friends, but I don't miss him as much as I should."

"People come and people go, and sometimes it's just time for them to go." It sounded so stupid and trite when he said it, but he didn't take it back.

"And when will you go?"

"Go? Did you want me to go?"

"No. No. I just wasn't sure how long you'd want to stay on my ship. I'm happy here, except I'd like to find the Professor. But once I find him and know he's all right, I'll head back to sea. I think I was meant for this ship."

"I'll stay as long as you like," he said. "Mr. De Leon is training me to take his place as bosun."

"He'll be leaving us when their contract is up, won't he?"

"Yes, he wants to retire."

"I've been thinking," she said. "About finding the Professor. We're becoming too well-known, and we know the Professor is on land somewhere. Might not our efforts be better spent in looking for him in cities? Miss Sanchez was from Los Angeles. We could fold up the ship and hide her for a while."

"What about the crew?"

"We'd have to take them home to Panama and sail back slowly, with just us two. We could do it."

"How long would it take?"

"I don't know. I'll have to ask Mr. Escobar."

"Or you could ask me," said a low, creaking voice from the front of the ship.

"Oh, you're up," said Hazel. Apparently she was unsurprised that the dragon had spoken. It still looked out to sea, and Neil watched its lower jaw move as it spoke.

"I would awaken if you asked me," said Skidbladnir.

"I thought you didn't like me," Hazel said.

"I do not. I do not like a filthy skraeling as my captain. But I must follow my captain's orders."

"Then I order you to tell me how long it would take to go through the Gulf of Mexico, overland through Panama and then to Los Angeles."

"Months," the dragon said. "I cannot say precisely as there could be delays."

"Thanks," said Hazel and then jerked her head toward the back of the ship. "She's a real delight," muttered Hazel as they climbed down the steps and opened the door to their quarters.

"You've spoken to her before?"

"Once, and she told me she slept most of the time, so I shouldn't bother her. She was not at all happy to have me as captain, as you can tell. Thinks I'm a skraeling."

"And what is that?"

"An Indian. But since I was born in America, I suppose she doesn't make any distinction."

She glanced over her shoulder where her lamp still burned. It was wasteful to leave it on and use the oil. Neil had a lamp on his own side of the room, though his night vision was so good that he only needed it for reading. But since he hardly slept, he did a lot of that.

"Did you mean it?" she said. "That we're best friends?"

"Yeah."

She touched his hand, only for a moment. And then she was gone, and the light shining around the edges of the Chinese carpet went out.

CHAPTER 26

July 12, 1864
Beaumont, Texas
Hub world

"Pirate Queen Eludes Local Law Enforcement," read McCullen. "That's the headline."

"Why are you reading that to me?" said Seamus, irritated at the interruption. He and McCullen shared a room in a hotel in Beaumont, Texas. With battles and blockades, they had been allowed to travel that far and no farther. They hoped the rail lines to Houston would open shortly, but it was a guessing game. McCullen had already made inquiries about getting a ship to take them through the gulf to Mexico, where they could reach Los Angeles from the south.

Miss Sanchez occupied an adjoining room, and since she was of Mexican ancestry, he had returned to the old routine they had used in New Orleans of claiming she was Seamus's Castilian cousin. McCullen, being white and Irish, easily passed for another cousin. It was unseemly for a single woman to be traveling with two men, but if they were all cousins and kept separate rooms, no one seemed to mind.

"Did you plan on asking this pirate queen to take us to California by sea?" Seamus asked, only half paying attention.

"Now, that's not a bad idea," said McCullen. "Her ship is reportedly very fast. But no, I merely found it amusing."

Seamus was struggling with his prototype of the prosthetic leg. Creating one was much more difficult than he had anticipated, and he was developing a healthy respect for the complexities of balance and musculature that the human body possessed. He was also becoming exceedingly frustrated.

"You could amuse yourself by helping me fasten these joints together," Seamus said.

"And interrupt your fun? Never. You're insufferable if you don't have a project to keep you occupied."

"At least I'm being useful."

"I'm being useful as well. See here. This woman supposedly sails a ship with a dragon's head and a red and white striped sail and has been smuggling escaped slaves north. I don't see her attacking any ships though, so I'm not sure where they get the idea of calling her a pirate. Or a queen for that matter."

"Sells more newspaper copies," Seamus said.

"Most likely. But can you imagine? A ship like that in this day and age?"

"The people in this world seem more superstitious than in my world," said Seamus around a long pin he held in his teeth. "They believe in spirits and all sorts of things."

"I noticed that too."

"So they're probably making this person and her ship out to be something fantastical."

Miss Sanchez knocked at the door and McCullen and Seamus called out simultaneously for her to enter.

"Excellent news," she said. "The train lines through Texas should be opened up by the end of this month!"

Seamus set down the ankle joint with a sigh. It would be impossible to have a final, functional version in fewer than three weeks. But though he might not have a final version, he might have a working prototype by that time. He might be able to send it to one of the men at a nearby hospital who had lost his leg above the knee. It wouldn't be pretty, true, but it would be a good sight better than hobbling around on a wooden leg or with no leg at all.

"That is excellent news," said McCullen.

"Oh, yes. Excellent," said Seamus and turned over the joint to work on the other side.

"Have you ever considered a job in piracy, Miss Sanchez?" asked McCullen. "It seems that women in this time are able to make quite a fortune smuggling slaves. Smuggling the slaves out of, not into, the South."

"Very funny. But how would slave smuggling pay anything? The slaves don't have money."

"A fine question! And one the article does not address." He handed the paper to Miss Sanchez who read it over. "And you may wish to see this. While our boy Seamus has been fiddling with mechanical body parts, I have made progress on finding us a ship, in case the train lines do not open up as planned. Also, I have been working on the time map. I have a good number of coordinates worked out for this universe. You and I won't need them, gods willing, but if there is any sort of difficulty, or if we can't reach California in time, we may find them of value."

"Don't even say that!" cried Miss Sanchez. "We're getting to California, and we're both going home."

The sharpness of her voice made Seamus glance up. Miss Sanchez was looking at McCullen's notebook, but he knew she was doing it out of courtesy. The numbers wouldn't mean much to anyone but McCullen and himself. Once they had clear coordinates and could list the dial settings, then the information would be useful to others. She handed the notebook and the newspaper back to McCullen and then came over to see what Seamus was doing.

"Don't worry. We'll get you home, lass," he said. "Come what may."

CHAPTER 27

July 18, 1864
Savannah, Georgia
Hub world

H AZEL LOST HER FOOTING ON a loose section of earth and fell forward, knees and palms scraping the ground. She froze and listened. Nothing. The moon was new, and it was so dark that without a lantern, it was impossible to see much of anything. Mr. Escobar and Mr. Grey were not having as much trouble. Mr. Escobar was close to the ground to begin with and had keen eyesight. Mr. Grey had excellent night vision as well.

She gasped when a person loomed in front of her and reached out, but then realized it was Mr. Grey. He was so silent on his feet that she felt like a lumbering oaf in comparison. She took his hand and allowed him to help her up, then brushed the dirt from her clothing and hands.

Mr. Grey had insisted that she start calling him Neil. He had not made any sort of fuss over it previously, but he said that using his surname had an element of formality that he did not like, especially from a friend. The crew still called him Mr. Grey, of course, but Hazel was learning to adapt. If she went about in men's clothing, then keeping to the formality of names was indeed unnecessary. He, in turn, called her Hazel except when addressing her in front of the crew when she was Captain Dubois.

He leaned in close to whisper in her ear. "Over that hill." He pointed.

She knew they would find Alma and the "conductor" who had brought her there in an abandoned cabin. They would take the young woman to a remote part of the coast seven miles south of Savannah. Once on the beach, Hazel would remove the folded cloth that was Skidbladnir from its place in her pocket. She had decided not to leave the ship docked, and though the monkeys could be folded up with the ship, all of them were leery of being trapped again. Hazel had agreed to let them have a few hours of shore leave to cavort in the wilderness, smoke, play dice or cards or simply relax. Once Alma and the crew were aboard, they would set sail for Long Island.

They crested the hill and saw the little cabin, a dim light glowing in the front room. Of course, the place probably only had one room, but the light appeared to be near the front window. It had no glass panes, as those were costly, but had slatted wooden shutters through which small horizontal bars of light shone forth.

"Shouldn't that light be off?" Hazel whispered. She did it so softly, that most people would not have been able to hear her, but she knew Mr. Escobar and Neil would. Most of the time when they approached a "station" the lights were off and it appeared to be abandoned. If any random person came by, they would pass by, none the wiser.

"Perhaps it's a new conductor," whispered Mr. Grey. "Hold on." He spun around, and Mr. Escobar did the same. Hazel had heard nothing, but she turned with them.

A line of lights appeared in the distance, then extended around them, the flames of lanterns being lit one by one. Within moments, men began to shout.

"Soldiers," growled Mr. Escobar.

Neil grabbed her hand and pulled her toward the cabin, away from the advancing soldiers who came running forward, lights bobbing. But the door of the cabin crashed open and three more soldiers emerged.

"This way," Neil said and pulled her in the direction

of the only dark part of the landscape, a copse of trees. But three lights bloomed there also. They were completely surrounded.

"The ship!" cried Mr. Escobar, either oblivious to the fact that regular people would hear him speaking, or else not caring. "Give me the ship. I'll see to its safety."

Hazel pulled out the folded cloth and gave it to him. He tucked it into an inner pocket of his vest and then turned, teeth bared at the jumping lights of the advancing men.

"Run, Mr. Escobar!" Hazel said.

"In good time," he said, and if she had not known better, she would have thought he was smiling. "For now, I stay with my captain."

"I'll get as many as I can," said Neil. "You run. Okay?"

"I'm not going to leave you behind," she said.

"We'll both get arrested if you don't. Now at the first chance, go!"

But the men had already advanced too far, and even if they had run at the first indication of trouble, it would have been too late. The lanterns were closer, showing a good twenty men, most with muskets. Why so many? There were only three of them and one, to their eyes, was nothing more than a pet monkey.

Neil broke toward a smaller group, only three men, and Hazel watched in amazement as two of them fell within moments and the third bent over double. Their compatriots rushed Neil, and he had two more on the ground before three others managed to hold him for a few moments. Mr. Escobar leapt forward, letting out an unholy shriek, and savaged the largest man's arm and neck. Hazel, refusing to allow her fear to petrify her, grabbed onto the man Mr. Escobar was attacking, kicking at the back of his knees until he lost his balance and crashed to the ground.

Free again, Neil was a whirlwind in the dark, felling man after man. He was not killing them, as some of them struggled to get up, but he was doing his best to disable them.

A man grabbed Hazel's arm, and Mr. Escobar leapt to her defense. She elbowed the man in his stomach and then smashed her head hard backwards into his chin. He loosened his grip enough for her to pull halfway free, but another man grabbed her, this one much larger, and enveloped her in a smelly, bearlike embrace. Mr. Escobar attempted to attack this man, but one of the other soldiers reached up and bashed him in the head with the butt of his gun. Hazel yelled in horror as Mr. Escobar dropped to the ground. Stunned, he staggered a few feet, then managed to leap up and race away. Hazel didn't think him cowardly for fleeing.

It was a little frightening, to see Neil in these circumstances. It was still dark, so she could not clearly see his expression, but he moved like a man altered, changed into a being of speed and strength. She had never seen him like this before, and it made him seem strange and unfamiliar. Alien even. He had warned her, had he not, that he was wanted for his abilities? She supposed she had not given enough credence to his claim, or had thought him merely a scrappy fighter, like the Professor. She had not understood that he was truly different from ordinary men. It frightened her.

A group enveloped him, and when they parted, she saw him silently struggling against three men who held him while other soldiers pointed muskets at him. She watched him as he looked for her, and once he saw that she was standing, he looked around at the men who held them, perhaps assessing their chances of escape. Hazel knew their chances were not good.

The men dragged her toward Neil, perhaps because she was the easier of the two to move.

"Name!" ordered one of the men, holding up his lantern so the light blinded her. She turned her head aside.

Neil made eye contact with her, and though he did nothing more, she knew he wanted her to stay silent. Sage advice.

"Name, I said!" The soldier, like her, had a southern accent. When neither of them responded, he slammed the butt of his musket into Neil's midsection, eliciting a grunt of pain.

"Leave him be!" she shouted.

"Tell us your name," he repeated and raised his gun to point it at Neil.

"Hazel Dubois," she said. There was no sense in making up another name. One name was as good as another, and if her guess was right, the conductor and Alma were locked away somewhere, or dead, but not before revealing what they knew about their small section of the Underground Railroad. Each conductor and passenger would only know the minimum amount, so as to keep the rest of the movement safe, but they knew Captain Dubois's name.

"And you, what's yours?" the man asked Neil.

"Samuel Clemens," he said, but with a wry gleam in his eye of defiance and amusement. Hazel saw nothing amusing in any of this.

The soldier spoke to a boy who looked younger than Hazel. "Private, tell them we have Dubois and her accomplice."

"Yes, Captain." He ran off in the direction of town.

The captain turned back to her and grabbed her chin, lifting her face up into the lamplight and turning it side to side. "You're younger than I imagined. Tell me a little bit about yourself."

"There's nothing to tell, sir," she said and saw the man's expression change slightly.

"You from the South, girl?"

Perhaps being a fellow Southerner may carry some weight. She couldn't hide her accent now anyway.

"I'm from Louisiana."

"Now that, gentlemen, right there, is a true crying shame. A good Southern girl, born and bred, now turning against her own countrymen. Her own kind. A real shame."

"As her countrymen, I think we have a duty to teach her a lesson," sneered a soldier with a thick, brown beard. "Maybe back in that cabin."

"You lay a hand on her, and I will hunt you down and kill you. Brutally," said Neil. His voice was low, calm and deadly serious. "I will find you, if it takes me fifty years."

"We'll do as we please," said the bearded soldier. "She's hurting her own countrymen, stealing their paid-for and legal property. She needs to learn a few manners, I say."

"Now, we're not doing anything of the sort," said the captain. "We're not savages. We're taking her into town, turning her in to the local sheriff and she'll be tried in a proper court of law."

They marched Hazel and Neil out to a narrow dirt road, and then toward the distant lights of Savannah. She glanced around occasionally, hoping to spot Mr. Escobar, but if he was following, he was so stealthy that she could not detect him.

"Will they hang a woman?" one soldier asked another.

"I don't know, but if not, she'll wish they had. She's young. She'll have a long life in prison."

"And the man?"

"Him? He'll be hanged."

CHAPTER 28

July 30, 1864
Beaumont, Texas
Hub world

"**A**REN'T YOU PACKED YET?" SIGHED Miss Sanchez from the doorway. "It's only two hours until the train leaves."

Seamus checked his pocket watch. "There's still time."

"Not the way you're going. You haven't packed a thing."

"Don't fuss, woman. I'll be ready."

Miss Sanchez set to clearing up some of the papers and items that littered the small area of the room that Seamus used to work on the prosthetic leg. The thing wasn't complete, not anywhere near to it, but he had decided to bring it along with him and see if he could get it to function eventually. McCullen's side of the room was much tidier, though he had left out a stack of books and newspapers, perhaps to peruse later. Miss Sanchez tossed some crumpled papers into the garbage. And after Seamus chased the meddlesome woman away from his table twice, she picked up a paper and sat down in McCullen's favorite chair.

McCullen was out, taking a constitutional walk, and Seamus was glad for his absence. Being trapped with him in a shared space reminded him too much of prison. He was also glad for Miss Sanchez's presence. She usually didn't make such a nuisance of herself as today when she messed with his belongings, except when he smoked his pipe and she reminded him, repeatedly, that it was detrimental to his health.

He wondered about her. She seemed to enjoy his company and even like him personally. She did not simply endure his presence as a means to get home. Sometimes, when he made her laugh, she would either playfully poke him with her elbow or bump her shoulder against his arm. And once in awhile, she would stand close, close enough for him to smell the faint, fruitlike scent of her hair. Or she would touch his hand. She never did those things with McCullen. Perhaps, in her world, that was how friends acted. In his world, it meant more.

Seamus sighed and began to pack up his things. There weren't many, as he had not brought much equipment and obtaining just a few necessary parts for the mechanical leg had been a struggle.

Would missing the synchronicity truly be such a bad thing? Sure, it was his duty to get Miss Sanchez home, but he still had the coordinates to his own world, where she could live quite comfortably. She wanted her own money and property and the right to vote, which he could now, after some thought, understand. If he imagined himself in her place, he could not be content. But despite these things, would spending her life in his world, perhaps with him, be so terrible?

Of course, there was the matter of her nephew. She needed to return home and coordinate the medical treatment that would save the child's life. Seamus would do all he could for the boy's sake. But once he was well again, what then?

"Holy hell!" Miss Sanchez shot up out of her chair and slammed the newspaper onto the worktable in front of him, sending a pile of screws clattering to the floor and a spool rolling away. The paper was opened to one of the inside pages, and there were several articles. Miss Sanchez jabbed her finger at one titled "Terror of the Confederacy: Pirate Queen Captured. Trial Pending."

"Why do you care—" he said.

"Look, it's her!"

He read the article through, and then read it again. A woman, Captain Hazel Dubois, had been captured near Savannah, Georgia, assisting an escaped slave. She and her accomplice, a Mr. Samuel Clemens, were both imprisoned and awaiting trial.

"She came through to this world!" he said. "How did she come through?"

"Neil Grey must have come for her. But why would they come here?"

"Ah, good Lord. She came after us, don't you see? She must have come to find us. But how?" Seamus ran his hands through his hair and began to pace.

"Well, if she came to find us, then why is she sailing around and helping escaped slaves?" said Miss Sanchez. "That doesn't make any sense."

It didn't, he had to admit. So why was Hazel here? Or was it, perhaps, an older version of her, like the woman he had met in 1961? It didn't matter, because either way, it was his Hazel. He had to help her.

"Throw McCullen's things in a bag," he said. "We're going to Savannah."

She looked over McCullen's possessions and then sighed. "We can't go to Georgia. We have to be in California."

"We'll do that afterwards, if there's time."

"If there's time?" Miss Sanchez said. "We've already lost enough time. No. I need to get home, and that's it."

"I'm not leaving Hazel to be hanged or to die in prison."

"You have a time machine. You can come back for her."

"Or we can get her and then use the machine to come back again and get to California."

Miss Sanchez glared at him. "I'm stuck here because of you and your little experiment with that peroxide engine. I've been as patient as I can, and you need to get me home."

He looked at her in shock. This was not the Felicia Sanchez he knew. She had cared for Hazel when she was eleven and had been hospitalized. She had been the one to insist that Seamus take in the child and give her a home. She loved Hazel.

"How could you leave Hazel? Answer me that," he said.

"I'm not leaving her. She gets out, obviously, or neither of us would have met her when she's older. Besides, Neil Grey is probably with her."

"You mean this Samuel Clemens person?"

"Maybe. He could have given a fake name. Oh! I think I understand. In my world, there was an author named Mark Twain, the pen name of Solomon Clemens. Maybe this was Mr. Grey's idea of a joke. Maybe in his home world, his first name was Samuel."

"A strange joke, as no one would know it unless they were from his world."

"McCullen and I would know it. That's assuming that a person named Clemens wrote the same books in his world. But yes, we're the only ones who would, unless there are other time travelers wandering around."

"So Neil Grey is jailed with her, and you still want to head off to California?" he said. "That's inhuman."

"No, it's not. Because we know they both get out. And because you can come back and try to bribe the guards or whatever you want to do. It's not like we can stroll in and unlock the prison anyway. Besides, the Union wins the war. She'll be freed after it's over."

"If they don't kill her first."

"We know she survives," she said. "They don't kill her."

"You're going to go to California then?"

"*We* are going to California."

"You and McCullen can go. Take the machine. I don't care. I'm not leaving Hazel."

"Don't be stupid. You'd be stranded here without a machine. You can come back for her."

"Maybe and maybe not. Who is to say if I can get back to help her? Maybe one can only go through a time once. Maybe Hazel spends twenty years in that place and I can only get her out when she's older. And there will be a machine available to me: the one she used to get here. You and McCullen can go to Los Angeles. He'll see to your safe trip."

He turned away from her and retrieved the screws and spool from the floor, hurling them into a box. He was angry, deeply angry, at himself, at Hazel, but more so at Miss Sanchez. How could she leave Hazel imprisoned, especially after scolding him about slavery being the great injustice of his time? If it was so terrible, then why wouldn't she help someone who gave everything to help the slaves?

If they could get to Savannah soon, then they could still reach Los Angeles in time for the synchronicity. Everyone would benefit. But if they went to Los Angeles first, Hazel might be executed or who knew what. Was the woman so hell-bent on getting to her own time that she'd sacrifice the girl to do it? Was that the sort of person she was? If so, Seamus wanted nothing to do with her. He saw her from the corner of his eye, simply standing there, watching him.

"Why are you still here?" he snapped. "Go find McCullen. Take the machine. Take the gold. I don't care a whit! Now get out!"

"Seamus, don't."

"Don't what? I spent six years, six entire years working to find a way to get you back from 1961. I gave up any sort of a normal life, living in that laboratory, for your sake. Because it was my duty. Do you understand that, or is duty some other idea that has gone out of fashion in your time, like manners and modesty? It was my duty to get you home, and you will get home. It is also my duty to look out for Hazel."

"First of all, it was your fault I'm here in the first place! It's only fair that you correct the wrong you committed. I've spent months of my life in this time, having people be nasty because of my race or treating me like an idiot because I'm female. You screwed up. You brought me through."

"And am I to do endless penance for it? And should Hazel suffer also? I thought you were some sort of kindly angel, healing the sick. You're a stubborn pain in my arse, sure, but you weren't like this, cruel and heartless."

"It's not heartless. It's practical. I need to get home."

"And there's that as well. Assuming you can get to your own time and save your nephew, you're still simply dying to leave us. You won't even entertain the notion of returning to us. You act as if being stuck here with me and Hazel is like being in the ninth ring of hell. Oh, aye, a comfortable home, food enough to eat and amusements too, but that's not enough. We're not good enough, the street child and the convict, for the perfect Miss Felicia Sanchez."

Tears quivered in her eyes, and he hated her for it, the manipulative woman. Did she think he was going to soften and pat her cheek and tell her that he'd go to California? Well, she had another thing coming. He was going to get Hazel, and nothing, not a woman's tears or the devil himself, would stop him.

"Get out!" he roared.

She rushed to the door, yanked it open and didn't bother to pull it closed behind her. Seamus threw things into a trunk and slammed it savagely. McCullen returned a quarter of an hour later, and Seamus informed him that he would be going to Los Angeles with Miss Sanchez while Seamus went to Georgia to see if he could free the Pirate Queen.

"I don't know about this," said McCullen.

"You're fond of Miss Sanchez. I didn't think you'd mind," growled Seamus. He hated doing this, entrusting Miss Sanchez to his worst enemy. But it was the only option open to him if he wanted to help Hazel and get Miss Sanchez back to her own time. He felt trapped by his lack of choices, and he felt like hitting something.

"Hazel is not your child, Seamus. Not even your niece."

"Do you people understand nothing? She's as much my daughter as any child born to me."

McCullen did not argue, but shook his head, put the last of his things together and set his luggage near the door. At four o'clock, when they needed to leave for the train to California, he took his bags and the trunk containing the time machine and shook Seamus's hand.

"Best of luck, brother," McCullen said.

"Safe journey."

McCullen picked up his bag.

"Before you go," said Seamus, "tell me. Did you have family? What are you returning to?"

"Yes, a family."

"Was there a woman?"

The words were out of Seamus's mouth before he could stop them. If there had been a girl, then she was probably married by now. McCullen had come through from his world when he was only twenty, and he was now in his mid-thirties.

McCullen only smiled. And then the man with whom Seamus had shared so much misery and so much triumph, left. Seamus dropped into a chair, flipping open a copy of *Harper's Weekly* that McCullen had left, but finding he could not read it. He tossed it aside.

He was in love with her. Nothing but love could tear at his guts in this way. From the moment the woman had stood outside his house, in her strange clothing with her strange accent, he had loved her. What a fool he was. He had fancied her a kind, noble being, albeit one with a tart tongue and an unnervingly strong will. Instead, here he was, facing what she really was. On one hand, he could tell himself that she wanted to get home to save her nephew. And that was true, as far as it went. But she had not shown any desire to stay with him after she reached her home. He was a temporary means to an end, a way to get home, a friend perhaps. Nothing more. He sat for a long time, perhaps an hour, looking out the window. He contemplated finding a pub, but no amount of drink would dull the hurt.

He put his head in his hands. Someone knocked at the door.

"Oh just a minute," he called. He had forgotten to pay the hotel for an extra day, and the person outside would want to know when he would check out. He needed to go to the train station and see when the next train left for Georgia. After that, he would find a pub. He located his coat and rummaged through the pocket, looking for his billfold. The door opened a crack.

"I said just a minute!"

"It's me." Miss Sanchez entered, her eyes and nose reddened.

"You've missed your train. What are you doing?"

"I told McCullen to go on without me. I'm coming with you."

CHAPTER 29

August 4, 1864
Savannah, Georgia
Hub world

HAZEL RESTED ON HER COT, staring at the little patch of night sky visible through her high prison window. The summer nights in Georgia were mild and she was not cold, even with only one blanket. The days were another matter, but she had lived in New Orleans long enough to be acclimated to heat. During the hottest part of the day, she imagined the cold ocean wind on her skin as she stood on the deck of Skidbladnir.

Her ship. She loved the very thought of it. The dragon at the prow didn't approve of her, but the crew seemed to like her well enough. She was more than willing to listen to Mr. Escobar's advice on managing them and had worked at being serious and respectable while not driving them to exhaustion and misery. Like Neil, the crew enjoyed listening when she played violin after supper. But unlike him, they did not sit with their eyes closed or look out over the sea. Some monkeys would sway and some would bounce up and down rhythmically. Others would leap up and dance in a twirling, hopping spin that no human could ever replicate.

Her violin was still on Skidbladnir, as was the time machine. The folded ship was still, God willing, in the possession of Mr. Escobar. Perhaps Mr. Escobar could open the ship, collect the crew and sail to their home on the island off the coast of Panama.

It was long after bedtime for all decent folk, as far as she could guess. She hadn't slept and knew that many hours had passed since sundown. The moon had risen and was now high in the sky, though occasionally obscured by drifting clouds. The other cell in the prison was empty, but guards stood outside. She was glad of it. One of the nights, a group of men had come to the prison door and Hazel had sat, cold with sweat, as the guards argued with them. After threatening murmurs she could not make out, eventually the men turned away.

She wished she knew where Neil was. Perhaps, because he was such a dangerous fighter, they had put him in chains and in a stronger prison. She imagined a place made of stone, like a castle dungeon, but there was nothing like that here in Savannah. Then the darkest thought of all came to her once again, and she imagined him tied to a post, hands behind him, glaring at a row of men aiming rifles.

But if he had come to see her when he was older, it meant that he would survive, didn't it? She remembered him as he had been when she was young, a quiet man in a long black duster. But though her memories were real, that didn't make him immune to death. He couldn't leap off a cliff and expect to survive. She wished she could talk to one of the people from the Time Corps, someone who would explain these things to her.

Something darkened the window, something very close, like a man's head looking in at her. It vanished. She jolted upright, unable to breathe. Then the window darkened again.

"Captain," it whispered, and she recognized the small, furry body, legs and long, curving tail. The bars were set close together, but Mr. Escobar maneuvered himself through them and hopped down to the foot of her cot.

"How did you find me?" she whispered. "I've been here for days. Why didn't you come sooner? Is Neil all right? And what about the crew?"

"I followed you. And once I knew where you were, I located Mr. Grey. And once I did that, I located the crew and notified them of the predicament in which we now find ourselves."

"Are they going to go back to Panama?"

"If that is where you would like to go next, but I propose that we have more pressing concerns at this time."

"I meant that they might want to go home, seeing as the ship has no captain."

"I do not understand," said Mr. Escobar. "You live, and until you sell or give away the ship, it is yours."

She wondered about that. Neil had stolen the ship from Mr. Van Dorn when it was in a bottle, so it seemed that theft was another way to gain control of the ship. But as Mr. Escobar said, she had more pressing problems.

"I fear they will be keeping me locked up for life," she said. "Either that, or they may execute me. I don't know."

Mr. Escobar nodded, considering. "I have spoken with Mr. Grey and the crew, and no one has any way to free you. The human men have guns. We do not. Mr. Grey cannot even free himself, and he is strong."

"Where are they keeping him?"

"Another prison across town. Not far, but hard to reach by daylight if one wishes to remain unseen. He has listened to his guards, and I have listened many times as well. It seems Mr. Grey will be executed, while you will be transported to Atlanta for trial. Mr. Grey says the trial will be a spectacle."

"I'm sure it will. It will make an excellent example of me. Now, tell me how Mr. Grey fares. Is he well?"

"Well enough. Not that it will make much difference. The time of his execution is set for tomorrow at dawn."

CHAPTER 30

August 4, 1864
Savannah, Georgia
Hub world

NEIL TRIED ONCE MORE TO get his wrists free of the heavy shackles. He had been locked into them after attacking three guards who had dared to enter his cell. They had to be dragged out, alive but injured, and he had been slammed against a wall and shackled, then beaten until he was bleeding from his nose and mouth and his ribs were heavily bruised.

The shackles were strong, he had to give them that. No amount of twisting or compressing his hands, short of breaking the bones where his thumb met his wrist, would free him. And the walls were too sturdy for him to kick through. He had tried. Repeatedly.

The notion of breaking his own hand bones was looking better and better. He didn't know if he would die by firing squad or by hanging, but he wasn't going to give up without a struggle. He'd take as many guards with him as he could. They could just as well shoot him escaping as tied to a post, so there was nothing to lose. He pressed experimentally against the bone in his left hand until the pain sharpened. He knew he had the strength to break the bone, but did he have the will? He would have to muster it. He would count to three.

One. Two. Three.

"You there!" said a voice through the horizontal slot in his door. "Stand up."

He obeyed, knowing already that if he refused, he would be hauled to his feet by a group of their strongest guards, beaten and perhaps not fed for the day. He backed against the wall and the guard unlocked the heavy door and pushed it open. The light from the lamp on the corridor wall was behind the guard, so the first thing Neil noticed was that the guard was alone. Foolish. Then he recognized him.

"How did you find me?" he asked.

Elliot Van Dorn put his finger to his lips and then closed the door. He grinned at Neil, but it was a vicious grin, full of unconcealed animosity.

"Turn around," Elliot said, holding up a key. At Neil's hesitation, he said, "Do you want to stay here? Now turn around."

Neil did so, and Elliot unlocked the shackles and slid them off, setting them on the ground so they didn't make any noise. Neil rubbed his wrists and flexed his hands.

"Thank you. How did you find me?"

"This is my home world, and I'm not doing this for you. You, young man, are a bastard and a thief. I do this for the man you will one day become, and for Hazel, who is my friend."

"How do you know Hazel?"

"Shut up and let's get out of here. The sleepy gas I sprayed the guards with won't work for long. I didn't want them to be brain damaged or anything so I gave them a partial dose."

Neil followed Elliot down the hallway and out the back of the prison building which was attached to the police station. They crept through the shadows along the edge of the town square and then rushed down street after street, stopping in a stinking alleyway where piano music and raucous laughter filtered through the back wall of a bar.

"I owe you one," said Neil.

"More than one."

"Why did you come for me?" Neil asked. "And what are you going to do with me now?"

Elliot chuckled. "I'm not doing anything with you. I'm leaving you right here in this alley. The first thing you need to know is that you are being hunted by someone a lot scarier than I am. He hasn't given up on you. But right now, if it were up to me, he could have you. I'm freeing you for Hazel's sake and because you'll be a better man, one day. Take this." He offered him a small canister, sleek and metallic.

"Sleepy gas," said Elliot. "Best I could do on short notice. They'll be transporting Hazel day after tomorrow to Atlanta. There's a small town along the way, about twelve miles out of Savannah. There's a pub there called the Raucous Raven. A friend of mine reminisced once, that he spent an evening there in this time. I suggest you go visit it."

"With this," said Neil, examining the canister, "I can knock out any guards traveling with Hazel and get her myself. I don't need your friend."

"Neil, you're not the only one who cares about Hazel. She's a great favorite among her friends, and there are those who would like to help her, and you, if you'll let them."

Elliot went to put his hand on his shoulder, and Neil jerked away.

"I don't need your help."

"Well then, perhaps you'd like to return to your cell where you were better off."

Neil had no reply to that.

"Fine," said Elliot. "Be a stubborn horse's ass. Oh, and one more thing. This is for stealing my time machine and the ship."

Elliot punched Neil hard in the face.

CHAPTER 31

August 4, 1864
Outside Savannah, Georgia
Hub world

S EAMUS RECOGNIZED THE MAN THE instant he saw him enter the Raucous Raven. Neil Grey was much younger now, only in his early twenties, but it was unmistakably him. For a moment, Seamus waited to see if Mr. Grey would approach him, but when he looked over the room and did not recognize him, Seamus rose from his seat.

"Where's Hazel?" he asked Mr. Grey.

The man spun around and Seamus braced himself for an attack. But Mr. Grey paused and looked him over, considering.

"Who are you?"

"A bit jumpy, aren't you?"

Mr. Grey did not answer, but Seamus knew the wary, watchful look of a hunted man. He had once been one himself.

"Tell me where she is," said Seamus. "Is she with you?"

"We're drawing attention to ourselves," said Mr. Grey. He seemed to relax a bit in regard to Seamus, looking over Seamus's shoulder at the rest of the room.

"Then let's go," said Seamus, tossing a few coins onto the bar to cover his bill. Miss Sanchez was upstairs in her room, as she hadn't cared to come down to the pub, so he had been enjoying a pint alone, thinking.

"She's still in jail, isn't she?" Seamus asked as soon as they were outside.

"You still haven't told me who you are," said Mr. Grey.

"Mother of God," he muttered. "I'm Seamus Doyle. I assume Hazel has mentioned me?"

"Yes."

"Now tell me where Hazel is."

"Still locked up."

"But she's safe?" asked Seamus.

"As far as I know."

"Please tell me you have a time machine. And friends from the time group of yours. I think we'll need some help."

"Sorry to disappoint," said Neil. "But I just escaped from jail." Seamus detected a note of humor in it. The man was filthy and unshaven, and he probably didn't have two cents to rub together.

The attack happened so fast Seamus almost missed it. One moment, they turned a corner to duck between two buildings, the next, a man leaped at Mr. Grey, pulling his arms back to restrain him. Mr. Grey pulled free, turned and grabbed the man under the chin, slamming him into the wall. When the man made a swing for Neil's face, he lowered him to the ground and slammed his head against the ground until he went still.

"Dear God," whispered Seamus. He had never seen such speed and ruthless brutality. When he had met Mr. Grey before, he had seemed such an average sort of man.

"This isn't a pickpocket," said Mr. Grey.

"A lawman, or a bounty hunter?"

If Mr. Grey had just escaped, no doubt people would be hunting him.

"Maybe the latter." Mr. Grey knelt and searched the man on the ground, going through his pockets and even checking in his mouth. "He's alive. I didn't kill him."

"I'm glad."

"No, not a bounty hunter. Not the kind you mean anyhow. This is a man from my own time."

"How can you tell?"

"He has white dental fillings."

"Well, who is he then?"

"He's after me, and he wanted me alive. He has no interest in you. No need to concern yourself."

"He's after you then? Why? What did you do?"

Mr. Grey pulled the man far back into the alley, laying him out flat near a wall. He stood and looked down at him, as if thinking.

"If you don't kill him, he'll come after you again, won't he?" asked Seamus.

"Probably."

Mr. Grey left the alley and Seamus followed.

"I'm a hunted man," said Mr. Grey quietly. "As long as Hazel is in jail, they'll know I'm nearby."

"All the more reason to get her out. And it seems we have that in common then. A man named Mr. March wants me dead, and according to a friend of mine, he can time travel without a machine. Have you heard of anything like this?"

"Yes, I have. He wants us both, and as long as Hazel is here, he'll know we will be too."

"Here's my hotel. Come inside."

Seamus made arrangements for Mr. Grey to have a room and asked for someone to send up a hot meal for him.

"Now," said Seamus when they reached his room. "Tell me how Hazel is."

"She's well, as far as I know. She'll be transported to Atlanta tomorrow. They'll be taking her on a road near here."

"That's not much time. I don't suppose you have any weapons or skeleton keys or useful things for getting Hazel free?"

Neil Grey pulled a metallic canister from his pocket.

"Just one."

CHAPTER 32

August 5, 1864
Outside Savannah, Georgia
Hub world

A GUARD OFFERED HIS HAND TO help Hazel into the police wagon and she hesitated before taking it and climbing in.

"Thank you," she said softly. He did not answer, but when she seated herself, she caught his eye and he looked away. She still wore her trousers and boots, though she had been offered a used dress while in prison. Once she went to trial, she would be sure to ask for something very ladylike, perhaps in white, something that made her look very young and innocent.

Did the guards know what had happened to Neil? She had asked the guards before, but none of them would tell her a thing. If he was dead, then why wouldn't they mention it? Were they afraid she would descend into hysterics, making their job of transporting a woman even more awkward? Two guards climbed into the wagon with her and sat on the bench across from her before the two doors clanged closed. She heard the lock being fitted into its place and snapping shut. Both of the guards inside with her were armed and also avoided looking directly at her. That couldn't mean anything good. Either they anticipated that she would have a grueling trial, which she had already accepted, or they knew something else she did not.

"Some people are coming," said a man outside, and through the two barred windows at the back of the wagon, Hazel and the two guards watched a group of men, perhaps the same ones who had come to the prison, approach.

"You all go home now," said a guard outside, and the wagon lurched forward. Some of the men in the group yelled and pointed.

"You'll be all right," said one of the guards across from her. "We have eight mounted men outside, riding along with us."

It was just after dawn, and if Mr. Escobar was correct, Neil was already dead. As the wagon bumped along, she silently said a prayer for the repose of his soul. If Neil was gone, then she was friendless in the world, except for Mr. Escobar, and only God knew where he was. If she was fortunate, he would be following along. And if not, then she might never see him again.

She refused to cry in front of the guards, and bit the inside of her lip hard, making tears come to her eyes, but for a reason she could control. She had done all her real crying back in her cell, and would do no more until she was alone.

She imagined her crew, fifty-seven capuchin monkeys, rushing the prison and tearing open the door, or leaping onto the gallows and freeing her, then bearing her away on their shoulders, like the tiny men in Gulliver's Travels. But that was a silly hope, as the monkeys would be shot and killed, or at least a few of them would, and she refused to be the cause of death for any of them. She had been unable to save Neil, but she could, at the very least, not cause any more death.

The trip to Atlanta would take days, and she would be kept under guard the entire time, stopping in the small cities along the way. She wondered if her journey was known to the locals. There might be other mobs waiting for her. She knew better than to ask the guards.

After four hours, she was sore from being bumped around in her seat. Then she smelled something sweet come in on the air through the window. It had a little tartness to it, like lemon pie. It wasn't a pleasant scent though, like food, but had another scent as well, sharp and medicinal.

The guards noticed it too, and one of them craned his neck to look out the window, as if he would be able to see the origin of the smell. Hazel felt tired, exhausted even, after such a long trip, and the guard across from her rubbed his eyes. She yawned and it felt like she could barely keep her eyes open. Taking a nap would be such a nice way to spend the trip. She leaned against the front wall of the wagon, letting her eyes close and sweet sleep take her.

Small sharp needles poked all along her back and neck, simultaneously itching and hurting. Her head felt fuzzy, but pleasant in a way, and she rolled onto her side to go back to sleep. But the needles were worse that way, stabbing her cheek, ear and even her eyelid, forcing her to roll onto her back.

Opening her eyes, she saw wooden beams, but they were far overhead, much farther than the roof of a prison cell or the wagon. She pushed herself onto her elbows and had a look around. It was a barn, and she was lying on a pile of grayish moldy hay. It was all over her clothing and when she reached into her hair, she found it clinging there also. The barn was dilapidated, with slats missing from the walls and a large hole in the roof at the far end. The place must be abandoned.

A tall, lean man with dark hair stood in the doorway, looking outside. His back was to her, but she knew him on sight.

"Professor?"

He spun around and hurried to her side, grinning wide. He knelt and embraced her. "Glad you're awake. We've been waiting for you. We need to get moving soon."

"What happened? How did you get me out?"

"We had some sleeping gas that made everyone, including you, go to sleep. Miss Sanchez was worrying herself to death, because this gas might be harmful, and as you were the smallest of the group, you'd be the most affected."

"You could have yelled for me to hold my breath."

"That would give away our position and alert the guards that they were being drugged, albeit in a way which would be strange to them. Mr. Grey insisted we do things quietly."

"Neil is alive?"

The Professor's eyebrows went up at her use of Neil's Christian name. "He's alive and well. He and Miss Sanchez should be back any moment. They went to scout out the area and make sure it's still empty. I won the straw pull to stay with you. They were both of them quite eager to stay with you, you see. And I think Miss Sanchez isn't going to forgive me for separating her from her patient any time soon. But I'm just happy you're alive."

Mr. Escobar sat in silent vigil off to one side and he nodded once when she looked at him.

"Where is the crew?" she asked him.

"Safe. Waiting."

"How long have I been asleep?"

"More than a day," said the monkey.

The Professor added, "Long enough for the guards to notify the authorities of your escape. We need you awake and then we'll take your ship and leave. You're now a fugitive from justice."

"Just like you. The apple didn't fall far from the tree, huh, Professor?"

"Ah, now you haven't killed anyone, so let's not go that far."

"We found two more," said Miss Sanchez, pushing open the barn door, letting Neil in and then closing it behind them. Then she spotted Hazel. "You're up!"

Miss Sanchez shoved an armload of what appeared to be clothing at Neil, who took it. He set two pistols on a crate in the corner as Miss Sanchez knelt beside Hazel, examined her pupils, took her pulse and asked her questions about how she felt.

"What did you mean, you found two more?" the Professor asked Neil.

"Two more lawmen," said Neil. "But I knocked them out and we stole their things."

"They'll be fine, I checked," Miss Sanchez assured the Professor, though Hazel knew that he probably wouldn't have minded if they weren't. Hazel managed to stand and set to pulling pieces of straw from her hair.

"Look at this," said Neil, showing one of the guns to the Professor. "A real Colt 1860 single-action revolver, muzzle loaded. The guy even had a pouch of bullets and gunpowder."

"Looks like something from a museum," said Miss Sanchez.

"I'm keeping this one," said Neil, taking a gun belt from the pile of clothing and fastening it around his waist. Then he found a long black duster, shook it out, swung it over his shoulders and put it on. He shoved his hands into the pockets. This was the long coat Neil had worn when they had first met him in New Orleans. Now, Hazel thought, he looked more like himself.

"The other pistol is a .44 revolver," Neil said to the Professor. "Looks like Union issue, so it might be stolen. It's yours if you want it, Mr. Doyle."

Hazel hadn't heard the Professor's real last name since the evening when he had told it to her and sworn her to secrecy when she was sixteen. In their world, he went by the name Seamus Connor. Among all the other Irish immigrants flooding New Orleans after the potato famine, he did not stand out with that name. But in this world, she supposed there was no reason for him to use the alias any longer.

"I haven't shot a gun in ages," said the Professor, but he went to examine his new prize. Neil found a milking stool and set to inserting gunpowder and bullets and tamping them down with a short stick and a piece of cloth.

"Is she well enough to travel?" the Professor asked Miss Sanchez.

"I'd rather she rest. But under the circumstances, I say she can travel."

"Mr. Escobar," Hazel said. "How long until you can assemble the crew?"

"Once we reach the shore, I can have them ready within a quarter of an hour."

"How close are we to the beach?" Hazel asked the Professor.

"An hour's walk."

"How did you get so far?" asked Hazel. "I was taken four hours inland in the prison wagon, and it would have been a long walk even without hauling me along."

"Mr. Grey carried you," said Miss Sanchez. Neil didn't look up or acknowledge the statement, but kept loading his gun.

"Mr. Escobar," said Hazel. "We will set sail in an hour and a quarter."

CHAPTER 33

August 7, 1864
Outside Savannah, Georgia
Hub world

SEAMUS WATCHED THE LITTLE MONKEY in a vest speak with Mr. Grey as he and Miss Sanchez collected the bags containing his equipment and their personal items. It was full dark, in the wee hours of the morning, and since they had no lanterns, they would be hard to spot unless they were out in the open.

"We'll take the main road," said Neil. "Going any other way will just slow us down. Mr. Escobar and I will scout ahead and watch behind, since we can see and hear any approaching people when they're still far off."

Seamus was about to tell them that he was just as able to detect any people or riders, but he was content to walk beside Hazel and Miss Sanchez. Hazel was alive and well and Miss Sanchez had proven herself remorseful for wanting to leave Hazel behind. He was still cross with her, but in time, he'd forgive her.

The important thing was that Hazel was safe now. They were together again, with Miss Sanchez. Having the young Mr. Grey and the bizarre talking monkey along was unreal, but Seamus did not consider it unfortunate. Both of them were decent people. If they weren't all fleeing as lawbreakers, the trip might have been pleasant.

"What on earth were you thinking when you decided to

wear trousers?" he asked Hazel softly when they were half a mile from the barn. "I haven't seen any other women in them in this world."

"Some of the artists in Spain and Italy wear them."

"I do hope you'll reconsider them. They're not entirely decent."

"Leave her be," said Miss Sanchez.

"It's not as if you have any say," said Hazel to Seamus. "I'm of age now, and I can do as I please."

"Oh!" said Seamus. "And that includes getting arrested and jailed? Did you know they called you the Terror of the Confederacy in the papers? The Pirate Queen?"

"I didn't commit any acts of piracy."

"They consider the slaves as property, so that's theft."

"They can say what they like, but slaves aren't property and they will continue to escape. The Railroad operators never let anyone know too much about the other stations or conductors. I only knew one name, the first name of the woman we were going to fetch, and the authorities already had that information. I hope she made it to Long Island by another route."

Mr. Escobar and Mr. Grey approached them, Mr. Grey from the front and Mr. Escobar from behind. They spoke to each other so softly that Seamus couldn't hear them and then split up again.

"You keep odd company," said Seamus to Hazel.

"I think they're fine company. Just wait until you meet my crew."

"And this ship is docked where?"

"Right now, it's right here." Hazel pulled a folded cloth from her pocket.

Seamus exchanged a dark look of concern with Miss Sanchez. The monkey had said that the cloth was a ship, but Seamus didn't think Hazel would have been so daft. Mr. Grey had not said a word on the topic, and Seamus dearly hoped that he knew where this ship might be. After all, he had not been subject to the sleeping gas. Nor was he a strange creature from a fairy tale.

"How fast is your ship?" asked Miss Sanchez.

"Fast," said Hazel. "Very maneuverable and swift as the wind. I love her, though she doesn't always return the sentiment. She's called Skidbladnir, by the way."

"What kind of a name is that?" asked Seamus.

"Viking. Oh, and tell the dragon you're from Europe. She doesn't like skraelings."

They walked on silently, and Seamus wondered about Hazel. Had the trip through time addled her brain, or had she not recovered fully from the gas? That must be it. These must be the lingering effects of the gas. He hoped it would wear off soon.

"How did you find me anyway?" Hazel asked.

"We were staying in a place in a little town outside of Savannah," said Seamus, "and I went down to a pub to have a think and a drink. Who should walk in, but a familiar face, albeit much younger than when last I had seen him. He knew the route and time you'd be passing, and the three of us set up a little ambush."

"How long would it take to get to California on your ship?" Miss Sanchez asked Hazel.

"I'm not sure," said Hazel. "How long do we have?"

"The synchronicity is the third week in September. We have six weeks," said Miss Sanchez.

"When we get on board, I'll consult with Mr. Escobar and set a route, then we'll see if we can make it."

"McCullen is going to wait, and if we get there in time, we can both get home."

"And if you don't?" asked Hazel.

"Then McCullen takes the machine and we keep trying," said Seamus. "Doesn't Mr. Grey have a machine?"

"He does, on board Skidbladnir." Hazel patted her pocket. "But we don't know how to use it. I suppose it's a lucky thing we found you."

"Or I found you, rather," said Seamus. "It interfered with our plans, and now we might miss the synchronicity altogether."

"That's hardly my fault. It's not as if you told me you were leaving. I would have gone with you! But you gave me no choice in the matter. You just left me behind, alone."

"Now, Hazel, that's not true," Seamus said. "We knew Mr. Grey would come on your birthday, and you would choose to marry Mr. Ross or do as you pleased."

"But you didn't ask me, now, did you?" Hazel wheeled on him. "You left me back there, with just a letter! I was worried sick about you."

"Well you needn't have worried, lass. We were safe as can be before we decided to break a foolish girl out of jail!"

Mr. Escobar dashed toward them and a few moments later, Mr. Grey appeared as well.

"Would you mind keeping it down?" said Mr. Escobar to Seamus. "We are hoping to travel undetected, if you had not noticed."

"I was just having a conversation with Hazel here."

"Captain?" the monkey looked inquiringly at her.

"It's all right. Carry on."

Seamus thought she sounded every bit a ship's captain. Hazel had changed, again, and Seamus didn't like it. It had only been a few months since he had last seen her, worrying about marriage. Now she was wearing trousers and ordering this monkey around like he truly was her first mate. She also owned a ship and had been able to elude the authorities for long enough to become something of a legend. That wasn't too shabby, if he thought about it.

"Maybe you didn't do so badly," whispered Seamus. "Your heart was in the right place."

Hazel didn't reply, but after a minute she muttered, "Thanks."

CHAPTER 34

August 7, 1864
Outside of Savannah, Georgia
Hub world

HAZEL UNFOLDED SKIDBLADNIR, AND SCRAMBLED aboard before it grew too large. Neil waited on shore with Miss Sanchez and the Professor and the few belongings they had brought with them after parting company with McCullen. Once the ship had grown to full size, Hazel asked the dragon to move as close to shore as she could. The dragon could control the ship, or, more properly, she could move herself from one place to another, albeit slowly. To truly make good time required the sails and oars.

"Are you able to lower your own gangplank?" Hazel asked Skidbladnir.

"I am."

"Please do it then."

The dragon lowered the gangplank into the shallow surf for the humans to board. Some of the crew scampered up with them while others merely scaled the ship's sides.

"I can't believe my eyes. You weren't brain addled," said the Professor, dropping his bags on deck and staring up at the great red and white striped sail, then at the prow. "And it has a dragon head too."

"Remember," said Hazel quietly to the Professor, "tell her you're from Ireland. She won't mind you as much."

Neil pulled the gangplank up once everyone was on board. The Professor and Miss Sanchez had many questions about the ship and crew, and while Neil answered them, Hazel called for the crew to immediately set sail. Lingering around shore, even in the dead of night, was suicide. She wanted to put as many miles between herself and Savannah as possible, for all their sakes.

They sailed for three weeks, stopping only in tiny port towns, never in larger ones, to take on supplies. By the time they passed around the tip of Florida and sailed into the Gulf of Mexico, the four humans had settled into a daily routine. Miss Sanchez had decided to take on Hazel's uniform of loose pants, since voluminous skirts on a ship were completely impractical. She performed small tasks around the ship, repairing boards, mending the few cloth items they had and cooking for the humans. The crew, for their part, ate mostly fruit, either dried or fresh, and occasionally hard tack.

The Professor spent his time working on deck, when weather permitted, or in his small compartment below deck that served as his sleeping area and laboratory. He was mapping time, using his equipment, and occasionally Hazel heard swearing from below, sometimes in English, and when things were particularly bad, in Gaelic.

Neil had moved out of the captain's quarters, making room for Miss Sanchez to share the space with Hazel. He took a tiny storage compartment near the Professor's, and hung a hammock inside. Most of the time, he was on deck, managing the crew along with the bosun, and occasionally taking an oar when they required rowers.

At the end of a particularly tiring day, Hazel lay in her hammock in the dark, listening to the soft creak of the ship and the splash of the waves against the hull. She loved this. The ship, the sea, it was as if they had been made for her, or she for them. The discontent and uncertainty that had tormented her in New Orleans made some sense now. She had not been intended for life there, but here. Sure, they were fleeing the authorities, but they were safe now, more or less.

She glanced over at the other hammock where Neil had once been and where Miss Sanchez now slept. When Hazel was eleven, she had wanted Miss Sanchez to stay in their time and marry the Professor. Now, with older eyes, she saw things differently. The Professor cared for Miss Sanchez, but he was also more distant from her, less eager to spend time with her, and also more critical at times. It was as if he was disappointed in her, though Hazel couldn't imagine why. Perhaps it was because he was preparing himself to lose her.

The ship rocked with the waves, harder than it should have. The wind was also picking up. It was hurricane season, and a storm could delay them or even capsize them, depending on its strength. She slipped out of her hammock, threw a coat over her nightdress, climbed the steep steps and walked out on deck.

Yes, the scent and feel of the air was different, there was no doubt. And the sky was clouded over with no stars visible. Even the moon was obscured. The crew was asleep in the rigging except for two monkeys who were on night watch, sitting awake at the top of the mast, where, on a human crewed ship, a crow's nest would have been.

She approached the dragon head and looked out ahead, west, but there was nothing but endless water and clouds all the way to the horizon.

"Skidbladnir?" she said.

"Captain," said the dragon.

"There is a storm coming."

"Yes."

"Can you tell how bad it will be?" She hated to ask the dragon this, as it revealed her ignorance. She was a competent captain, but not a seasoned one, and Skidbladnir was hundreds of years old. Even Mr. Escobar was not so knowledgeable.

"The sea folk I have spoken with today say the storm is moving in from the southeast. It is strong."

"Sea folk?"

"That is what I said."

"What are the sea folk?" asked Hazel.

"The people who live in the sea."

"I don't understand. What do you mean? Mermaids?"

"The sea people. The ones who live in the sea. How else should I put it, ignorant skraeling?"

"Now, that's enough of that. It was an honest question. I've never been to this world before. Talking ships and monkeys don't exist where I come from. And if there are real mermaids or talking fish, I want to know about it."

"The storm will hit us by morning, unless we sail west."

"Can we outrun it?"

"We can, if I have sails and oars working together all night. But I cannot do it alone."

"I'll rouse the crew."

First she found Mr. Escobar sleeping low in the rigging and woke him. She ordered him to wake the crew and sail due west. Then she lit a lantern and padded down the steps to get Neil, the Professor and Miss Sanchez. The monkeys, though small, were as strong as large men, perhaps due to whatever enchantment made them able to speak. Hazel had asked once, but Mr. Escobar simply said they had always been like that, as had all their people. But even with all of them either managing the sail or rowing, four humans at the oars could only help.

There was no door on Neil's compartment, and she held the lantern aloft as she stepped silently inside. He was asleep, which was rare for him, and his head was tipped far back, his mouth open wide. He looked so vulnerable, almost sweet and childlike, though a few days' worth of beard stubbled his face. Then the light caught something, a dark thing at the top of his mouth. No, it must have been a trick of the lamplight and shadow. But still, she looked closer. It was not an illusion. There was something black on the roof of his mouth. She moved the lantern to get a better look. She had seen animals, cats and dogs, with dappled upper palates, pink and black. But no human was like that, were they?

The mark was symmetrical, three times as wide as it was high, and consisted of three roughly equal symbols. They were shaped almost like musical notes with stems joined at the top, but they definitely were not notes, not in any musical notations she had ever seen. The first two marks were not identical, but both were shaped like arches, although with pointed upper corners, like calligraphy or script. The last was like a stylized X.

Before she could pull back, faster than any person should have been able to move, Neil's hand shot out and grabbed her wrist, squeezing painfully. His eyes opened, and a moment after she squeaked in pain and shock, he let her go.

"What is it?" he asked.

"A storm is coming. We need all hands on deck. We'll be sailing all night."

He nodded and swung his legs over the edge of the hammock. He would need to change into his clothing, and she gave him one more glance over her shoulder before going to the Professor's compartment to awaken him.

All night, the humans and monkeys rowed and worked the sail. They exhausted themselves, all but Neil, with his strange ability to work for long periods of time without fatigue. Hazel thought about telling him about the mark in his mouth. Perhaps he already knew about it. After all, who had not used a mirror to look inside their mouth? He was a taciturn man, and he might feel she had invaded his privacy by studying him in his sleep.

But if he didn't know, then she ought to tell him. It might hold a clue as to why he had uncertain memories of his past and why he was so physically strong. Another thought came to mind. If he didn't know and she told him, he might run off through time to find out why he had the mark, leaving her on her own. The thought of it was too painful to contemplate.

By dawn, rain was falling, but it was light and the winds were not the wild, buffeting wind of a storm, but rather a strong sea wind. At noon, they were clear of the storm and everyone ate a well-deserved meal. Hazel considered playing violin for the crew, but her arms ached from rowing and she was too tired after a night without sleep. Perhaps there was an uninhabited island close by where the crew could have a few hours of shore leave. She would have to consult her maps.

Everyone else was as exhausted as she, except for Neil who was, even now, adjusting the sail. He must have felt her watching him, for he turned toward her and met her gaze. His expression softened a little around the mouth and eyes, which for him, she knew, passed for a smile.

CHAPTER 35

September 15, 1864
California coast
Hub world

S EAMUS SWORE AND THEN SLAMMED the steel box that housed the time sensor down on his makeshift worktable. He immediately regretted it. The blasted thing was delicate, albeit entirely confounding at the moment. It wasn't able to detect the fine changes that made one time differ from the rest and it was maddening. He opened it up and checked it for damage, finding none. But he would only know for certain when he tried to use it again.

He had worked for weeks now, as the ship sailed through the eastern half of the Gulf of Mexico, stopping at an island, but only for half a day, for everyone to enjoy shore leave. Everyone except him, that was. He was too consumed with mapping the timelines in this world.

After sailing south past the western tip of Cuba and straight south through the Caribbean, they reached the Estado Libre del Istmo, or the Free State of the Isthmus. Mr. Grey and Miss Sanchez called it Panama and said that one day men would dig a canal through the narrowest part, connecting the Atlantic and Pacific oceans. They hired four horses and began to cross the narrow strip of land. The monkeys traveled over land by their own way.

Riding across land was the worst part of the journey,

as Seamus couldn't work or study, but had to guide his horse over trails and hills through the towns, some rough and some pleasant. At night, when they stayed at various small inns, he could work. But it was not enough. It was never enough. He hoped his work would not be necessary, not to Miss Sanchez at least, as his mapping of time would be for his own use, unless she chose to join him. If they reached California in time, his work would be nothing to Miss Sanchez. But the days slipped by and their progress toward Los Angeles was so frustratingly slow. Miss Sanchez was growing more grim and quiet by the day, speaking only when necessary or when they needed her to speak Spanish to secure a room at an inn or hire fresh horses.

Mr. Escobar spoke Spanish also, and he tried whispering in Hazel's ear, but the translation took time and her pronunciation was awkward. Seamus saw as the monkey and Hazel became close to inseparable, and Mr. Escobar was especially fascinated by her feet, which he thought resembled his own, at least compared to the feet of every other human in this world, save Seamus himself. Mr. Grey explained to them that a man named Darwin in his world had laid out an idea that monkeys and humans had a common ancestor. Seamus's mother would have said it was all stuff and nonsense, but Seamus didn't know what to think of the notion.

They finally reached the coast and set sail, the monkeys happy from their time leaping through trees or feasting on fruit or whatever they did while the humans plodded along on land. The humans were more subdued. The night of September twenty-fourth, the day of the synchronicity and the earthquake in Los Angeles, they were just passing Cabo San Lucas at the tip of Baja, California. Miss Sanchez did not eat any of her supper, but went down to her quarters without speaking. Seamus watched Hazel and Mr. Grey exchange a look, but neither of them went to follow her. He didn't wish to go either. What would he say? That he was struggling to map this time? That Oren McCullen had now left this time with the machine and that they were stranded here, with no home and limited money?

Hazel put her hand on his arm. "I know you'll find a way," she said. "And you're both welcome with me as long as you like. We can hire ourselves out and run cargo up and down the coast, from San Diego and Los Angeles to San Francisco, all the way up to Seattle and Vancouver. We could earn a living that way."

"I'm not much use to you on the ship," he said.

"It's no bother. You can stay as long as you like."

He had said as much to her not too long ago, but the feeling of taking Hazel's charity galled him. Seamus had trouble sleeping that night and the following nights. They finally arrived in Los Angeles, and a few miles south of town, they disembarked. Hazel was the last to leave, and Seamus watched from shore as she stepped into the surf and pressed her hands against the ship's planks, about three feet apart. She pressed inward, and the ship folded. She continued this folding motion until Skidbladnir was a small square piece of brown cloth. They headed into the town of Los Angeles.

"Do you know any of the streets or landmarks?" Mr. Grey asked Miss Sanchez as they moved into the city proper. They were both originally from this city, albeit in the future.

"Not a thing. It's completely different," she said.

"Dirt streets, no cars, just farms and outlaws." Mr. Grey didn't sound particularly unhappy about this, and he seemed to be almost enjoying himself. He walked along, hands in his pockets, taking in the rough buildings and rougher people. Farms stood farther out and buildings, including houses and shops, clustered around a few central streets. Carriages and men on horseback passed, but the streets were dusty and unpaved, and even the wooden sidewalks, what there were of them, were missing boards here and there.

The earthquake had severely damaged many buildings. Some of them were surrounded by work crews and others stood forlorn and empty, some with collapsed ceilings and others tipping dangerously, ready to collapse at any moment. After speaking with a few people, they learned that it wasn't only buildings that were damaged, but storehouses and wells, leaving farms and sections of town without water. The damage would take years to repair, and yet the city would remain, and Seamus knew it would grow.

"I suppose we ought to find out where we can ask around for any shipping jobs," said Hazel.

Miss Sanchez paused to look in a store window, but as it was full of farm equipment, Seamus understood that she wished to avoid the conversation about life after missing the synchronicity. He didn't speak to her, leaving her to her own thoughts.

"We just need to find the port," said Mr. Grey. "There are usually jobs wherever ships dock."

"Agreed," said Mr. Escobar from his perch on Hazel's shoulder.

Hazel and Mr. Grey discussed their options for shipping cargo. Before, they had only taken on family heirlooms with limited amounts of larger cargo. Now, they might be shipping dry goods, bolts of cloth, building supplies, anything at all. How would they load the goods without the monkey crew being seen? And how would they pay human dockworkers to do that portion of the work? It would be difficult, and word of a dragon-headed ship would spread, even to Georgia. The law might catch up with them.

"Once we save up enough, we could do a cross-Atlantic trip, perhaps," said Hazel.

Seamus listened in, but making a living running cargo was not something he wished to do. He followed Hazel and Mr. Grey toward the dock, checking behind him to make sure Miss Sanchez was coming along. She was. He saw her wipe her eyes with the back of her hand. He wanted to comfort her, but seeing as he was the cause of her trouble, he thought it best to leave her alone.

Sunset was coming, and after asking around, a man told Mr. Grey that the shipping office was already closed. It would open in the morning. Nearby stood an inn where sailors often stayed. The walls were grayish and the place had no sign out front at all.

"We might as well eat here as anywhere else. I'm famished," said Hazel.

Seamus had misgivings, as he was uncomfortable exposing his female companions to itinerant sailors. But dressed as they were, their motley group could not expect to be welcomed into any finer establishments.

The inside of the inn was tight, cramped and almost empty. No one played at the weathered piano to one side, and only one woman was on duty, serving whatever passed for a meal here. In one corner sat a group of three men, all of them muscled and deeply tanned, either farm workers or sailors, Seamus guessed. Mr. Escobar hopped onto a chair beside Hazel as they took their seats.

In the corner sat a lone man who leaned back, his legs crossed at the ankles. He was tall with tawny hair and the kind of face and physical build that women always liked. There was a feeling Seamus had about him, the sense of a man completely at ease with himself. But it went beyond that. He was a man completely comfortable about his place in the world. Seamus had never seen that before, not if he thought about it. Men were always striving and filled with discontent and even in their quiet, happy moments, there was still an undercurrent of unease. But not with this man.

"Ladies," the man said to Hazel and Miss Sanchez and, since his hat was on the table, he dipped his head for a moment in greeting.

"Something is off about that man," said Mr. Grey, very

softly to Seamus. "Mr. March could send someone else after me, and that's just the sort of guy he would send."

"How do you know?"

"Because I used to do the same work. Look at him. Boots are dirty but not worn down. The shirt is bright white, even the hat is in perfect condition, though covered in dust. If he's wealthy, what's he doing here? And if he's not, why the nice clothing?"

Mr. Grey was right, but the man was only quietly drinking a beer. The waitress came over to tell them that the inn was serving only cold sandwiches. They asked for five, and though the server glanced at Mr. Escobar, she didn't refuse.

The tall man at the table set down his glass, folded his hands over his middle and closed his eyes, as if taking a catnap. When they were halfway through their meal, a rotund man with a white beard entered, looked around and took a seat across from the younger man. He ordered a sarsaparilla.

"How was the visit with your brothers and sisters?" asked the younger man.

"As well as can be expected. It's family." He shrugged. "Our brother is being difficult."

"What are you going to do? Kill him?"

The older man didn't look shocked at this line of conversation, but just shook his head and glanced out the window. "No. Family, you know. But your help is appreciated, I can tell you that."

The younger man ordered another beer. Seamus caught him studying Hazel and Miss Sanchez, and Hazel took one too many sidelong looks at him.

"That's not the sort of man you'd want to associate with," whispered Seamus.

"Oh, do you think he's dangerous for me?" Hazel whispered back with a wicked twinkle in her eye.

"Do you know where your brother is?" the younger man asked the older one.

"Not yet. March is a slippery devil."

Hazel gasped and looked at Mr. Grey who was as still as a statue. Seamus thought Mr. Grey looked like a coil, too tightly wound and ready to snap. Mr. Grey turned in his chair to face the two men.

"I couldn't help but overhear you speaking about Mr. March," he said.

"Do you know him?"

"I might."

Foolish man! Seamus wanted to haul Mr. Grey out of the room by his ear. If he was being hunted by this Mr. March, then alerting his associates of his identity was madness. Although, if Seamus thought about it, there might be some sense in it. If these men knew anything about Mr. March, then Mr. Grey might need to know it too, if only to avoid the man.

The older man studied Mr. Grey and then asked. "Are you Neil Grey?"

"I am."

The good-looking man at the table chuckled, then smiled at Miss Sanchez and Hazel. "It looks like we have a common acquaintance, then."

No one at their table answered, but when the man smiled at Miss Sanchez, her cheeks pinkened slightly.

"I am Santiago," said the younger man, "and this is my friend Julius."

"You said you were Mr. March's brother, right?" Mr. Grey asked Julius.

"Sadly, yes."

"And are you like him? Can you, you know, do anything?"

Well, Mr. Grey hadn't wasted any time with small talk. But the older man didn't seem to mind.

"I can do plenty of things. But more to the point, I want to find him, and you wish to avoid him. Even though we have disparate goals, I think both of us would like to know his current whereabouts."

"And do you have any idea where he might be?"

"I do not. But I think I'll stay close to you. If he's looking for you, he's sure to find you, one way or another."

Seamus didn't like the sound of that one bit. Mr. Grey was not the only one Mr. March was hunting.

"We should go," said Hazel. "Right now. We can pay and leave and head down to Mexico, to South America. We can work there. Or even go to Europe."

"I'm tired of running," Mr. Grey said softly. "He'll hunt me to the ends of the earth. This earth, or another one. I've known that, but I hoped it wasn't true."

The man named Santiago pulled over his chair, flipped it backwards and sat straddling it. The other man, Julius, stayed at his table and pulled a small book from his pocket. He sat reading and sipping his sarsaparilla.

"So, what brings you to town?" Santiago addressed Miss Sanchez, who hadn't spoken a word through their meal.

"We're looking for shipping work, carrying cargo," she said.

"And you just arrived in town, I presume?" he said. "You don't seem like locals."

"We're only here until we can get work, then we leave," she said. "March or no March."

"And do you have someone for whom you are working?"

Seamus wasn't at all comfortable with giving this man information, and he wanted to stop Miss Sanchez. More than that, he wanted this man to get away from the table. Every instinct in him shouted that Santiago was not a good sort of person.

"Do you know of someone?" Miss Sanchez asked. Good girl, don't give him more than you need to.

"Yes, in fact. As I'm sure you know, an earthquake recently struck. There's a man who has been in town only a few months, though by now he knows the name of most every man, woman and child in the city. He's helping with the reconstruction, and is supervising some of the import of construction materials, even funding some of it, at a hefty interest rate, I'm sure. He's an Irishman, name is McCullen. He'll have work for you. His office is only a few blocks away. I could walk you over, if you like." This last line was addressed solely to Miss Sanchez.

"McCullen?" she said. "He's here in town? He didn't leave?"

"So you know him? Curious, don't you think?" he said. "How many acquaintances we share?"

CHAPTER 36

October 1, 1864
Los Angeles, California
Hub world

NEIL STUDIED SANTIAGO, THE MAN who might be a criminal, a bounty hunter or even an assassin. Seamus looked on impassively. Neil knew that Seamus was wearing his poker face, and that he welcomed Santiago to the table like he'd welcome the bubonic plague. But if this man held information they needed, then the four of them, five if you counted Mr. Escobar, had to endure his presence. Two of the five, the female two, were not having as hard a time of it. Santiago was joking with them, telling them a highly improbable tale involving the daughter of a farmer who purchased a dog that turned out to be a coyote. Hazel laughed, and Neil could tell it was her real laugh, not her polite one. He wanted to punch Santiago in the face.

"So the coyote hid up under the girl's enormous hoop skirt," said Santiago, "while her father looked everywhere for him. And when he was gone, the coyote ran off into the hills, never to be seen again."

"As delightful and amusing as that tale is," said Seamus, "we need to be seeing Mr. McCullen. Can you direct us to him?"

"I will take you there personally, if the ladies would care to accompany us."

"Fine," said Neil. "Let's go." He stood and stalked out the door, leaning up against the front of the building until the rest of the group emerged. The man named Julius, who was decidedly less irritating than Santiago, decided to come along. If Julius and Santiago wanted March dead, then that suited Neil just fine. The enemies of his enemy might not be his friends, but they might be useful.

Santiago guided them through the streets, making sure he was sandwiched between Miss Sanchez and Hazel the entire time. The two women seemed not to mind his company, and if they were playing along to get him to cooperate, Neil couldn't fault them for it. Seamus still looked as serene as the moon, even when Miss Sanchez laughed hard at something Santiago said.

The house Santiago indicated was modest, but if McCullen had only been in Los Angeles a few months, he had done very well for himself. The man who opened the door was in his mid-thirties with sandy brown hair and he seemed clearly delighted with the group assembled on his doorstep.

"Ah, Seamus my boy," McCullen clapped Seamus on the shoulder. "And Miss Sanchez," he took her hand. "And Miss Dubois, I am glad you are free of your ... legal entanglements."

"Could we come inside?" asked Seamus. "I'd rather us not linger about on the streets."

"Yes! Do come in. Do come in." McCullen let them inside. The house was furnished in what Neil knew from previous experience was upper middle-class furniture and decorations, slightly nicer than warranted by the exterior of the house. McCullen rang for a servant and ordered tea.

"I don't think I've had the pleasure," he said to Neil.

"Neil Grey," he said and shook his hand.

"Ah yes, I have heard of you. But I had thought you were a bit older."

Neil didn't answer, but he knew McCullen was clever enough to guess that time travel was involved.

"Have you eaten?" McCullen asked the group. "Do you have a place to stay?"

"Never mind that, Oren," said Seamus. "Why are you here? Why didn't you go? The earthquake was a week ago."

McCullen waved his hand in a magnanimous gesture. Neil got the impression that he liked offering them things they needed, that it put him in a position of power, although with the patina of gentility and generosity.

"I simply couldn't leave you behind," he said to Miss Sanchez. "It would have been so ungentlemanly, and with Hazel in prison, I had no way to know that you would be able to get the second machine. You could have been stranded here, and that would be unconscionable."

Miss Sanchez looked puzzled and flustered. "You stayed ... for me?"

"Now don't feel uneasy about it. It was simply a friend helping another friend. Both of us were accidental travelers, and I think we should look out for one another, just as Seamus and I, as fellow countrymen, have assisted one another in the past. Besides, the people here seemed to need me. This city, it's so new, so rough. Nothing like the Irish cities that have been there for centuries, or even the cities of the Eastern United States. Those are all so civilized. Out here, it's lawless and wild. Wouldn't you agree, Santiago?"

"That's just how I like it," he said with a wolfish grin.

"Speaking of lawless," said McCullen, "an old friend of mine contacted me. And when I say 'friend' I use the term very loosely. For this is the man who left me stranded in 1961."

"If you were of no use to him, he would have abandoned you," said Julius. "It's my brother's way."

Neil was all at attention now. He knew from Seamus and Hazel that McCullen had claimed to have known Mr. March and had even been assisted by him in making engines that produced unnatural amounts of energy. But if Mr. March was now contacting McCullen again, the web around Neil was tightening. And he didn't like that at all.

"Mr. March has it out for you, Seamus," said McCullen. "He doesn't like us working on the time machines. I assured him that I would not do such a thing. But he wouldn't believe for a moment that you wouldn't be relentlessly studying the machines and trying to make them useful to you."

"He's right about that. But even if I work a lifetime, I'll never be able to travel at will. Why, with just a thought, he can create time holes."

"Warrens," said Santiago.

"Pardon?"

"He makes warrens. Interconnecting tunnels, some going one way, some another with openings in unexpected places. That's what he is, like a hare, darting in and out of them, eluding those who hunt him. He's not a Door, properly speaking, but he's similar."

"Why are you looking for him?" Neil asked Julius. "If he's your brother, what has he done that is so terrible?"

"He's interfering with the timelines. And he's interfering in the affairs of people. See, our kind are under an agreement, as loose and difficult to enforce as it is, not to perform certain actions. We do not kill people. We are not to overly influence events."

Santiago snorted. "And they all become lawyers when it comes to defending themselves, because almost all of them do just that."

"That's enough," said Julius, looking pointedly at Santiago. "We are what we are."

"And what is that?" asked Hazel. "What are you, exactly?"

All eyes turned to Julius, and Santiago was half smiling, as if anticipating a treat. When Julius simply shrugged, Santiago said, "Just tell them, old friend. I'm all ears as well."

"We have a common purpose, and that is to locate my brother," said Julius. "Let us focus on that."

"The Twelve are very secretive," said Santiago, waggling his eyebrows at Hazel. "Some are good, like true-hearted Julius here and his sister September. Some are cruel, like April. Some have more, shall we say, situational principles, like Augustus."

"You know Mr. Augustus? He's here?" said Hazel.

"He is. But no one ever truly knows what The Twelve are up to."

Yes, thought Neil, who knew? If the Twelve were not allowed to kill people, then it made sense that Mr. March had needed him to do it. He had been used, just as McCullen had, as a cat's paw, harming people and influencing events to fit Mr. March's purposes. McCullen and he did the things March did not wish to do himself. They were useful pawns. That had been bad enough, but to be hunted by Mr. March, to not be free of him, and to have his very presence endanger Miss Sanchez, the Professor, and most especially Hazel was too much.

He wanted to leave, to flee, to draw Mr. March away from all of them and keep them safe. And if that meant his death or enslavement, then he would choose death. He would be no one's tool again. He would live free or die, as the saying went.

"As I was saying," said McCullen, taking a tea tray from the serving girl and setting it on the table, "Mr. March paid me a call. He believed me, I think, when I said that I was not working on mastering the use of the time machine. However, he would not believe the same of you, Seamus. He was convinced that you were going to figure it out and make use of the machines, perhaps even creating more. Before, you could only move through time, but now you can go between worlds as well. This, to him, cannot be. He will not allow it. I fear, my friend, that he aims to kill you."

"Well that's not going to happen," said Hazel. "Not while we're around." She looked at Neil. "Right?"

He nodded once. Hazel loved the Professor like a father,

and if it mattered to her, it mattered to him. Besides, he had grown to like Seamus. The man was generally good-natured and frighteningly intelligent in the area of mechanics and physics. He was also irritating and sometimes talked too much, but he cared a great deal for his loved ones, and Neil had to respect that.

McCullen found them rooms upstairs, and the next morning after breakfast, Hazel and Neil went for a walk to get out of the overcrowded house. Mr. Escobar stayed behind, which suited Neil just fine. He liked the little primate, but having some time with just Hazel was a luxury nowadays.

They went out to the beach and sat on the shore.

"We could go, right now," said Hazel. "I have Skidbladnir in my pocket, and though the dragon is not as fast when she doesn't have a crew, she can move. We could go and sail somewhere. Never be found."

"You'd never leave the Professor and Miss Sanchez."

"No, I wouldn't," she sighed. "Or Mr. Escobar and the crew. Mr. March wants you either dead or obeying him, and he seems to just want the Professor dead. And if he thinks that's going to happen, he can think again. He'll kill the Professor over my dead body."

"And if he wants to kill you, then he'll have to kill me first. And I think Mr. Escobar might try to protect you too."

She chuckled. "He'll be very busy with all the killing."

They sat for a while in silence. Neil couldn't tell what Hazel was thinking, but when she was happy, she usually talked or sometimes sang or hummed. This time, she just looked out at the waves. Eventually, they decided to head back. They turned the corner onto McCullen's street when they saw a figure waiting outside.

"My God, it's him," said Neil. "He's found us."

CHAPTER 37

October 1, 1864
Los Angeles, California
Hub world

HAZEL GRABBED NEIL'S ARM, AS if she could keep him from progressing toward Mr. March. Neil was strong, unnaturally so, but Mr. March was something inhuman. In a fight, she didn't know which one would win. And if Mr. March could open his time warrens, he could slip away, appear somewhere else and attack Neil that way. Or at least, she imagined he could. In her mind, the man had been built up into a monster, brilliant, ruthless and powerful.

"Don't go," she hissed, pulling him harder. It had no affect on him physically, but he still paused instead of dragging her along with him.

"He could have done something to Felicia and Seamus," he said.

Hazel's hesitation vanished, and she walked forward with Neil, wanting to run into the house and shout for the Professor. But she kept her gaze level and her stride strong. Inside, she might be terrified, but she would not allow anyone to harm the Professor.

"My boy!" shouted Mr. March, and hurried toward them, arms outstretched.

Then Hazel heard shouting, two men yelling at each other in Gaelic, and then Miss Sanchez yelling at both of them in English. They were all right then. They were safe and alive. Mr. March had not harmed them. That meant he had not gone inside to kill the Professor, but was instead waiting for them, or rather, waiting for Neil. She would be an afterthought if she was thought of at all.

When Mr. March drew closer, Hazel saw what a slight man he was. He was taller than she was, but not by much, and was rather narrow across the shoulders for a man. He was exceptionally fair, one of the lightest-skinned people she had ever seen, even lighter than the redheaded Irish people she knew back in New Orleans. His eyes were pale blue and almost looked lavender, as if a drop of pink had been added to the blue of each.

"Mr. March," said Neil, and Hazel detected a touch of warmth in his voice. Neil had told her how March had cared for him and had been like a father. A part of her wanted to leave them alone, feeling like she was invading their privacy, but she couldn't leave Neil.

"I've been looking everywhere for you," said Mr. March. "I've wanted so much to see you." He was within a few feet of them now, and without hesitation, he wrapped Neil in his arms and embraced him. Neil reached around and hugged him back, but then stepped away.

"Please come back," said Mr. March. "I've missed you. Our work, it suffers without you. No one I've hired holds a candle to you. No one. And not simply because of your skills. It's who and what you are. I don't want to continue on without you."

"Then maybe you shouldn't. You're doing things you shouldn't be doing. And you sent someone to kill me near Savannah."

"Let's discuss this," said Mr. March. "I want to be completely honest about everything and clear up any misunderstandings. Please."

And with that, he slipped between her and Neil, putting an arm around each of their waists. She was about to pull away, but Neil hadn't. In fact, he was looking down at Mr. March with something akin to affection. Mr. March's touch was light, not groping or uncomfortable, and since his attention was focused on Neil, she felt like he was including her out of good manners.

"Now, I know you left word with September Wilde that you no longer wished to continue in my employ. And I respect your autonomy and the good reasons you think you have. But I want to make my case. The work you are doing, it is good work."

"You had me kill innocents."

"No, I did not. I have the proof right here."

He pulled an object from his jacket pocket, about the size of a book, but much thinner and with a sheet of glass on one side. It glowed, and he touched it here and there. Hazel wondered if it was a computer, for it matched the descriptions that Neil and Miss Sanchez had given her. Whatever it was, he used it in plain sight of everyone on the street. Neil must have noticed also, because he steered them to a quieter street and they stopped in a deserted area near what looked like a run-down park.

"Boston Applied Robotics," said Mr. March. "Right there. Weapons program. Very covert. I have documentation, files and files of it. You can look through it whenever you like. And in Las Vegas, I had an investigator confirm that the girls were dead. Then I had the bodies autopsied with modern methods, not the 1980's kind, and DNA samples of the killer matched Rick Gallo in each case."

Neil glanced at the computer, or whatever it was. "How do I know you didn't falsify the information? I have no way of knowing."

"Well," said Mr. March, and his tone hardened just a fraction, "you can always ask your little friend here."

"What do you mean?" asked Neil, but he stiffened visibly, and every instinct Hazel possessed told her that he knew exactly what Mr. March meant. When she was young, she had stood in the doorway of her house in New Orleans and Neil Grey had been outside. He had given her a newspaper and had pointed out something in it. Her uncle had died suddenly on a train.

"Andrew Dubois was her uncle," said Mr. March.

The world dropped away as both Neil and Mr. March looked straight at her. The smaller man was assessing and cool, but Neil was focused completely on her. His eyes were brown, a plain, unvarying brown without flecks of color. And they were surprised and pained.

"I thought—It's a common name," he said. "I didn't think ..."

"You killed him?" she asked, her voice soft.

"I'm sorry! Oh, God, I'm so sorry. Mr. March told me he was a child molester, and I believed it. I didn't know. Please."

Child molester. Was that what her uncle was called? He had come to her in the night when she was in her room and done terrible things, things she still dreamt of now and then, waking shaking and nauseated. She was younger then, and had run away from him and the only home she had left in the world after her parents' deaths from influenza. She hadn't run because of what her uncle had done to her. At the time, she had blamed herself. With time, she had begun to understand that what he had done was not because she was a wicked, evil girl. But she also knew that something was wrong with her, that she was not like other people, other girls. That knowledge would not leave her, not now and not ever. She had run away because her uncle had snapped the neck of her beloved little dog. The man had been dead for six years, and now he was back in spirit to haunt her.

"You promised me," she said. "You promised me that you didn't kill him. I asked you, and you said it."

"No I didn't. I never said that."

"But you did! You will! You swore to me that you weren't

on the train, that you were in New Orleans. Oh God, you didn't lie, but you did lie. You did both."

"Hazel," he took her shoulders, looking at her unflinching. "I didn't tell you that."

"You did, when you were older and I was younger. You said that you weren't on the train. That you were in New Orleans the night before. You told the truth but you lied, because it was you who killed him."

"I'm sorry. I didn't know. March told me that man was a child molester. That he was hurting kids."

Kids. Not baby goats. In Neil and Miss Sanchez's time, it was a word for children. Neil only slipped into slang when he was upset or emotional. She pulled his hands from her shoulders.

"He was a bad man." She looked away, afraid to look him in the eye to see his pity or revulsion or whatever other emotion he would show her. "He was not kind to me."

"Are you saying that Mr. March is telling the truth?"

"Hang Mr. March! You murdered someone!"

"I murdered many people. You know that."

"But not someone I knew."

And that was it, wasn't it? It was someone she knew. Her uncle was a terrible man. He had killed her dog, Mandy, by snapping her neck like a chicken. The dog had been her best friend, and her uncle knew it. And though she had wanted him dead herself, looking into the face of his killer, a person who had murdered, made her feel disgust. When Neil had told her before that he had killed people, well, it had seemed more abstract. But she knew a victim, a man who had been sent to hell with all his sins on his head, and it was no longer so abstract.

"Leave me alone," she said. "Just go."

She didn't spare a glance for Mr. March who stood to one side, his fingers on his mouth in shock or perhaps concern. Maybe it was mock concern.

Neil looked stricken. He opened his mouth to speak,

but said nothing. And then he looked down at the slats of the wooden sidewalk.

"Now, my boy," said the older man. "You see, I told you the truth. All killers, molesters, warmongers, bad people. Every one of them."

"I don't care. I'm not working for you, now or ever again."

Hazel knew she should leave, run down the street, go to her bed in McCullen's house and throw herself onto it. But she stayed. Mr. March looked out down the street, and when he turned back to Neil, tears quivered in his eyes.

"Then allow me to leave you with this: You can return to me and the purpose for which you were created, or you will die. You have one day to decide. I love you. Do not forget that."

He turned and walked away, but Neil stayed looking down at the sidewalk, his hands in the pockets of his long coat. She wanted to walk away, to get far from this killer, this murderer, this strange man with the writing on the roof of his mouth and his preternatural physical abilities. He was terrifying and alien. And yet, he was Neil, her Neil. Her crew member. Her best friend.

"You can go on without me," Neil said. "I understand. I won't follow you."

She thought about it and almost stepped away. She could leave him here, go with Miss Sanchez and the Professor and leave behind McCullen and Neil. Neither of them were fit company for decent people.

But the Professor had killed a man, killed his brother-in-law in anger when he had beaten his sister. And Hazel held no animosity toward him. So why did she feel so ... so angry? No, it wasn't anger, not the white hot kind, but more of a slow simmering emotion, dark and painful.

Betrayal. That was it. She had trusted him, trusted the older man who had stood in her doorway when she was eleven and had given her a beautiful violin and had showed her that her uncle would never harm her again. She was safe. He had meant it as a gift.

But this man before her was not yet that older man. He was the raw clay from which that man would be formed.

"I'm not leaving you," she said, and he glanced up. She didn't know what else to say, so she turned and headed down the street, in the opposite direction from the one Mr. March had taken. Neil came up beside her and they turned down McCullen's street. "We'll set sail tonight maybe," she said. "We won't worry about finding work. We have enough rations to get us through a week, ten days if we eat sparingly."

She reached into her pocket to touch the folded cloth that was Skidbladnir. The pocket was empty. She checked the other pocket, then all her pockets. Twice.

"Where is it?" she cried. "Where is the ship?"

"Does Mr. Escobar have it?"

"No! I've been keeping it myself. Where is the blasted thing?"

"Stolen," said Neil. "He stole it. He must have picked your pocket."

"Why didn't you warn me?"

"I didn't know. I didn't know he knew how, or that he'd know about the ship."

"Well, we have to get it back," she said. "Where do you think he is? Do you think he made one of those time warrens?"

"I don't think so. I talked with Julius last night when he couldn't sleep, and Mr. March can't make warrens one right after the other. They take effort and energy. So if he's going to be here tomorrow to hear from my own lips that I won't work for him and to kill me, then he'll be staying around."

"Then we have to find him. I need my ship back."

"And what about Mr. Escobar and the crew?"

She ran the rest of the way home, crashing through the front door and rushing from room to room until she found the Professor.

"Where's Mr. Escobar?" she asked. "Is he all right?"

"He said he had to go," said the Professor. "It was strange. He hopped up from a nap and said to tell you he had to go. And that he was very sorry."

CHAPTER 38

October 1, 1864
Los Angeles, California
Hub world

S EAMUS WATCHED AS HAZEL WENT from confused to frantic.
"We have to get him back, Professor!"
"Get who back?"

"Mr. Escobar. He's with the ship. Here, take your coat. We have to go find him." She pulled his coat from the coatrack and tossed it to him. "Where is Miss Sanchez? Never mind, she can't help. What about McCullen? Can he shoot?"

"Stop!" he said, and when Hazel ran from the room to find McCullen, he looked to Mr. Grey for an answer.

"Mr. March stole the ship from her pocket. It's now his, by whatever laws govern the transfer of things of that nature. He stole it, and now the crew and the ship are his. That's why Mr. Escobar had to leave."

"And the time machine you had? Was it on the ship?"

"Yes. But McCullen has the other."

"That wasn't what I was concerned about. Mr. March will have the machine and he'll be able to make warrens too. I don't like that one bit."

"And he wants us both dead. Don't forget that."

"I haven't forgotten. Do you have any idea where the man might be?"

"If I had to guess, he'd be trying out his new toy.

Assuming he knows what it is, he would want to open it up and take it for a spin. He'll stay close by, as I have one day before he comes back and kills me."

"You're awfully calm about it."

"I don't plan on dying easily."

"Go get Santiago and Julius and tell them to bring a few guns. McCullen can shoot, as can I. The women can stay here."

"Don't you think they'll resent that, just a little?" said Mr. Grey. "It's Hazel's ship, after all. And Miss Sanchez doesn't want either of us killed or the ship stolen either."

"Miss Sanchez is a healer, not a killer. And Hazel is a good girl."

"She can shoot," said Neil. "I taught her myself."

"Even so, she doesn't belong there."

Apparently, Mr. Grey didn't find the topic worth arguing over, and he left to get Santiago and Julius. While he was gone, Seamus explained the situation to McCullen and Miss Sanchez. Hazel was beside herself with worry. She was convinced that Mr. March would be cruel to her crew and to the ship itself.

"Professor? Is it possible for him to take Skidbladnir through time in the same way we put the machine into the rowboat?"

He considered. "Yes, I don't see why not."

"So he could be anywhere by now. He wouldn't have to make a warren, but could use the machine!"

"No, not quite. Not unless he already knew how to operate it."

"September Wilde gave you coordinates," said Hazel. "That's what you said, isn't it? So maybe her brother knows things of that sort too."

"All the more reason we leave immediately," said McCullen. "We need to catch him before he goes anywhere. If this is my chance to be free of that man, I'll be happy to take care of him."

Mr. Grey returned with Santiago.

"Where is Julius?" Seamus asked Santiago.

"He's gone to find his brother and he'll tell us where he is."

"And Julius is at peace with you killing his brother?"

"That's why he called me."

"And what about Mr. Augustus and September Wilde? Have you seen them?"

"No, but I know they're around. They're not too fond of their brother either. It's not that they want him dead, per se, but they do want him stopped. And that's what I aim to do." He checked a gun and handed it to Hazel. "Here you go."

She thanked him and Seamus put out his hand to take it. "Give that to me. I'll not have you shooting anyone."

"He wants you dead, Professor. And Neil too. And he stole my ship and threatens my crew. Of everyone here, I have the most reason to want the man gone. You can't leave me unarmed."

"You'll be unarmed, and you'll be here with Miss Sanchez."

"Like hell, Professor. You aren't going to stop me. I'm taking back my ship, like it or not."

"Christ, Hazel. Do you not understand? The man can kill you. He's not a straw-stuffed dummy that will sit there while you shoot at it."

"He's right," said McCullen to her. "I know you want your monkey friends to be safe, and you want your ship back and your Professor and Mr. Grey safe. You're willing to kill for them. I understand that desire. But Santiago, Mr. Grey and Seamus and I will handle this. It won't weigh on us like it will weigh on you." He gently took the gun from Hazel and turned back to finish loading his gun. For that moment, Seamus was grateful to the man.

Seamus put his arm around Hazel's shoulder. She was so small, and he wished he could make her stay home and keep her safe, like he had when she was younger. But she was grown, and he couldn't keep her safe, not by leaving her in New Orleans or by any other means. The world was dangerous on its own, but by inventing the time machine, he had put her in more danger than he could have previously imagined.

"Hazel, you're more likely to get shot than to shoot that man. Besides, the three of us, Mr. Grey, McCullen and I, we've killed before. And Santiago perhaps has also. If you were to kill a man ... it changes you. It weighs on the mind and on the soul. I would not put that on you."

"And if I'm in danger? If he does something? Am I to be defenseless?"

"You will be safe here, so it's not a concern."

"Professor," she said quietly. "I know you want to protect me, but I'm no longer a child. I have people, my crew, depending on me. I am a woman grown with a woman's responsibilities. They're my crew. It's not the loss of property that bothers me, although I do want what's mine. It's my crew and the dragon. I don't want them misused. Not to mention Mr. March's intent to kill both you and Neil. I can't stand by while the people I love are killed. Not if I have the remotest chance to save them. And in what other circumstance are we going to know where March is? If we lose him this time, he could bolt to another time and pop up to kill you both in your beds."

Mr. Grey silently handed her a gun and a holster which she fastened on. It was too large and hung low on her hips.

"God, Hazel. You're a stubborn thing," Seamus said. "And foolish to boot."

Mr. Grey looked grim, even for him, and Seamus supposed he was no happier about it than he was.

Julius came to the door to speak with Santiago. He looked over their group grimly.

"You folks aren't much to look at, are you?"

"Well, Julius," said Santiago with a cocky grin, "you're welcome to do this yourself."

"I didn't mean anything by it. Just two women, criminals and a dog. That's the best we can do?"

Santiago pulled one of his pistols from his holster and offered it to Julius, butt first. The older man sighed heavily but did not take the weapon.

"He's at the dock," he said. "And don't think for a second that he doesn't know you're coming. Oh, and Santiago? I presume we will talk when this is over? Assuming you survive?"

"Surviving is what I do best."

Julius turned away, and Seamus thought that he looked like a man with the weight of the world on his shoulders. A wicked or drunken brother would be a burden, but a brother like Mr. March was a hundred times worse.

As they were heading out the door, Seamus put his hand on Neil's shoulder and whispered into his ear. "You protect her. I've seen what you can do, and you keep my Hazel safe, you hear?"

Mr. Grey nodded once. He was about to close the door behind him when Miss Sanchez pulled it back open. In his concern for Hazel, he had neglected to talk with her and give her what reassurances he could.

"I suppose I ought to say good-bye," Seamus said, "in case that bastard manages to shoot me dead."

"You can do that with your dying words, as I'll be there to hear them."

"You can't come along."

"Oh, can't I? I think I'm the only one Mr. March doesn't want dead, in fact, he might not even know I exist. Besides, who else is going to put you back together when you're all bleeding from monkey bites and bullet holes?"

"Am I speaking into the wind here?" Seamus cried. "Is there no sense in your head, woman? You can't shoot, you can't fight, and he'll kill a woman dead as quick as he will a man. Is it not enough that Hazel will be there?"

"Now you listen to me, Seamus Doyle." He blinked in

surprise at her address. "I'm not sitting here worrying myself while you are out getting killed. I'll be there with you, but I'll stay back and out of the way. I have a small measure of common sense, you know."

"Seamus!" shouted McCullen from down the street. "Come along!"

Seamus glanced at Miss Sanchez, who he thought was being as stubborn as a she-mule, and then trotted to catch up with the group.

They were fools, he knew, the lot of them.

CHAPTER 39

October 1, 1864
Los Angeles, California
Hub world

HAZEL STOOD AT THE END of the dock, her heart pounding in her chest and her palms clammy with sweat. She wiped them on her trousers. She had a terrible sense of being trapped, of the inevitability of the minutes to come. Everything led to this, and there was nothing she or any of them could do about it.

Skidbladnir was tied up at the end of the dock, the only vessel in sight. It was full dark now, and any daytime dockside workers had all gone home. A few lights illuminated the windows of nearby buildings, but no people were out.

"Something isn't right," said Seamus, and Hazel had to agree.

"Too quiet, no people, and the ship is sitting there waiting for us?" said Santiago. "What could be wrong?"

As they got closer, it was clear that no people were on board and no monkeys scurried about on deck. They couldn't be asleep yet, as most of them preferred to sleep up high in the rigging, and that was empty. The sail flapped gently in the wind and the ship creaked. It was a soft, familiar sound, and Hazel wanted to run to the ship, to leap on board and flee with it. It was hers, her home, her livelihood and her joy. She simply had to get it back.

Then came a high-pitched twanging. Out of the corner of her eye, Hazel caught McCullen and Miss Sanchez exchanging a confused glance.

"My violin," she whispered. She would know its sound anywhere. It made a painful *twooong*, as the person who held it plucked hard on the lowest string, making it vibrate too hard. Oh, that was too much. To steal her ship was despicable but understandable. It was valuable, rare and beautiful to boot. But to mistreat a musical instrument was monstrous. She fought the urge to leap on board, snatch the violin from its abuser and smash in his face. She wouldn't do it with the violin, as that would damage it. But her fist or foot might work well.

Neil must have noticed her distress, for he touched her arm. "He's trying to goad you," he whispered.

But why do that? There was no purpose in it aside from sheer spite. Did Mr. March hate Neil so much that he would torment his friends just for the fun of it? Or was he jealous of Neil's affection for her? Perhaps he wanted to anger her, and maybe the others. An angry enemy made mistakes.

The gangplank was down, and it rubbed rhythmically against the dock as the ship rose and fell with the waves. The sound of the violin being plucked came from the prow of the ship, but as the tide was high, they couldn't see on board.

The Professor whispered something to Miss Sanchez and then he put his mouth to Hazel's ear. "Stay behind us and run if anything happens. It's clearly a trap, but it's our only chance at finding him. We won't get another."

Hazel couldn't agree more. The whole situation stank of a setup. But before anyone could form and discuss any plan, Santiago rushed down the dock, leapt up the gangplank, silent and graceful. He hopped on deck, gun drawn and fired off a shot. Hazel couldn't see if it hit its mark.

Before she could recover from the surprise, Neil was already up the gangplank with McCullen and the Professor following. Hazel came up behind them while Miss Sanchez waited on the dock, rightly concerned with being in the center of any gunfire. Hazel crouched at the top of the gangplank and scanned the empty ship, but the only living thing was Mr. March and two monkeys. March sat on the deck leaning back against the prow holding the violin by the neck, his pink-lidded eyes closed. He opened them lazily and twisted one of the tuning pins far too hard, and though the violin made no sound, she could feel the strain on the string. She jumped on board.

The Professor, to his credit, did not hesitate, but raised his gun and shot at Mr. March. An instant later, the Professor gasped and touched his ear, which dripped fresh blood. A tiny piece had been shot out of the edge of it.

"Don't," said Neil, holding up a hand. "He must have made a small warren to take in the bullet and then redirect it toward you. That was a warning. Since the warren was so small, he can most likely make more."

"Very good, Neil," said Mr. March.

Tiny warrens that could make pathways for bullets? Hazel had never considered the idea before. It meant that weapons were useless against the man.

And then, two thoughts came together and she understood something that had not made sense before. The McCullen engines, the machines that were based upon the Professor's stolen peroxide engine designs, were able to produce far more energy than they should have. According to McCullen, Mr. March had assisted him in creating them. The engines required a catalyst to operate, and the Professor had used silver. But McCullen had added a second catalyst, matter from another universe. Specifically, air from another world coming through tiny pinpricks between worlds. Mr. March must have provided the technology to do it. Or the magic. Hazel was not sure where the difference between the two lay, but the Professor had never fully understood the use of the tiny vial of bluish liquid inside each McCullen engine.

Mr. March plunked another violin string and looked at Neil. "Are you here to come back to work with me or not?" He stood up and set the violin down on the deck carelessly, causing it to make a painful bonging sound.

"I won't," said Neil. "I'd rather die."

"Such sacrifice. But I would not kill you, not unless I truly had no choice. And right now, I do still have a choice. Neil, pick up this monkey." He pointed to one of the two monkeys beside him.

To Hazel's astonishment, Neil picked him up.

"What are you doing?" she asked.

He didn't answer, but held the monkey, one of the younger ones whose name was Jemmo. Hazel remembered that Jemmo liked mangoes and dancing, and that he liked sleeping curled up in a group with others. The little monkey looked uncertainly from Mr. March to Neil and back again, but because he knew and trusted Neil, he did not try to escape.

"Miss Dubois," said Mr. March. "I understand that you are quite attached to your crew. If I order it, Neil will kill this animal."

"Are you mad? Of course he won't."

"Yes, I will," said Neil. He was still and relaxed. He didn't look troubled or unhappy, just ... nothing. Almost blank. It chilled Hazel's blood, for this was Neil, but altered. Neil didn't look at her when he spoke again. "If he says it, I'll kill Jemmo."

Hazel held her hand up to stop Santiago, the Professor or McCullen, if any of them were thinking of stepping in. Something was terribly wrong, and she wouldn't allow one of her crew to die for the sake of an impetuous mistake.

"Good boy," said Mr. March. "Now, tell me if you will come back to me."

"I won't. I won't kill any more innocents."

"And that is where you are wrong. Because you have one right there, do you not? And you will kill him if I say it."

"Neil? What is going on?" Hazel said, but he did not look at her.

"We're talking right now, Miss Dubois," said Mr. March. "But on second thought, you may be able to assist me in making my wayward child understand the error of his ways. You see, Neil, you care for Miss Dubois. And yet, with one bullet, I can remove her from your life."

"Oh, don't you dare touch a hair on her head," said the Professor.

"Neil, silence Mr. Doyle."

Neil walked over to the Professor, transferred the monkey to the other arm and before the Professor could react, punched him hard in the mouth. Neil stepped back and the Professor touched his fingers to his mouth. When he pulled them away, Hazel saw the blood.

"Oh, is that it, Mr. Grey?" said the Professor, aiming his gun at Neil's chest. "Have you been working with Mr. March all this time? Is that it?"

"No, Professor!" said Hazel. "It's not his fault! March is doing something to him."

"You see, Neil?" said Mr. March. "You can obey me willingly, and we can be father and son. Or you can refuse, and we'll do things by the old-fashioned rules. So be a good boy, and you won't have to do the same to your lady friend here. Or worse."

"How are you doing this to him?" Hazel cried. "What is he?"

"He is mine, that's what he is. He belongs to me."

"One person can't own another," she said. "Each man is his own."

"That's very sweet, Miss Dubois. Very admirable to believe that all men are equal, especially in this country at this time. But I have seen the eugenics experiments and the duplicate hoards of the centuries to come, when men are truly equal. And there are new and horrific ways people find to divide themselves and kill each other. Men are indeed unequal, and it is best they remain that way. Listen, Miss Dubois, I recommend you do nothing, or I will order Neil to kill Jemmo and then do the same to you." Then he turned toward the prow of the ship. "Now, Mr. Escobar!"

A rush of monkeys swarmed up from below decks. They circled Santiago's ankles, and he immediately pointed the gun at one of them, then another and another.

"No!" screamed Hazel. "No! Don't hurt them!"

To her relief, Santiago seemed to be reconsidering it. The monkeys did not touch him, but circled in tight, looking up at him with their somber little faces. Their nostrils twitched, and they spoke to each other in a language not Spanish or English, but their own native tongue. They were agitated, she knew that much, and under the circumstances, she didn't fault them.

Other monkeys circled McCullen, the Professor and herself. Miss Sanchez had remained on the dock, which was for the best. Hazel wondered if she was still there, or if she had fled. The monkeys pressed forward until each of the humans were ringed with five or six monkeys, each group easily capable of pulling them to the ground and holding them there.

"Stop," Hazel said to the monkeys. "I order you to back away."

A few of them looked at her, with flickering, ashamed glances, and then looked to Mr. March. More monkeys emerged, until the entire crew stood on deck. Mr. Escobar waited to one side, and he did not look away from Hazel when she tried to catch his eye. Instead, he placed his hand on his chest, over his heart and lowered his head for a moment. Hazel understood him. He was bound to the ship, at least for the duration of his contract, and had to obey the captain.

"Take their weapons," said Mr. March, and the monkeys leapt, quick and strong, tearing their guns from their holsters. Hazel allowed them to do it, not wanting to hurt any of them. They did not take Neil's weapon, but if he was under Mr. March's control, there was no need.

"Don't you hurt them," she yelled to McCullen, who looked like he was ready to start kicking at the little creatures. "Or you either," she called to the Professor.

Santiago folded his arms and let the monkeys take his weapon. The Professor and McCullen tried to pry the monkeys off, but though they managed to toss a few away, they jumped right back at them. There were too many of them and they were strong. Eventually, the monkeys managed to snatch their guns away also. The monkeys collected the weapons and placed them in a pile beside Mr. March.

"Now restrain them," said Mr. March. At that, McCullen and the Professor did fight, but when Mr. March rose lazily, pulled the pistol from Neil's holster and pointed it at Hazel's head, the Professor and McCullen went still. Hazel never would have thought that McCullen cared enough for her to do so. Santiago looked like he was doing some sort of internal math as he looked from Hazel to Mr. March, but he eventually quit struggling and allowed the monkeys to take him to the mast, where he crossed his arms and leaned back. He looked utterly comfortable and at ease. Perhaps he was trying to deny Mr. March the pleasure of intimidating him. She wished she could do the same, but she knew there was no disguising her fear.

Other monkeys came with rope and tied their wrists together. Each crew member was an expert sailor and they tied knots so well and so tightly that Hazel knew none of them could ever get free of them. Mr. Escobar himself tied Hazel's hands, and when he was finished, she felt him pat her arm gently. McCullen and the Professor had their wrists tied behind them, while Santiago was tied to the mast. Hazel wondered why he was singled out for such restraint.

Once everyone was secured, Mr. March slipped the gun back into Neil's holster. He sighed, picked up the violin and looked it up and down. "I have no idea how to play this thing," he said. "But seeing as it's mine now—"

"It's not yours. It's mine," said Hazel.

"It was on the ship, and now I own it, along with the crew and that lovely machine in the trunk below deck. All mine."

"Saying something doesn't make it so," she said. Mrs. Washington had said that so many times as Hazel was growing up. Hazel almost told Mr. March that he didn't own the crew, but then stopped herself. Let him think it. They were bound to obey him by duty, but not by ownership. Her only advantage in all this was their affection and potential loyalty to her.

"I can't say I'm happy to see you again, Coyote," Mr. March said to Santiago. "It's fascinating that you are assisting my siblings. I must admit I am a little surprised that you are here to kill me. The penalty would be steep."

"I've searched for you for many years."

"Ah yes, the Coyote hunting the Hare. But in half the stories, you know, the Hare wins."

Santiago grinned, but it was a grin full of malice and hunger, as if he wanted to tear Mr. March's throat out.

"And Mr. Doyle," said Mr. March. "You are like a magpie, always wanting to play with shiny things. And the time machine must have been the shiniest thing of all. You just had to play with it, didn't you? Speaking of which," he turned to McCullen, "where is Felicia Sanchez?"

"Not here," said McCullen.

Mr. March cocked his head to one side. "Now how is that going to work?"

"I kept my end up. Now it's your turn." McCullen pulled his hands from behind his back. No rope hung from his wrists or lay on the ground. How could that be? Hazel gasped. The monkeys had never tied him up.

The look Hazel saw the Professor give his former friend would have frightened her if she wasn't already scared out of her wits. It was a look of pure hatred, but Hazel knew him well enough to see pain and betrayal there too. He must have hoped that his old friend had changed. Or at the least, robbed of his former power and wealth, that he could behave in a way resembling that of a decent man. Perhaps men like McCullen didn't change. Perhaps they couldn't.

If he hadn't been tied up, she knew the Professor would have been on McCullen in an instant. Both she and the Professor knew that McCullen was a snake, and though they had never trusted him completely, they had been fooled into thinking he had been defanged. They had believed that he hated Mr. March, and perhaps he did. But since when did McCullen's feelings toward a person interfere with him using them to get when he wanted? They had been played for fools.

Santiago laughed. It was a hearty, happy sound, and Hazel looked at him in shock. He was thoroughly enjoying himself, even if he was tied to a mast. He noticed her disapproving look.

"What? It was so well done. You must admit that it was exceptionally well done."

"Yes, Santiago," said Mr. March. "You of all people would enjoy a good double cross." He turned back to McCullen. "Here it is, per our agreement," he said and handed him a slip of paper from his jacket pocket.

McCullen unfolded it, read it, then tore it to pieces and tossed them over the starboard side of the ship, the side farthest from the dock. Hazel watched as the scraps floated down like confetti onto the water, rested there and then began to sink. McCullen looked back at Mr. March, and the two of them regarded one another. Out of the corner of her eye, Hazel saw Mr. Escobar climb up the dragon's neck and speak into her ear. The dragon's wooden head remained immobile, and Mr. Escobar swung from her lower jaw, landed lightly on the gunwale and dropped to the deck where he took up his former position near Hazel's feet.

"It is finished," said Mr. March. "What you do with the information is your concern."

The paper must have contained coordinates to another time or world, most likely McCullen's own. Perhaps having missed the synchronicity, McCullen had made a bargain with Mr. March to deliver the Professor and the machine to him in exchange for the coordinates. But that made no sense. Why had McCullen waited at all? He should have left when the earthquake synchronicity occurred.

Then the answer came to her: Miss Sanchez. McCullen had always been obsessed with her, wanting to spend time with her years ago in New Orleans, making her Mardi Gras queen, even taking her along in his monstrous machine to destroy the city of New Orleans. And now, after acting like a decent man for months, he had waited for her in Los Angeles. Hazel had known that the Professor loved Miss Sanchez, but McCullen had been more reserved about showing his feelings. Or perhaps they weren't truly feelings, but maybe a desire to possess and control, to take what was the Professor's, or might have been his, and make it his own.

The Professor glared at McCullen. "Don't you even dare speak to her, you animal."

"Now Seamus, I have never, ever asked Miss Sanchez to do what she did not want to do." He called out over the port side of the ship, "Have I, Miss Sanchez?"

He looked out over the port side, and Mr. March did the same. Hazel couldn't see anything from her vantage point, but Miss Sanchez must not have been there, because Mr. March said, "You brought me Mr. Doyle, but didn't bring your own prize?"

The Professor moved over to the side of the ship, and the monkeys allowed it, perhaps as curious as he was. Hazel felt small hands touch hers, and then a piece of rope was pushed into her palm. A moment later, Mr. Escobar was beside her, just where he had been before. She felt along the rope and then began working at it as best she could while Mr. Escobar looked dutifully at Mr. March.

"I'll find her," said McCullen. "But first, I'll be taking the machine that you have."

"I thought you already possessed a machine," said Mr. March.

"I do. But the one down there is a later model."

Mr. March considered. Hazel wondered why he would allow McCullen to have a machine if he would not allow the Professor to have one. Perhaps McCullen could not create any more machines, while the Professor could. After all, the Professor had made a machine that could travel through time within his own world. McCullen had only contributed a stronger power system. It made her proud that her Professor surpassed the wicked McCullen in his abilities.

"So long as Mr. Doyle doesn't have one," said Mr. March. "And that won't be a worry in a few minutes."

Mr. March was going to kill the Professor. Hazel worked hard at the rope, wiggling it and trying to push the untied end through to loosen it. The rope was prickly and hard and her skin was raw from the friction, but she kept at it. McCullen headed to the stern of the ship, pulling a small book from his inner jacket pocket. It was the book of coordinates that had come with the machine with Miss Sanchez from 1961. He now had a newer machine and all the information contained within the book's pages. He went below deck and Hazel saw the flare of light from the dark hole as he lit a lantern.

"So you plan to do me in?" asked the Professor. "Well, you're welcome to try. You wouldn't be the first. Now, untie my hands, and we can see who is the better man."

Mr. March looked the Professor up and down. March was small, and the Professor was thin, but he was also six foot three. In a fair fight, the Professor would win, even against a man his own size. He had older brothers who had taught him to fight, and Hazel knew he was able to handle himself, even unarmed. Mr. March would never be so foolish.

Mr. March again took the pistol from Neil's holster and pulled back the hammer.

"No!" Hazel screamed and jumped forward. The monkeys held her lower legs, forcing her to her knees. She would have crashed face-first into the deck, since she couldn't use her hands to break her fall, but the crew caught her, and eight tiny hands helped her to a kneeling position.

Mr. Escobar wasn't even looking at her, but was watching Santiago. What Hazel saw next made her doubt her own sanity.

One moment, he was a man tied to a mast, and in an instant, his face stretched out to a pointed snout. His arms grew very thin and furry and once his hands narrowed, he slipped them free of the ropes that bound him. His back hunched and as his body folded over, his arms reaching to touch the ground. A lean, tawny, yellow-eyed canine shook himself free of Santiago's clothing and snapped at the monkeys surrounding him, nipping one of them. They leapt away, chattering and shrieking, and Santiago, the coyote, ran and leapt at Mr. March.

He got hold of March's arm and shook his head side to side, growling. Mr. March yanked the gun up at him and Hazel flinched at the gunshot. The coyote yelped, crashed to the deck and scrambled feebly, dragging himself away. A long dark red streak appeared where his belly slid along the wood planks of the deck. The sight was utterly pitiable, and Santiago made little whining sounds as he went.

"The rope," said Mr. Escobar, very softly. "He's giving us this chance." But he was not speaking to her. Small hands worked at the ropes around her wrists, and then they were gone. The entire action had only taken seconds, and all eyes were on Santiago as he continued to pull himself across the deck.

From her position, Hazel could see the stern of the ship, while Mr. March faced the prow. She had to try very hard to keep her eyes on him, as she saw a familiar figure climb up over the side of the ship, drop to the deck and slip down the hatch. It was Miss Sanchez, and she had climbed up the rope ladder. But the ladder had not been down when they had first come to the ship. The gangplank was the only way on board. The dragon could have lowered the ladder herself, and barring a contradicting order from the captain, she would take an order from the first mate, Mr. Escobar. That was what he must have told the ship to do when he climbed up onto her neck.

The Professor didn't see Miss Sanchez, which was a blessing. He had what was called a good poker face, but when it came to McCullen and Miss Sanchez, his emotions ran too high. He was still staring, agape, at Santiago.

"What in the name of all that is holy ..."

"He's a Coyote, Mr. Doyle," said Mr. March. "The monkeys talk, the ship is alive, and there are doorways through time. Clear? And in a moment, I will have you killed and you can see what is on the other side of death."

"Didn't your mother teach you manners? You and all of your siblings? There are twelve of you, correct? Where are the rest of you? And what exactly are you?"

"Always asking questions, aren't you? You truly are one of the more interesting people I've encountered. So few humans would ever be able to understand the time machines, let alone build one. Such a loss, but an unavoidable one. Neil, put down the monkey and take Mr. Doyle."

Neil set down Jemmo, who scurried off into the crowd of other monkeys. "Where will I take him?"

"I'm fond of this ship. Let's do this on the dock. Take him there. Oh, and bring Miss Dubois as well."

Neil grabbed the Professor with his left arm and Hazel with his right. She tried to keep her untied hands clasped behind her back and keep her back to Neil's body so Mr. March would not see that she was unrestrained. And for the most part she managed it. The Professor, his ear dripping blood down his neck and collar, was cursing colorfully in English and in Gaelic, drawing most of Mr. March's attention as March led the way down the gangplank.

It was so quiet, with just the four of them, and the water lapped at the dock's pilings with a soft hissing sound. They moved down the dock toward the shore, away from the ship, and then Mr. March made a motion with his hand. The air at the point where the dock met the land shimmered. Then a door opened.

The Professor's description of the void wyrm was nothing compared to the actual thing. Its head was huge, white, almost luminous, and featureless save for the gaping slash of a mouth that split open, scarlet and slick. An instant after she registered the horror of the hungry, eyeless monster, the air surrounding them pulled at them, tearing the hats from their heads and making her braid fly out toward it. If Neil hadn't been holding them both, she thought the Professor and she would have immediately been sucked into the void wyrm's terrible mouth. Neil appeared unaffected, as did Mr. March, who stood looking at the thing as if it were a curiosity at a traveling carnival.

"Throw Doyle in," he said.

Neil's arm around the Professor loosened. "Stop, Neil!" Hazel yelled. "You have to stop! You don't want to do this." She struggled and tore at his other arm, the one that restrained her, trying to get free. She managed to get herself facedown, but Neil's arms still held her like a vice.

"No, I don't want to," Neil said. "Shoot me."

"What? I can't shoot you."

"Kill me, or he'll make me kill you both." He was speaking softly, and his voice would be muffled by the wind. Mr. March could not hear him.

Neil took a step toward the void wyrm, which lifted its head slightly, as if sniffing. All the air was sucked from her lungs, and Hazel had to labor to breathe. For a second, she thought about the ship, and she was glad that Mr. March valued it and the crew. It meant that they were safe.

"Get his gun!" said the Professor. His arms were pinned hard to his sides, and he was still tied up, whereas her hands were free.

"I can't kill him! I won't!" she cried.

But as she said it, she wriggled the arm that was trapped between Neil's body and her own. His grip seemed to soften a bit, and he let out a little moan of pain. He was fighting against his master, or whatever Mr. March was, and it was costing him.

She got her arm loose enough to snake it around Neil's waist, toward his left hip, where his pistol was holstered. It was the one he had stolen when she was unconscious in the barn. Her fingers touched the butt of the pistol.

"Stop her!" ordered Mr. March, and Neil's grip around her body tightened. He tossed the Professor to the ground, where he landed on his backside, scrambling to get a purchase with his heels, clawing at the boards behind him with his useless restrained hands. He slid a few feet toward the void wyrm.

"Kill her," yelled Mr. March, and Neil let out a moan, low and dark, like something that comes from under the earth, crying in its pain. It was inhuman, lower than his normal vocal register, but she did not stop to ponder it. He was trying to resist, hurting himself to let her have a few moments. She would not waste them.

She pulled the gun free, worked with her thumb to pull back the hammer, aimed it at Mr. March and fired. No bullet hit him, but neither did one come zinging out of the air to hit either her, Neil or the Professor. Perhaps he could only make one warren at a time.

The gun only had six shots, and she had used up one. "Kill her! I order it!"

Neil pulled her out in front of him, as easily as a boy would draw out a doll, and he moved his hands, one just under her jaw and then the other beneath it, to the base of her throat, suspending her over the ground. She clawed at his hands in a mad panic, trying to keep hold of the gun. She managed it, but just barely, and her eyes focused on his face now, contorted in pain, his mouth open in agony. She could not see the roof of his mouth, and she wished she had told him what she had seen there. Would he have known the meaning? Would all of these events not have come to pass?

She had one choice and one only. She wouldn't kill Neil, but neither would she die at his hands. He moaned again as he lowered her, slowly, until her toes touched the ground. She could support a bit of her weight, and she used the advantage to stop ripping at his hands and pull back the pistol's hammer. She held the pistol to Neil's wrist, pointing it away from his body, and fired. His arm jerked back, the bone shattered, and she staggered back as he released her. She hit the ground and slid a few yards, past the Professor who had managed to turn onto his stomach. He yelled something at her, but she could not make it out.

Flipping over, she made sure to keep a grip on the gun. Neil held his wounded arm which was covered in blood. His hand hung limp and useless at the end of his wrist, and when he met her eyes, she wanted to cry. He looked grateful, infinitely pleased and grateful.

She clawed her way away from the void wyrm, driving

splinters into her hands, digging her boots into the wood and scraping herself along on her stomach.

Mr. March moved beside Neil, and examined his wrist. He shouted at him, but Neil did not react. Hazel got a good purchase on the wood with her feet and braced the gun against the dock. She pulled back the hammer and lowered her head to use the sight, just as Neil had taught her. Mr. March was too close to Neil to risk a shot and she glanced backward at the Professor. He was precariously close to the edge of the dock. The water was still deep at that point and if he fell in, he would surely drown, sinking to the sea floor, hands bound, struggling in the black.

There was no more time. She aimed again and waited until Mr. March threw up his hands, stepped back and pointed at the void wyrm, shouting at Neil. She fired.

Mr. March lurched and touched his stomach. She had hit him! She aimed again and fired, landing another shot. Still the shimmering hole pulled the air around them, though it seemed to pull with less ferocity. Hazel did not turn to see how large the doorway was. Mr. March fell to his knees and Neil stood to one side, unmoving, watching his master.

Hazel crawled forward, so slowly, wanting to make her last two shots count. And then a naked man ran down the gangplank and stood over Mr. March. It took her a moment to register that it was Santiago, as beautiful a male specimen as she thought she would ever see. He was the same color all over, not more tanned around the face and neck like most men who spent time outdoors. He was unarmed, of course, but he didn't hesitate to yank Mr. March's head up by the hair and punch him. Then he hit him again.

It was enough to distract Mr. March, perhaps, because the wind pulling on her stopped completely. She didn't look back, terrified that the Professor was already gone and knowing what she had to do. Mr. March might open another warren at any moment. Scrambling to her feet, she pounded up the dock.

As she went, she thought about the silver and pearl bracelet that Mr. Ross had given her, sparkling and lovely. She thought of a life by the fireside, with children and tea, needlepoint and walks in the botanical gardens. There would be talks with her lady friends about what lace to use to trim a parasol or what committee to assist at church. That life was gone, as was the person she might have been. So too the scrawny girl who had lived in abandoned buildings and played violin on street corners. That frightened girl was gone as well.

She was a new creature, but what kind? She glanced up at the ship, where Miss Sanchez ran toward the gangplank and where monkeys clung to the rigging, watching. She saw Neil, blank and almost dead-eyed, staring at his bleeding master.

And she knew what she was. She was Captain Dubois of the dragon ship Skidbladnir. And she would not let anyone harm the people she loved.

The inevitability of the moment hit her. Everything had to occur in just this way. Santiago, the Coyote, was beating Mr. March, but would not be the one to kill him. Because if he did, he would be the owner of the ship. She would not allow that to happen. It would be her. It had to be.

She stopped in front of Mr. March, who clutched his bleeding stomach. She pointed the gun at his head. He simply raised his face, his lip bloody from Santiago's beating, and looked her in the eye. Her resolve flickered, and she wondered if he would open another warren, one that would redirect the bullet into her.

"If you do this, my blood is on your hands. Do you truly—"

Hazel pulled the trigger.

March's left eye and the upper part of his face exploded.

She pulled back the hammer again, for the Professor, for Neil, for all her terror and rage. The rage was the strongest. With it came a calmness, a dark serenity that gave a sense of purpose. Peace. She pulled the trigger again, barely registering the kick of the weapon. The loud crack of the gunpowder was distant. This time, she hit him in the jaw, tearing off the lower half of his face. He fell backward, almost softly, crumpling into a white and red semicircle on the dock.

She kept pulling back the hammer with her palm and pulling the trigger, the gun making clicking sounds, but nothing more. Santiago put his hand over her wrist and pushed her arm down.

"It is finished," he said.

She turned to him, this strange unclothed man, who looked into her face, completely unaware of his nudity, or more likely, not caring about it. He was a Coyote, Mr. March had said, and animals had no human sense of modesty. Even Mr. Escobar only wore vests because they had useful pockets.

His golden eyes were beautiful, and she felt a sense of peace come over her. He took the pistol from her hands, which were shaking hard, and then he whispered something to her and took her hands. She felt like she could stay with him like this for a long time, delaying forever the need to look back at the curled body. He said other things to her, things she could not recall later. And then he leaned forward, smelling of sea wind and wild brush, and kissed her forehead.

"That's enough," he said and released her hands.

"Hazel!" cried the Professor and swept her up in an embrace that pulled her feet up off the ground. Neil stood behind him and tossed torn rope fragments into the water. One arm still hung useless and bloody at his side. Had he torn the Professor's rope with only one hand? Over the Professor's shoulder, she saw that the void wyrm was gone, the door closed.

When the Professor put her down, he turned to Miss Sanchez, but the instant the woman saw Neil's injury, she was at his side, examining him and asking questions.

Hazel wanted to go to Neil, to embrace him or at least speak with him. But she was afraid as well. She looked at the body, at the wounds. The white skull bone was jagged and exposed, fringed with red, shredded flesh. Spattered brain material, blood and tissue were all over the dock. There was a smell too, metallic. Blood. And other odors also.

She knelt at the edge of the dock and vomited into the water, where the contents of her stomach swirled with the tide and were carried away. She stayed looking down at the movement of the greenish black water, the darkness beneath. Everything that went into it became mixed with the whole ocean, until it disappeared. A man was dead, and she had killed him. She sat for a while, watching the water.

Neil was the one who eventually pulled her up, gently, with his good arm. "Thank you."

"I need to get him home and get that bone set before the swelling gets worse," said Miss Sanchez. If she was horrified by what she had seen, she did not indicate it. If there were injuries, she would treat them and be efficient about it. Hazel knew she would confront the horrors later. For now, there was work to be done. Miss Sanchez led Neil away, toward the town.

"Where's McCullen?" Hazel asked the Professor.

"Miss Sanchez says he took the machine but she convinced him to leave the second machine for us. For her, rather, but it's the same thing really. She says Mr. March gave him a way to use the machine without needing a synchronicity, that he made adjustments inside it and then used the coordinates that Mr. March had given him."

"And she just stood there while he stole it?"

The Professor sighed and looked at Miss Sanchez's back as she walked beside Neil.

"She says he wanted her to go with him, and she refused. But she tried to memorize what he did to the inside of the machine. Without her, we'd have no hope. But I have to wonder if she was tempted to go. He would have taken her home, perhaps."

Santiago was looking up at the sky, squinting, perhaps in concentration, as the only light was from the moon. His nostrils twitched. He was still nude, but Hazel no longer cared one way or the other. With everything that had happened, it seemed like such a minor thing.

"Santiago?" said Hazel. "What happened? You were shot. We saw it. Was that some sort of trick?"

"Of course it was. And a good one too, as I was able to distract March enough for you to shoot him."

"Why didn't you shoot him yourself? You could have taken one of the weapons that he left on the deck. You could have done it yourself."

"Ho, ho, no. Not for all of Solomon's gold would I have the blood of an otherkind, especially one of the Twelve, on my hands."

"What are the Twelve? And what will happen to me because I killed one?"

"To you? Nothing. You're a daughter of man, and you killed in self-defense. The only authorities you're subject to are the ones of your people, and I'm not seeing any police officers coming." He looked toward the shore where two figures approached, a man and a woman, though Hazel couldn't make out their faces.

"I like you, sugar tart," said Santiago. "I like you a lot. But even I couldn't stop the plans the Twelve had for you."

"What plans?"

"Well, you can ask them yourself. It looks like Mr. Augustus and September Wilde are coming this way."

CHAPTER 40

October 1, 1864
Los Angeles, California
Hub world

NEIL SAT ON THE FLOOR across from Hazel in her quarters on Skidbladnir, an old trunk with two glasses and a bottle of whiskey between them. It was late at night, and the crew was asleep. The Professor and Miss Sanchez were staying at McCullen's former house, and the ship was still docked. A single lantern lit the room and the Chinese curtain that had bisected the room was absent. Hazel had not asked him to leave.

Hazel was drunk and Neil used his good arm to move the bottle of whiskey away from her, but she scowled and pulled it back, then filled her glass, sloshing some onto the trunk.

"It'll only make you feel worse," he said.

"It feels better right now, and that's what matters."

"I wish you would stop."

"And I wish I wasn't a murderer. I killed a man, and it was easy. So very easy. I just shot him, and I didn't even feel bad about it. Is killing like that?"

He didn't want to go down this line of questioning, but he also didn't want to lie to her. "Sometimes," he said. The fact was that most of the time, it was very easy. But that was back when he had been deceived into believing that he was working for a just cause. He wondered if there was such a thing.

"It was so easy ..." she said and emptied her glass.

The ship moved with the water, and he wondered if Hazel would fall and hurt herself if she tried to get up. Or if she would vomit everywhere later, maybe on him. And yet, he stayed. He couldn't leave her like this, alone, drunk and tortured.

A slip of paper sat in his pocket, depicting the lettering on the roof of his mouth. While she was still sober, Hazel had made a copy. He had no idea what the letters meant, or how they might be connected to his strange memory. He had memories of another man's hands doing coin tricks. There were others, of places and events, seen through eyes that he was now certain were not his own. If his memories were a composite of other people's pasts, did that mean he was a composite as well?

"How's your wrist?" Hazel asked.

"It'll heal."

"How fast? Will you heal in a day?"

"I'll heal at the fast end of normal, if my past injuries are an indication."

"Do you have any notion of what you are, precisely?"

"No."

"I'll tell you what you are. You're the same as me. A murderer."

"Stop it."

"I won't! Think about it. The Professor killed a man. You killed many men, and maybe women too. And I killed a man. Murderers. Now Miss Sanchez, think about her. She heals people. Helps them. Doesn't shoot anyone. She's a good person. I can see why the Professor loves her."

"Miss Sanchez is good-hearted and gentle, but if you hadn't shot Mr. March, you and the Professor would be dead and I'd be March's slave, under his control for life. Sometimes virtue is impractical. Sometimes, you have to crack some heads."

"Crack some heads?" she giggled, and then, finding the

phrase inexplicably hilarious, she laughed and laughed until tears squeezed out of her eyes.

"Your head is going to feel cracked if you keep drinking this." He pounded the cork in with the heel of his hand and set the bottle behind him. "You're not a bad person. You need to stop torturing yourself."

"And how would you know? You've killed so many people, it's probably normal to you."

That hurt, and Neil looked down at the trunk between them for a while before answering. "It's not like that."

"I'm sorry," she said and put her hand over his. "You're good. I know you are. Even if you're a strange monster from a fairy story."

Was that what he was? A monster? If he was a killing creature, enslaved to an evil man, then that was precisely what he was. Like Frankenstein's monster in the old movies, an unnatural creation. But then, the monster wasn't evil, not really.

"I'm the monster," she said, rested her forehead on her folded arms and sighed a long and weary sigh. Then she started to cry.

He scooted around beside her and put his arm around her. Leaning his head against hers, he smelled the stink of her breath and the warm scent of her hair.

"You're not a monster. You're a good person. You are a good captain to the crew and you helped those slaves. And me. You saved us all."

"And I killed someone. Someone non-human, but it still counts. There are so many non-humans around."

"Speaking of which," said Neil. "What did Mr. Augustus and September Wilde tell you about killing Mr. March?"

"Not much. They were more concerned with removing his body. They said they weren't upset with me, that nothing would happen to me. They were very nice."

"Well of course they were!" came a voice from the doorway. Santiago stood there, fully dressed this time. "You did just as they wanted."

"And where have you been?" asked Hazel. "I haven't seen you since they took the body."

"I had a few things to take care of. And then I had to talk to Miss Sanchez about a wound I have. It's in a tender location and I needed it to be examined. In private."

"I need you to tell me something," Hazel said.

"For a glass of ale, I'll tell you a tale."

"We have whiskey," said Neil and shoved his own glass across the trunk toward Santiago, then filled it. Santiago sat cross-legged on the floor, apparently perfectly at ease with their humble setup.

"A tale of adventure or a tale of romance?" he asked Hazel and winked.

"No tales," she said. "The truth."

"Oh, now that's another matter entirely." He drained his glass and motioned for Neil to refill it. He obliged.

"You said the Twelve had plans for me," said Hazel. "What did you mean?"

"Well, as you know, Mr. March was interfering with the natural unfolding of events. His siblings wanted to stop him, but were having a great deal of difficulty. So they needed him dead, for now at least. But killing an otherkind isn't so simple. I certainly wouldn't do it."

"But you led us to believe that you would," said Neil. "We thought you wanted to kill him."

"If you think back, I said I wanted him dead, but not that I would be the one to kill him."

Neil thought that Santiago would have been quite willing to lie to them, but he didn't think it was diplomatic to say as much.

Santiago continued. "I wanted to be there when it happened, because Mr. March is a craven bastard and watching him die was immensely gratifying. And since you did it, things are clean and simple. If one of the Twelve killed him, it would be bad. Blood of your brother on your hands, you understand. There are penalties. Ugly ones."

"So they needed a human?" asked Neil.

"That's right. And Hazel here was just the right human."

"How could they know?" she asked. "How would they be able to predict what I'd do?"

"Well, some of the Unseelie have farseers, but I don't think the Twelve need to consult with the likes of them. I think they can see some things just fine on their own. They don't exactly confide in me, you understand, so this is all purely speculation. But I think they just needed a human to kill him. It could have been you, the Professor, McCullen or Miss Sanchez. Using your affection for your crew, your love for your Professor and your—" he waved his hand to indicate Neil, "friend here, well, it was a touch of genius. Most likely the only way someone like you would kill."

"But that was Mr. March's doing," Hazel said. "He stole the ship and the crew and created the danger for the Professor and Neil, which forced me to act."

"All true. You had free will and complete agency, as did Mr. March. That's the beauty of it. No one was forced to do a single thing. Well, except for you, Neil. You were forced a bit there. But in the end, Mr. Augustus and Miss Wilde gave the coordinates for this world to the Professor and you, and from what I understand, they've both known you for years. Who knows how long they took to set this up?"

"I've known Mr. Augustus since I was young," said Hazel. "He met me when I was only eleven. I've worked with him at his music shop."

"Don't hold it against them. They're really not so bad as far as otherkind go. Being used as a cat's paw is quite mild in comparison with other things that can happen to you. Some of our kind are much, much nastier."

"And what are you, exactly?" asked Neil.

"Me? I'm Coyote. Singer of songs and teller of tales. In fact, I have a story I recently heard about a young virgin and a sea serpent. Would you like to hear it?"

"Maybe later," said Neil.

"Whatever you are, you don't have much sense of fun," said Santiago.

"Do you have any idea what I am?" Neil would not tell him about the lettering on the roof of his mouth. He did not trust the man.

"No. You smell human. And yet, clearly, you are something else."

They sat in silence for a minute, Santiago drinking and Hazel looking off out the window.

"Why didn't Mr. March simply kill Seamus?" asked Neil. "He could have found him at any time. He could have found him as a baby or child and killed him."

"March was watched," said Santiago. "The Twelve keep watch over one another. That's sort of their special purpose, watching. And Seamus was probably watched as well, if they knew what he was able to create. So March had McCullen watch Seamus, and the Twelve watched March. If March killed him, they would have known. I have no idea why he didn't have you kill him. Maybe he planned to. Maybe that's why he wanted you back. He managed to get Seamus to shoot at him, and the Twelve are allowed to kill in self-defense. Maybe that was his plan. Or maybe he didn't care if he got caught killing a human. In the end, perhaps the only thing he cared about was you."

"I don't think he is capable of caring."

"Now, don't misjudge him. Otherkind are just as capable of love as humans."

Neil didn't want to think about Mr. March and his affection for him. For though he knew that March was wicked, he had been kind to him. Neil had loved him as a father, and if he went into the quiet part of his soul, he still did. But it was too late at night and he had drunk too much whiskey for these thoughts.

"You said that the Twelve used Hazel as a cat's paw, just as Mr. March used me," said Neil.

"Yes. And he used McCullen to keep an eye on the Professor," said Santiago. "Or did McCullen use Mr. March to get home? I can't keep track."

"What I mean is, what else are the Twelve going to do?"

"Now that, my strange friend, is an interesting question. A little bird told me that Julius has been talking with the Professor, and that friendships and alliances are being forged."

Neil wondered about this. He would have to ask about it in the morning. Hazel was leaning on the trunk, eyes closed. She certainly wouldn't remember this so he would have to fill her in come morning. Once Santiago left, Neil would lift her into her hammock and put a blanket over her.

"Thank you for the hospitality," said Santiago. "But it's a beautiful autumn night and I think a good run and a good hunt are just what I need. I'd invite you, but I don't think you could keep up."

"I'd rather not anyway."

"If you ever find out what you are, please tell me. I'm dying to know. The world is filled with so many strange things."

"You're telling me."

CHAPTER 41

February 12, 2014
Los Angeles, California
Hub world

SEAMUS CLUTCHED SKIDBLADNIR'S MAST AND tried hard to keep from vomiting. Hazel and Miss Sanchez huddled together near the prow, also sick. Hazel leaned over the edge to vomit into the water. Skidbladnir lurched with the waves, and Seamus nearly fell to his knees as the world spun out of control, the sky undulating and the lines of the sail and rigging twisting, evil and serpentine.

"Mr. Escobar, pull her around," commanded Neil, the only one of the non-monkeys who was not affected by what Seamus had decided to call Time Sickness.

They had required a synchronicity to travel to this time, but since they were traveling forward in time within the same world, it had not been too difficult. A few minutes later, the ship came to shore on a deserted beach.

The ship moved herself as close to land as possible, and Seamus packed up the time machine and pulled the trunk down the gangplank with Neil's assistance. Everyone else, including the monkeys, disembarked. The monkeys scattered out on the beach to enjoy their shore leave, except for Mr. Escobar who stayed with Hazel on deck. Hazel clutched the gunwale and looked like she wasn't going to be able to descend without tumbling headfirst into the surf.

Seamus felt better now, with only a slight nausea troubling him. "Come along now," he called. "Time for the captain to leave the ship."

When she vomited into the water again, he went back for her.

"If you hadn't drunk yourself into insensibility, you wouldn't feel so terrible." He spoke softly enough that the others would not hear. He knew better than to shame a captain in front of her crew.

"Don't punish me, Professor. I feel bad enough as it is."

"I expect you do. And a good lesson for you it is, too."

She allowed him to take her elbow and lead her down to the shallow surf, where she folded the ship and handed it to Mr. Escobar who put it in his vest pocket. They headed up the beach, Neil and Seamus carrying opposite ends of the trunk containing the time machine. He didn't want to leave it on the ship again. It was bulky and difficult to drag about, but he could not chance loosing it. Once on the sidewalk, which Seamus noted was made of white concrete, he dug in his pocket.

"Take this," he said and handed Miss Sanchez a piece of paper. "I've memorized it already, and I suggest you all do the same. It's the address of Julius's house in this time."

She read it and handed it to Neil who then gave it to Hazel.

"I don't know what the numbers at the bottom are," he said. "Some sort of coordinates, but they don't match up to the ones our machine needs."

"They're a phone number," said Felicia, smiling at him. "And the first three numbers are a Los Angeles area code. Once we get settled, you two need to learn to use phones and the Internet and everything." She turned to Neil. "Do you know where that address is located?"

"No. It's a residential street, I assume. And we don't have a GPS or a phone or anything."

"We could always see about buying a paper map," said

Felicia and then chuckled as if she was making a joke. Seamus could tell she was happy to be in her own time, even if it was in a different world than her own.

"I'm not sure where we would even get one in 2014," said Neil. "But if we can find a phone, we can call him collect."

"Finding a pay phone might not be easy, but either way, we need modern money." Miss Sanchez looked down at her clothes and sighed. She was in trousers, which was the current fashion, though he supposed her outfit would be out of place here. He was in outdated clothing also, as was Mr. Grey. Even Mr. Escobar did not fit into this time. The little capuchin monkey sat on Hazel's shoulder, taking in the marvels around him.

Miss Sanchez unfastened a gold chain that was twined around her ankle. "First a pawn shop, then to find a phone or a map."

They walked into town, and just as Miss Sanchez had described, women were almost all in trousers, everyone was hatless, and everyone seemed to be in a hurry to get somewhere. A huge truck roared past, and Hazel flinched. Another car drove by with the music player inside turned to a high level, causing the air around them to pound uncomfortably until it passed. Other cars stopped in long lines at the colored electrical lights that told cars when to stop and when to proceed. To Seamus's eyes, it was not too different from New Orleans in 1961, though the cars were more rounded and the women's clothing more revealing. They passed a newspaper machine, and saw that the date was Wednesday, February 12, 2014.

Seamus rattled the machine's door, testing the mechanism, until Miss Sanchez touched his hand to remind him not to act strangely. He had done the same for her, years ago, when she had come to his time. He left the machine alone, but wanted to insert coins to see how it opened.

"There, an old pay phone in front of that liquor store," said Neil. "And it still has a phone book."

The book was tied to the structure that supported the telephone, and Neil looked through its pages. He must have found what he was looking for, because he told Miss Sanchez which streets they needed to take to get to the pawn shop. Then he held the phone to his ear and pressed the zero. He punched in the phone number that had been on Seamus's slip of paper and spoke to someone, presumably Julius.

"This is marvelous," said Hazel softly to Seamus. "Don't you agree?"

"I do." Talking over a long distance with this device was indeed marvelous, as were the internal combustion engines within all the multitude of cars that zipped up and down the street. A building with a cross on top sat on the far corner with a mostly empty parking lot.

"Is that a church, do you suppose?" asked Seamus.

Hazel squinted at it and said that she thought it might be. Neil hung up the phone and said he knew which way they needed to go. As they got closer to the building, Seamus could read the letters on the concrete and metal sign out front. Saint Faustina's. He had never heard of this saint.

"You two," said Seamus, indicating Miss Sanchez and Neil, "tell us how to get to Julius's and you go on ahead without us. Hazel and I are going to have a little time alone."

"What are you talking about?" said Hazel. "We need to get to Julius's house. I'm hungry and tired."

Seamus lowered his voice and spoke into her ear. "You've killed a man, and you're going to confession."

He looked into her eyes, and after a moment of defiant anger, she looked down. "I know I ought to. But I don't want to. Perhaps another day."

"Hazel, I've killed a man too, you recall. And you need to go get this weight off of your soul. Mr. Grey and Miss Sanchez love you, but you and I are not like them in some ways. I know you, and you need to go."

Hazel glanced at Miss Sanchez and Mr. Grey who stood side by side, neither encouraging or discouraging her.

"We're not in any real hurry," said Miss Sanchez. "The pawn shop is only two blocks away. We can meet up here after Neil and I go there to get some money."

That seemed to help Hazel make up her mind, as she turned back to Seamus.

"Will you come with me?"

And for an instant, she was that little scruffy girl who came to his house, wild-haired and filthy, frightened to go out for fear of encountering her monster of an uncle in town. The man was dead, and Seamus's only regret was that Mr. Grey had taken the privilege of killing the animal from him. But that was no thought to have before entering a church.

Mr. Grey went with Miss Sanchez to find the pawn shop and Seamus rolled the trunk across the street, Hazel by his side. Confession hours were posted on the sign on the church's side door, and there were no confessions on Wednesdays. The rectory was behind the church, and they knocked on the door. Mr. Escobar leapt from Hazel's shoulders and scampered up a tree at the edge the property. A small, brown-skinned man opened the door.

"We need to see a priest about confession. It's urgent," said Seamus.

The man looked from one of them to the other, and then opened the door and invited them inside. The building smelled like boiled cabbage and aging upholstery. The small front room had a sofa, and they sat together while the man left and then returned with a purple stole around his neck.

"There's a room down the hall we can use," he said to Seamus.

"I'm the one who wants to confess," said Hazel, and she disappeared through the door with the priest.

Miss Sanchez would be down the street, but he would

wait here. She had aged, he thought, though physically she was less than a year older than when he had first met her. Her manner was different, more weary, but perhaps stronger. She had grown quieter since missing her synchronicity, and he wondered if she was losing hope. Hope in finding a way home. Hope in him.

And how different Hazel was now. In bits and flashes now and then he saw the little girl she had been, but now she was a woman grown. He had thought to walk her up the aisle at her wedding, but she was married to the ship now, in a way, and the hoard of little monkeys were her children. He had hoped to dandle her babies on his knee. Uncle Seamus, they would call him. Or perhaps Granddad. He could teach them a bit of Gaelic, and like the Irish children, they could call him Daideó. Or perhaps another name for a grandfather, Athair Críonna, Father of the Heart.

Well, there was still time, and Seamus had seen how Mr. Grey looked at Hazel, and how she sometimes looked at him. Seamus wasn't sure about the man. He knew Mr. Grey would grow into a good man, but the person he was now was largely unknown. Even after weeks on the ship together, he did not know how the man's mind worked. More importantly, he didn't know what the man was. He wasn't human, that was certain. Was he a creature like Santiago or Mr. Escobar? Or perhaps like the Twelve? Seamus knew that Mr. Grey would age. He had met the older man. But how long, exactly, would that aging process take?

Too restless to stay put on the sofa, Seamus went outside and stood on the front step. The inside of the building felt confining, and he liked being under the open sky. It was sunny here, as it supposedly always was in Southern California. It was the complete opposite of Ireland in that way, and it felt and smelled different than New Orleans too.

He felt like he too had aged over the last few months. The world was nothing like he had imagined it to be, an intelligible place that could be understood through science and reason, exploration and experimentation. It was a place of wonders, like a foldable Viking ship, and horrors like the void wyrm. And other things, like the Twelve. Julius had mentioned something about his siblings. They were watchmen, and they stood on the ramparts, whatever that meant. What they guarded against or watched for, Julius would not say.

Well, whatever stood in his way, Seamus would find a way to get Miss Sanchez home to her family and to her sick nephew. He would erase the worried, tired expression on her face and replace it with one of joy. And in doing that, he would redeem his mistake in bringing her from her world, and in creating the machine in the first place. They were headed to Julius's house, and he knew what, or who rather, waited for them there. Today was a momentous day. For now, he and Miss Sanchez were lost. But that would change.

As for Hazel and Mr. Grey, the two of them seemed to prefer it on the ship, with no home and no set destination. They were lost also, but they seemed to like it that way.

CHAPTER 42

February 12, 2014
Los Angeles, California
Hub world

THEY PAUSED AT A CROSSWALK, and Hazel insisted on pushing the button to tell the illuminated sign that they wished to cross. To her delight, it changed from an image of a red hand into a walking figure.

"Miss Sanchez, would you teach me to drive a car?"

"Call me Felicia. It's going to sound strange if you keep calling me Miss Sanchez."

"I'll do my best. But might I drive a car?"

Hazel glanced at the Professor, just in time to see him smile and then try to hide it.

"You can learn," said Miss Sanchez. "But first, you need to be a pedestrian for a while."

"What about a bicycle?"

"Yes, that's fine."

Hazel wanted to go fast, to try flying through this world the way she flew over the waves on Skidbladnir. The ship was in Mr. Escobar's pocket. According to the rules of its possession, if it was stolen from him, it still belonged to Hazel. But if someone took it from her directly, then it became theirs. Odd the way things worked.

The priest had been kind enough, but when she said she had killed a man, he hadn't seemed to believe her. He gave her an easy penance, a few prayers, but she didn't feel any better. She was still a killer, forgiven or not. The act had left an indelible mark on her. The Professor had been right.

Half an hour later, they moved off of the main street and into a neighborhood full of matching houses.

"These were built in the early twentieth century," said Felicia. "It's an older neighborhood."

Fragrant pepper trees ran up and down the street, providing shade, and the footsore travelers stopped to rest. Felicia checked the addresses painted on the curbs or on painted metal on the front of the houses.

"That one," she said, indicating a yellow and white two-story house across the street. Hazel loved it on sight. It had a wide front porch, not as large as the galleries on their house in New Orleans, but still roomy, with painted steps leading up to it. A driveway ran along one side, leading back to a garage. A silver car sat parked in front of it. They climbed the steps and knocked on the front door.

Julius answered and shook each of their hands before showing them in.

"I'm glad you got here when you did. It gives us a little time before the rest of the guests arrive."

"Who else is coming?" asked Felicia.

"A few of my siblings and some other people you may know. It's an auspicious day. But first, let's get you situated in your rooms upstairs. You must be exhausted."

For Julius, more than a century had passed, and yet he was unchanged. They left the time machine downstairs near the kitchen door. Julius led them up the stairs, and Hazel took in the details of the house. There were books, hundreds of them, on bookshelves, which was perfectly ordinary. There was a television, or perhaps a computer, in the living room. She would have to ask about that later. The bathrooms had hot and cold running water and flush toilets, just like her house in New Orleans, but she knew that this system was more efficient and didn't require the Professor's homemade water heater to operate.

"You're welcome here as long as you like," said Julius. "As I said back in 1864, I'll be here for a while, and you can always come here. September said the same about the New Orleans house back in your home world. Whatever time you're in, you have a place to stay."

Hazel thought she'd rather stay on Skidbladnir than in a strange house, but she would never be so impolite as to refuse an invitation of hospitality, kindly offered. Felicia and Hazel were shown to one room, while the Professor was given his own, presumably because he liked to make messes and work on projects that would disturb a roommate.

"You and Elliot sometimes share a room," Julius said to Neil. "But that's only when we have a full house. Most of the time, various ones or the others of you all are in and out, so you can have your pick of the rooms. Today, I expect a full house."

"What is he talking about?" Hazel whispered to the Professor while Julius showed Neil the closet where he hung his black duster.

"You'll see," he said. "Once the other guests arrive."

"Who is coming? McCullen?"

"Lord, I hope not. No. But I believe Mr. Augustus might come by."

She wasn't sure what to think of that. She liked Mr. Augustus, but was wary of him now. How much of his friendship had been manipulation and how much was sincere? Mr. Escobar jumped from her shoulder to go explore the house, including the trees in the yard. Once Hazel's coat was hung and she had flipped the electrical light on and off a few times for fun, she hurried downstairs to the kitchen. Hazel knew what the refrigerator was, but still opened it and the freezer.

"Ice cream!" she smiled at the Professor. "They have ice cream."

"Oh yes," said Julius. "And cold milk, central heating,

so many cable channels I can't even keep track and wireless Internet connection."

She understood these things from conversations with Neil and Felicia.

"And if you want, you can even take a hot bubble bath later," said Julius.

Oh, she hadn't had a hot bath in ages. She imagined that it would feel just like heaven. Neil was watching her, with that look of his that was almost a smile.

"Don't tell me you don't like seeing marvels like this," she said.

"On the contrary. I know exactly how you feel."

"He just thinks it's cute how you think ice cream and a bubble bath are the height of excitement," said Santiago. He must have slipped into the kitchen without her noticing. He hadn't changed in the slightest, from the faint lines around his eyes to the tawny yellowish color of his hair. He wore blue canvas pants, which Hazel knew were called jeans, and cowboy boots.

"Did you travel through time also?" asked Hazel. "Julius said we'd be seeing some people we knew."

"No, I don't bother with that. I just live one day right after the other. There's enough trouble to get into without all that time travel business. Besides, meeting the void wyrm once was enough for me."

"Yooo hooo!" called a woman from the entryway. She hadn't bothered to knock, but had come right into the house. Hazel went to see who it was. September Wilde stood with a plate of cookies, along with Mr. Augustus, both of them dressed in twenty-first century clothing. The white cat that had been at Miss Wilde's house snaked between them and walked into the living room, tail high. A raven sat on a perch behind a chair in the front room, and it made a *tok tok tok* sound at the cat.

Others came. There was a blond man in his mid-twenties named Elliot Van Dorn. Neil whispered in Hazel's ear that he was much younger than when Neil had known him. Elliot wouldn't remember punching Neil in the face or Neil's theft of his machine. Behind Elliot was a young woman, also blonde, who looked very much like Elliot, but did not speak. A woman who might have been Native American came and embraced September. Hazel thought she caught the name May. A few minutes later, two Asian women arrived. The older of the two, June Yee, was a sister to Julius, September, Mr. Augustus and the woman named May and went into the dining room to speak with them. The younger woman did not give her name, but when she saw Mr. Augustus, she went pale. Then she caught sight of Santiago and glared. He winked at her and went to talk to her.

"Neil!" said Elliot. "You have to come see this art book I got in 2126. There's this artist who is a hybrid, and she does amazing work. The book is up in our room."

Neil followed him upstairs, leaving Hazel alone. Various clusters of people spoke together, all of them apparently familiar with each other. Even the Professor was speaking with Felicia and the five members of the Twelve that were present. Hazel wished Mr. Escobar was there, but he was off exploring.

Hazel went into the kitchen and poured herself a glass of cold iced tea. She leaned over the sink and looked out the kitchen window, into the world that she had longed to see for so many years. But there was more than just the wonders, the technologies and the food. And it didn't end even with the vehicles, marvelous as they were. The world was so much bigger than she had ever imagined.

"It's time," said Julius, poking his head in. "They're meeting in the dining room."

"Time for what? I don't even know these people."

"You will, I'm sure. And as for what, it's the first official meeting of the Time Corps."

The Time Corps. That was the name of Neil's time

traveling group. And here she was, about to meet some of its members.

"Tell me something," she said. Julius must have caught the seriousness in her tone, as he let the kitchen door swing shut behind him. "What are you?"

"My siblings and I are watchers. We keep an eye on things."

"But March did more than watch."

"Precisely. He chose a side, and sadly, it was the wrong one."

"Side? There are sides?"

"There always are. An old war with new battles. Good and evil. Though, of course, both sides claim to be good. But don't worry, September and I are on the right side."

"And Augustus? And what about June and May? And the others?"

"Augustus has chosen to remain neutral, but seeing as he's not against us, I have no reason not to trust him. As to the others, they make their decisions, just like your kind do. It's not too much different."

"If March was on the bad side, why did he send Neil to leave a message with September? They're not on the same side, right?"

He looked thoughtful. "At that point in time, September knew March was violating some of our rules, but she didn't know the extent of it. And he would have counted on her good nature to faithfully deliver a message. But let's set this aside for now. It's time to join the others."

Hazel decided to ask him more later, but she wondered how forthcoming he would be. She found the dining room which was equipped with a long wooden table. September had set out cookies on a few plates and Santiago grabbed one before pulling a chair away from the table, shoving it into a corner and flopping down onto it.

"I'm not a member," he said to Hazel.

"Then why are you here?"

"This is my territory, my land. I like to know what's going on, especially if it involves strange happenings and strange folk. And you lot are the strangest. Well, some of the strangest."

The Professor, Neil, Felicia, Elliot and everyone else took a seat. Hazel found herself next to Elliot and June Yee. The white cat leapt up onto the table and the raven perched on a seat back. No one seemed to give these things a second thought, and Hazel wished Mr. Escobar had come. After glancing at September, who gave a small nod, the Professor spoke.

"I'm glad to meet you. I'm afraid I'm at a bit of a disadvantage, being where I am on my personal timeline, but I've been assured by my friend," here, he nodded toward Julius, "that you will not mind. You are, most of you, the members of the Time Corps, and you are used to asynchronous events."

"What do the Time Corps do?" Hazel whispered to Elliot.

"I'm about to answer that," said the Professor, overhearing. "You're early in your timeline also, as are Neil and Felicia. The rest of you, I understand, came as early in your timelines as you could manage. Our purpose, our official purpose, is to mend the problems that I have caused by the creation of the time machine. I have ripped holes in time, attracting the void wyrm at some points, and at others, allowing people to come through from other worlds who did not wish to do so. I take full responsibility for these actions, and I will dedicate my remaining years on this earth to correcting the problem. I will set events right that have been pushed out of place. We will identify time loops and make them into stable timelines. Our first job will be to work with Miss September Wilde to permanently stabilize the time rips in New Orleans. I am not sure how we will accomplish it, but that seems to be the modus operandi for the Time Corps."

Hazel glanced around the table, but everyone seemed

to be content with this answer. They must understand things she did not.

"We have safe houses, open to any member, in Los Angeles, New Orleans, New York and elsewhere in this world and others. There are also gold reserves, emergency mailboxes and other resources for the teams who travel to dangerous times and places."

Hazel looked at Felicia, and wondered what she was thinking. Was she a member of this Time Corps? She thought Felicia wanted to return home, and would do so at the first opportunity. Felicia met her eyes, and Hazel saw the uncertainty. Yes, she still wanted to get home. Any help from the Time Corps would be a means to that end.

September Wilde took a turn speaking, assuring them of the assistance of some of her siblings, who had an interest in keeping the world stable and progressing along standard timelines, whatever they were. June Yee talked about bank accounts and land acquisitions, stock investments going back generations and other things that didn't interest Hazel. She only jolted to attention when the word "Skidbladnir" was spoken. The raven tilted his head slightly, as if in recognition of the name, and the cat glanced up and blinked at him.

"Can we list it as an asset?" asked June Yee.

Hazel didn't know what to say, so she looked to the Professor.

"It would remain yours, of course," he said. "But if the Time Corps needs it, can we ask you?"

"Yes, I'll help when I can."

June smiled at her. The discussion droned on, and Hazel wanted to leave. Eventually, the guests got up and started saying their good-byes. Elliot squeezed Neil's shoulder in a brotherly farewell and he and the girl who looked like him left. The young Asian woman walked out alone, but Santiago got up and followed her. Only the five members of the Twelve, Felicia, the Professor, Neil and Hazel remained.

Neil jerked his head to the side an inch, asking with a glance if Hazel wanted to go. She nodded once. They rose and headed for the kitchen. Neil got down two bowls and dug in the drawers until he found an ice cream scoop. Then, he put two large scoops into each bowl and set them on the kitchen table. Hazel dug in.

"Quit watching me eat," said Hazel. "It makes me uneasy."

He shrugged one shoulder but continued to steal glances at her.

"Are we members of this Time Corps now?" she asked. "I'm not even sure what we're signing up for."

"Me either. But we can leave when we please. I think our first trip should be sailing up the coast to San Francisco. We can visit the San Francisco house."

They finished their ice cream and Neil put the bowls into the dishwasher, laughing when Hazel got on her knees to see the inside where the water shot up to clean the dishes.

"Now look at this," said Neil, taking a key ring from a set of hooks beside the kitchen door. "This looks like a car key."

"Do you think it belongs to the vehicle outside?"

"I do." And then he smiled, just a little. "Would you like your first driving lesson?"

"Oh, I don't know. Won't Julius be cross with us?"

"We'll only drive it up and down the street."

"I'm not sure."

"Don't tell me you're afraid. You're Captain Dubois, of the ship Skidbladnir. Time traveler, sailor of fierce seas, player of sweet songs and liberator of the oppressed and the enslaved."

"Don't say that. I'm just a girl."

"Yes, you are."

And with that, he leaned in and kissed her. His mouth was warm, and he tasted like vanilla ice cream and smelled like warm male. She slipped her arms around him, not caring what he was. Or rather, she knew. He was Neil Grey, time traveler, liberator of slaves, bosun of the ship Skidbladnir and a free man.

He pulled her against his body and her thoughts all vanished. A minute later, he let her go, and before she could speak, he pulled open the kitchen door and headed for the car.

"You still coming?" he called.

"I'll be there in a minute. Let me tell Mr. Escobar where I'm going."

She ran to the backyard, spirits high and heart free. The world, or rather, many worlds, were wide open. Hers for the asking.

Anything could happen.

AUTHOR'S NOTE

I love hearing from my readers. To drop me a note or to learn about my other books, please visit www.heatherblackwood.com.

If you enjoyed this book, please post a review on the retail site where you purchased it.

www.ingramcontent.com/pod-product-compliance
Lightning Source LLC
Chambersburg PA
CBHW030026180626
46810CB00001B/228